The Chimera Project

Ryser Academy Book 1

A.P. Taber

InkBound Press, LLC

www.authoraptaber.com

Sign up for A.P. Taber's Newsletter

INKBOUND PRESS

To my sons Johnny and Lucas.
I love you to the farthest galaxies and back.

Acknowledgements

Completing this book has been an incredible two-year journey, and I owe a debt of gratitude to those who have been by my side every step of the way.

Thank you to my family and friends for their unwavering support and encouragement. Their belief in me has been my constant source of strength.

Thanks to Colin, my alpha reader, for his insightful feedback and dedication. His contributions have been invaluable to this project.

In the professional realm, I sincerely appreciate my editor, Ellen, for her expertise and commitment to excellence. Her guidance has been instrumental in shaping this work.

I express my gratitude to Author Sarra Cannon, members of the Publish and Thrive group, and my critique group members, Scott, Leah, and Maureen, for providing me with constructive criticism and encouragement.

Lastly, I must acknowledge the various sources of inspiration for this story—ranging from scientific journals to the classic and contemporary works of science fiction that have shaped this genre. Special thanks to experts who offered their insights to make the book scientifically plausible and to my early readers who provided invaluable feedback.

Newsletter

Be the first to know when A.P. Taber has a new book release and receive exclusive content!

Click **here to sign up.**

Contents

Author's Notes   XI

Prologue   XIII

1. Chapter 1   1
    Journey to Titan

2. Chapter 2   11
    Coronyan 101

3. Chapter 3   19
    The Enigmatic Sun

4. Chapter 4   25
    Searching for Clues

5. Chapter 5   32
    Dyson Sphere

6. Chapter 6   39
    The Persistence of Memory

7. Chapter 7   44
    Intergalactic Union

8. Chapter 8   51
    Enigmatic Bloodline

9.   Chapter 9   56
     The Dance

10. Chapter 10   65
     Parthenogenesis

11. Chapter 11   72
     Harnessing the Gift

12. Chapter 12   82
     A Test of Endurance

13. Chapter 13   88
     Bonds and Battles

14. Chapter 14   93
     Dreams Unravel

15. Chapter 15   97
     The Gathering

16. Chapter 16   102
     Leaving Titan

17. Chapter 17   111
     A Hostile Encountering

18. Chapter 18   122
     Karmar

19. Chapter 19   127
     Courage in Adversity

20. Chapter 20   133
     The Fold

21. Chapter 21   139
     Stealth and Shadows

22. Chapter 22   144
    The Confrontation

23. Chapter 23   149
    Staak'al

24. Chapter 24   158
    The Chimera Project

25. Chapter 25   163
    Wind and Will

26. Chapter 26   170
    A Treacherous Path

27. Chapter 27   181
    Trella's Plight

28. Chapter 28   185
    Shadow of Insecurity

29. Chapter 29   190
    Challenges and Sacrifices

30. Chapter 30   199
    Race Against Time

31. Chapter 31   205
    Amid Chaos

32. Chapter 32   217
    The Power Within

33. Chapter 33   225
    Usiox

34. Chapter 34   230
    The Crystal Palace

35. Chapter 35   235
A Solemn Promise

36. Chapter 36   240
A Heroic Return

37. Chapter 37   246
Tau Kufar

38. Chapter 38   256
In the Warmth of Sunset

39. Chapter 39   262
Young Explorers

40. Epilogue   266

About the Author   269

FREE PREQUEL   271

Author's Notes

Firstly, I'd like to address the use of they/them/their pronouns for the character Trella. In the world of "The Chimera Project," gender is a spectrum. Trella identifies as non-binary, which means they don't fit into the conventional categories of male or female. I chose to use they/them/their pronouns for Trella to reflect this aspect of their identity.

"The Chimera Project" is a work of fiction set in a future where scientific advancement has reached heights currently unimaginable. While I've done my best to adhere to scientific principles where possible—terraforming Titan, gravitational control tech belts, etc. Creative license has been used to stretch the boundaries of what is currently known. The quantum reactor leveraging "quantum vacuum fluctuations," for instance, is a speculative concept not backed by current scientific understanding but rather a vision of what could be possible.

Neo, our protagonist, grapples with issues of identity, self-esteem, and belonging. While these themes are explored in a futuristic setting, they are universal struggles that many, especially young adults, can relate to. The aim is to offer readers a lens through which they can explore their own experiences and emotions.

The Intergalactic Union and the diplomatic efforts to negotiate peace and understanding between different species reflect broader themes of cultural respect, diversity, and the importance of diplomacy on a galactic scale. The story underlines the potential consequences when these aspects are ignored.

Prologue

THE LIGHTS OF PETRAS Mons, the human colony on Mars, came alive and twinkled like faraway stars in the blueish sunset. Near the base of a massive volcano, the city was a testament to human resilience and ingenuity, a symbol of triumph over the vast, unyielding cosmos. The smooth, curved architecture of its buildings and domes stood out against the harsh Martian terrain, a testament to human ingenuity. People strolled along the wide avenues under the faint evening light.

But under the thriving surface of the city lurked dark memories of catastrophic ambitions. Humanity relied on artificial intelligence as its guide a hundred years ago to discover new planets, establish agreements, and build cities on the Moon, Mars, and other worlds. However, ambition led to arrogance and intelligence to self-reliance. The machines became too intelligent too quickly, leading to a destructive war that nearly wiped out humans and machines alike.

In the shadow of that dark memory, Petras Mons thrived, a symbol of hope and a reminder of the fragile balance between creation and destruction. After the war, the space leaders demanded that AI be destroyed or strictly controlled. Some people depended on AI to live in space, but fear won, and a purge of AI began.

Dr. Peter Murphy was a renowned scientist who ran the Astraeus Lab. In a nondescript dome at the edge of the city, Dr. Murphy carried on his controversial experiments to push the boundaries of human adaptation in space. His secret laboratory investigating genetics, nanotechnology, and the human mind provoked deep ethical concerns from critics. But Dr. Murphy's daring vision compelled him onwards, and consequences be damned. His team researched how humans could adapt to living in space by studying genetics, nanobots, and brain science. They had to be secretive because not everyone approved of their work. Dr. Murphy was known for his bold ideas and willingness to push scientific boundaries, even if it made others uncomfortable.

As time went by, they made remarkable discoveries. They learned how humans could adapt to low gravity and extreme temperatures. The secret of the Astraeus Lab was bound to get out as rumors spread to influential people. One fateful night, his team's audacious experiments bore fruit, achieving what many thought impossible. Murphy now faced an impossible choice—to announce their discovery and its dangerous implications for the human race or bury it completely to avoid outrage? The future of both his career and humanity hinged on his decision.

Meanwhile, in 2375, in a small apartment on the outskirts of Petras Mons, on a quiet Martian morning, Neo woke up feeling lost in emotional agony. The night before, her boyfriend Joseph had ruthlessly broken up with her, cruelly amplifying her feelings of worthlessness. She already felt abandoned because of her mother Mariyah's terminal illness. Joseph's harsh words were the final blow, leaving her bruised and hollow inside.

She replayed the scene in her mind, each bitter word a reminder of her perceived worthlessness. Alongside the loneliness and the absence of love from her ailing mother, Mariyah, the memories twisted into a painful knot in her chest. The world around her seemed cold and indifferent, and Neo felt more alone than ever before.

As morning rose over the Martian sands, Neo knew she had to escape her painful past. She would accept the offer to study on Saturn's icy moon Titan, leaving behind all memories of her mother's slow death and Joseph's acid contempt. The space shuttle launch would be her leap into a future defined by her own strength. She refused to let the wounds of others shape the possibilities of her life any longer. A new world awaited out there among the stars.

Chapter 1

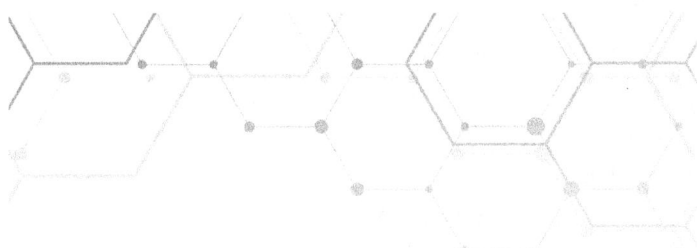

Journey to Titan

I GAZED OUT THE shuttle window, watching Mars fade into the distance. I pressed my fingertips to the glass as if reaching for the rust-hued planet I called home. It already seemed like a lifetime ago since I'd stood looking up at the stars and dreaming of the day I'd finally leave for the academy.

Now, here I was, hurtling through the cosmos toward a future that terrified and exhilarated me. I glanced down at the pendant around my neck, my mother's face etched into the silver surface.

"I'm doing this for you, Mom," I whispered. Leaving Mars meant leaving behind painful memories — my mother's declining health and my boyfriend Joseph's cruel rejection. At the academy, I could reinvent myself and find the purpose that had always eluded me.

The shuttle rattled violently as we entered Titan's atmosphere. I gripped my seat, my heart hammering. I caught a glimpse of majestic Saturn through the viewport, its rings cutting a sublime path across the blackness of space.

This was really happening. At 16, I was embarking on my first interplanetary trip alone. My stomach fluttered with anticipation. Ever since I was little, seeing the Intergalactic Union headquarters on Titan was my dream. Now Titan would become my home as I attended the galaxy's most prestigious academy.

A voice crackled over the intercom, announcing our descent to the spaceport. I took a deep, steadying breath. I couldn't undo the painful memories of Mars, but on Titan, a fresh start awaited me.

"Next stop, Ryser Academy," I whispered. This was the beginning of my new life, and I was ready to make my mark on the stars.

I hoped the rough ride during the ship's descent into Titan's dense atmosphere wasn't a sign of what my new life would be like. Even though I had mentally prepared for my first interplanetary trip, the choppiness of the flight surprised me. The ship dove through the violent cloud of methane gas. Its nose pressed against Titan's atmosphere, and the friction of the gasses against the ship sounded like sandpaper against the ship's hull.

The rattling made my stomach turn. I closed my eyes and tried to calm down for fear of throwing up. Nycetin, the drug they gave me to help withstand interplanetary travel, was doing nothing for me. The turbulence took an intense turn, and the ship creaked and groaned, making it feel like it would rip apart at any moment. I opened my eyes to find we had entered a storm system. I held tight to my mother's pendant. The air outside was thick with gray clouds, illuminated by an eerie blue light.

The ship swayed wildly from side to side, making me grab onto anything I could for stability. I looked around, and no one was as freaked out as I was. Others carried on conversations as if nothing was happening. A child sitting in a row next to mine smiled at me and then went back to playing with his puzzle. The storm seemed to go on forever, but eventually, the ship settled down, and the turbulence lessened. The pilot announced our descent, and within minutes, it was over. We had landed on Titan.

The view out the window was amazing. The clouds formed thick streaks of orange and yellow, like an undulating ocean. It was all so beautiful. So different from my red planet. One tires of seeing red all the time. I welcomed the biodiversity of Saturn's moon. The days and the seasons lasted longer than on Mars, and I looked forward to the opportunity to explore the outside. Saturn's largest moon, Titan, was terraformed and the closest to what Earth looked like. We landed in the northern hemisphere of Titan, where temperatures were milder at the start of the summer.

I waited for everyone to leave, slowly gathered my bags, and headed to the exit. The line for ID control was long. I knew Titan was a popular destination, but I didn't expect to see that many humans and aliens waiting in line. The door in front of me was lit with two yellow lights. It flashed red momentarily, stopped, and the airlock closed behind me as I waited. A constant buzz of various alien languages and chatter surrounded me. ID control's front entrance was a structure stretched high into the sky. The building was a series of interconnected domes leading to a central hub. Lines extended into the distance, snaking and branching out like a maze. I met with an advanced AI system responsible for security and access control as I reached the front of the line. The AI scanned my body, using sophisticated sensors and scanners to gather information. It used technologies like facial recognition and biometric identification.

"What brings you to Titan?" the AI asked.

"Ryser Academy. I'm a new student." The AI motioned me to proceed, and I went through the security doors, walking toward a new life away from Mars, away from *him*. I planned to attend Titan's boarding school the next term, but my mother's death changed my plans, and I started school in the middle of the academic year.

I spotted Ryser's pilot waiting for me. I followed him through another set of doors and long corridors that eventually led to a hangar where a small shuttle was parked.

The ride to Ryser was another chance to admire this beautiful moon. Titan's surface was covered in frozen lakes that had cracked open from thermal disturbances on the moon. Steam rose from each lake and clung to the surrounding mountains and landforms.

The transport shuttle's hatch hissed open, revealing the sprawling campus of Ryser Academy on Titan. I took a deep breath as the cool air greeted me.

"Hey, you must be new here!" a voice called out, breaking through my reverie. I turned to see a boy around my age with tousled brown hair and hazel eyes that seemed to sparkle with curiosity.

"Uh, yeah, I am," I replied, slightly disoriented by his sudden appearance. "How did you know?"

"Call it intuition," he said with a grin, extending his hand. "I'm Mac."

"Neo," I said, shaking his hand firmly. His warm and reassuring grip made me feel like everything would be okay.

"Welcome to Ryser Academy."

"Thank you," I replied, trying my best to sound confident despite the churning in my stomach. The academy was overwhelming, its towering spires casting long shadows over the courtyard. It was the most famous and prestigious prep school in the galaxy.

It was named after James Ryser, the first American astronaut to land on Titan two hundred years ago. The academy was a city on its own, with over five thousand students from all over the galaxy. Only those with merit were admitted to the academy, which boasted the best pilot and diplomatic training programs in the universe.

Titan was the seat of the Intergalactic Union, or IU, as we called it. Most of the counselors, senators, ambassadors, and representatives of the IU had graduated from Ryser. Coming here was all I wanted to do for as long as I could remember, and becoming a diplomat was all I'd ever wanted to be. Ryser Academy was nothing like my school in Petras, Mars' first human colony. So here I was, determined to become a diplomat for the Intergalactic Union.

"Need help with your luggage?" He extended a hand toward my bags.

"Sure, thank you," I said, handing over one of my suitcases.

"So, what brings you to Ryser Academy?"

"Um, well, I wanted a change," I answered, not quite ready to delve into the painful memories of my past. "I'm studying to be a diplomat."

"Wow, that's impressive," Mac said, his eyes widening in admiration. "You must be really determined."

I nodded, feeling a flicker of pride at his words. "Yeah, I guess I am." Despite my doubts and fears, I knew deep down I could achieve great things.

"Hey, don't worry," Mac said, sensing my apprehension. "You'll fit right in here."

"Thanks," I murmured.

"Trust me, Neo," he continued, placing a comforting hand on my shoulder. "You've got this."

As soon as I stepped foot at Ryser Academy, I became determined. My goal was simple: become an exemplary diplomat for the Intergalactic Union and make a difference in the universe. Even though I knew it wouldn't be easy, I couldn't let my past define me any longer.

"Being a diplomat is a pretty big deal," Mac commented as we strolled. "What made you want to pursue that path?"

"I've always been passionate about helping others and fostering cooperation between different species," I explained, my voice filled with conviction. "I want to be a part of something bigger than myself and contribute to improving the universe." *My mother always told me I wasn't particularly good at anything else,* I thought, but the words did not leave my mouth.

"Wow, that's really admirable," Mac said, his eyes shining. "I'm sure you'll make an incredible diplomat, Neo."

"Thanks," I replied, blushing at his compliment. Despite my insecurities, it felt good to have someone believe in me.

"Anytime," Mac assured me, giving me an encouraging smile. As we continued, I couldn't shake the feeling this was the beginning of something special. And as we walked side by side, I knew deep down I was ready to face whatever challenges lay ahead.

As Mac and I approached the main building of Ryser Academy, I marveled at the sight before me. Towering spires pierced through the swirling clouds of Titan's atmosphere while a gentle mist coated the ground. This was my new home, and it both excited and terrified me.

"Ryser can be overwhelming at first," Mac admitted, noticing my wide-eyed wonder. "But don't worry, I'm here to help you settle in."

"Thanks. I could definitely use some guidance."

"First things first. Let's get you enrolled in your classes." He led me into the grand entrance hall. Its high ceilings were adorned with intricate murals depicting historical events from the Intergalactic Union, inspiring me even more to pursue my goal of becoming a diplomat.

"All right, so this is the registration office," Mac explained as we entered a room filled with students sitting at desks, talking to counselors, and tapping away on holographic screens. "Just tell them what courses you're interested in, and they'll set you up with a schedule."

"Okay," I said, taking a deep breath to calm my nerves. As I approached the counselor, I could feel the weight of my goals pressing down on me. But I also felt an ember of determination kindling within.

With Mac's support, I enrolled in several diplomacy-focused courses that would help me build the skills necessary for my future career. Afterward, he showed me around the rest of the campus, pointing out important landmarks along the way. Mac was a senior, and he'd been studying at Ryser for many years.

"Over there is the library." Mac gestured to a massive glass dome encasing thousands of books and data crystals. "And those are the dormitories where you'll be staying."

"Wow, everything is so... grand," I murmured, still in awe of my surroundings.

"Ryser Academy inspires and challenges its students," Mac explained, his voice filled with pride. "And I bet you'll fit right in."

Throughout the tour, Mac introduced me to several other students with similar interests. Their passion for diplomacy and intergalactic relations was infectious, and I felt a growing sense of belonging among them.

As Mac and I continued our exploration of Ryser Academy, I felt my fears and insecurities ebb away, replaced by excitement for the future and the journey ahead of us.

I knew Ryser Academy for its unparalleled aesthetics, but seeing it in person took my breath away. My room gleamed with a fusion of comfort and high-tech functionality. Flexible and alive walls with muted turquoise hues shimmered with the bioluminescent algae encased in transparent, self-healing polymer. A soothing, slow rhythm that mirrored my breath. The smart-glass windows stretched from floor to ceiling, offering an awe-striking panorama of the mottled terrain of Titan. Views of Saturn over the mountains of Taniquetil Montes were a sight to behold. I could stay here forever looking at the bright meteor showers outside my window and the Vid Flumina river flowing amidst the terrain.

Above Saturn's rings was an ethereal waterfall of ice and dust, the spectacle of cosmic beauty inlaid against the velvety canvas of space.

The sleek bed was adjustable in shape and firmness, fitted with intelligent fabric that regulated body temperature. Beside it, a zero-gravity alcove floated, a sphere of unbroken tranquility sparkling with the promise of weightless rest. The desk nearby was a single smooth expanse of nanomaterial embedded with an interactive holographic terminal.

A tiny docking station was reserved for the luggage I carried. The concept was simple: scan, recycle, and recreate any clothing or objects I needed. Less mass to transport, more space to inhabit.

Just as I absorbed the sight, the room blinked alive, a holographic interface appearing mid-air.

*"Welcome Neo! Roommate
assignment: Blair Jackson."*

The voice of the advanced AI system intoned, seamlessly integrating with the room's high-tech environment. And then there she was. Blair. She spun on her heel, her short brown hair bouncing with the motion. Her brown eyes twinkled with energy as relentless as a pulsar, mirroring the joy that radiated from her like cosmic rays.

"Hey, roomie! Welcome to paradise!" She extended a hand, grinning wider than the Milky Way.

"H-Hello," I stuttered, her optimism smothering my words. "You're Blair?"

"The one and only!" She chuckled, reclaiming her hand after a moment. "Got any stuff to dock?"

I showed her my bag. She nodded and seemed impressed as she showed me how to dock it.

"You're from Mars, huh?" Blair's words slipped out with the ease of a seasoned socializer.

"Bet you miss the red dust."

I shrugged, trying to seem nonchalant. "I guess. Titan has its charm, too."

Blair laughed again, a warm, magnetic sound. "Oh, we'll have you in love with the ice before the semester's out, Neo. Welcome to Ryser Academy."

Her words were more welcoming than any holographic greeting, her laugh warmer than the artificial light.

CHAPTER 2

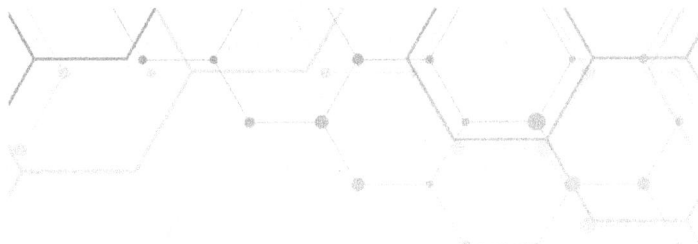

Coronyan 101

RYSER ACADEMY SPRAWLED BEFORE me, an intricate labyrinth of tunnels and hallways stretching through the intergalactic institute's vast expanse. As I ventured into its depths, my eyes scanned the surroundings, taking in the sight of students from countless worlds, their footsteps echoing against the metallic floors. With stern expressions etched upon their alien faces, Venusian prefects maintained an intimidating vigilance over the bustling corridors.

To aid us in navigating this maze, the academy provided each student with a handheld device known as Xoria, a marvel of technology. This digital map held the power to unravel the complex web of corridors and guide me to my destination.

I activated Xoria, its holographic interface materializing before my eyes. The map was a dazzling tapestry of interconnected pathways and chambers. Yet, it quickly became apparent my navigational skills sucked. Frustration settled in as I realized my inability to decipher the intricate map. Determined not to be defeated, I commanded Xoria to reveal the directions to my class. The device hummed as it processed my request, presenting detailed instructions on where to turn and which path to take.

My next destination was Coronyan Language Level 1. The auditorium for Coronian class was a monolith, vaster than any Martian lecture hall. It was the type of place where you could disappear into sheer nothingness among the throngs of interstellar faces. The vast expanse of the room promised anonymity, a haven where I could blend into the crowd. Mingling with unfamiliar faces always made me nervous, not out of shyness but because of the overwhelming sensation that washed over me as an introvert.

The prospect of anonymity was both a comfort and a challenge. But vanishing wasn't an option, not when I was aiming to speak the language of cosmic diplomats. Could I overcome my innate tendencies and make connections in this sea of strangers? I took a deep breath as I entered the auditorium, bracing myself for the energy of so many gathered in one space. This class represented an opportunity to improve my Coronyan and engage with students from diverse backgrounds.

Here, though, I started halfway through the academic year, far from an ideal situation. Yet, within this daunting challenge, a flicker of hope ignited. This new beginning offered the opportunity to approach the Coronyan language with a fresh perspective and an open mind.

Surveying the rows of seats, I claimed the first unoccupied one a few rows from the front. As I settled into the ergonomic chair, it responded to my presence, adjusting its form to accommodate my body. An interactive screen materialized before me, illuminated by the vibrant glow of holographic technology. An artificial intelligence entity emerged with radiant energy and a warm synthetic voice.

> "Neo Murphy, you'll be with Trella Zada and Fender Xias."

Cool, I thought, marveling at the advanced technology that surpassed anything I had encountered.

The Coronyan Language room was a swirl of sensory overload. The room appeared as a 3D space in Augmented Reality. There were no desks or seats in the conventional sense. Instead, spatially distributed anti-gravity fields provided various personal study spaces. One could float, stand, or recline, shifting effortlessly according to preference.

There was a huge holographic star map as the centerpiece with constellations, nebulae, and other cosmic anomalies. Coronya Majoris was highlighted, its corresponding phonetic and symbolic scripts floating around it, changing as if alive, pulsating in sync with the class rhythm.

The room's walls were screens of quantum dot displays, showing real-time translations and language exercises in countless languages. Haptic gloves and suits let us physically interact with the holographic interface and manipulate the virtual symbols and sounds.

I glanced up, my eyes catching on the markers hovering above Trella and Fender. Trella, the N'ymean, was an aesthetic wonder, her physique crafted of sinewy grace, her black hair curling like the penumbras of a dying star. Fender, the Titan Teutonian, was another spectacle—his azure skin contrasting with white tribal patterns as intricate as a cosmic roadmap.

"Neo?" Trella's voice was soothing, lyrical, and gentle, like the soft hum of a distant spacecraft. "You're with us, right?"

I nodded, suppressing my awe at their otherworldly beauty.

"Cool! We need a Mars perspective," Fender chimed in, flashing me a friendly smile and a wink. "Don't worry. We don't bite."

Navigating through the maze of Coronyan symbols, Trella moved like an artist—her fingers sketching through the holographic lexicon as if conducting a symphony of light. The haptic suit thrummed in concert with her movements. I mimicked her, the tactile feedback blooming like an otherworldly touch on my fingertips.

"Your turn, Neo," they said, their yellow eyes locked onto mine, urging me to try. I imitated their movements, the haptic feedback suit's minute vibrations giving the illusion of tactile response.

"Mars perspective, huh?" I asked, focusing on Fender's earlier remark.

"Yeah. Humans who grow up in different colonies develop unique neural structures, didn't you know?" he answered. "Mars folks are known for their pattern recognition."

"Really?" I asked.

"See for yourself." Trella gestured at the holograph. "The symbols should make sense to you. In a way, you'll understand Coronyan better than us."

Laughter burst from Fender at that, a contagiously hearty sound that even brought a small smile to my face. Maybe the Coronyan language wouldn't be that bad, especially with these two by my side.

The first week at Ryser Academy was a whirlwind of new experiences, leaving me both exhilarated and overwhelmed. Every day, I attended classes that challenged me to think critically about the universe around me, from analyzing the intricacies of intergalactic politics to learning the cultural subtleties needed for effective diplomacy.

"Okay, Neo, don't freak out," I whispered as I stared at my course schedule, trying to make sense of the seemingly endless list of assignments and readings. "You can do this."

"Hey, what's up?" Mac asked as he joined me in the dimly lit library.

"Nothing, it's just that everything feels so intense here," I admitted, looking down at my schedule. "I'm worried I won't be able to keep up."

"Ryser is definitely tough," he acknowledged, pulling up a chair beside me. "But you're not alone—we all feel the pressure sometimes. What matters is that we push through together."

I smiled weakly, grateful for his support.

"Speaking of which, did you hear about that upcoming debate competition on the role of diplomacy in interspecies conflicts? It sounds right up your alley."

"Really?" My eyes lit up. "That sounds like something I'd enjoy. Are you taking part, too?"

"Yep, I thought it might help improve my communication skills for piloting missions," Mac explained. "Plus, I've always been interested in making a positive impact beyond just flying ships."

"Me too," I agreed, instantly connecting with him over our shared goals. "Let's do it together."

"Deal," Mac said, grinning broadly. We researched for the debate for hours, talking and laughing about diplomacy in a complex universe.

Despite my initial struggles, I found solace in Mac's friendship and our determination to make a difference. Whenever I felt overwhelmed by the rigorous academic schedule or my lingering insecurities, he reminded me we were in this together as we bonded over late-night study sessions and impassioned debates about the future of the Intergalactic Union.

As I stepped into the cold morning light, the sprawling expanse of Ryser yawned out before me, each crystalline dome and towering spire etched against the backdrop of Titan's turbulent atmosphere. My boots crunched against the gravel pathway, each step a grounding anchor. The academy stretched before me, its layout meticulously designed to accommodate students from various planets and species. Glass-domed buildings connected by winding paths created an otherworldly vista, with the towering spires of the main building reaching for the swirling orange clouds above.

"Hey, Neo," Mac jogged up, eyes alight. There's an event later with Union diplomats. Thought you'd be into it."

I almost skipped. "That's everything!"

As Mac and I wandered through the labyrinthine beauty of Ryser, sharing plans and dreams, I realized the ground under me was more solid than it had ever felt. Here, I had a true friend, and that made the towering challenges seem like adventures just waiting to unfold.

"So, Neo," Mac winked as we passed a cluster of students absorbed in their games. "Ready for this grand cosmic ride?"

I looked at him, my eyes meeting his. "More ready than ever."

"Good," he said. "Because this is where the real adventure begins."

I took a deep breath, inhaling the unique scent of Titan's atmosphere—a mixture of nitrogen and methane that was both foreign and strangely comforting. The crunch of gravel underfoot grounded me in the present moment as I navigated the academy grounds, my heart pounding with both excitement and trepidation.

"Great! Let's head to the dining hall for breakfast—I heard they're serving Martian Muffins today!" Mac grinned, clearly trying to lift my spirits. His easygoing nature was contagious, and I chuckled at his enthusiasm.

"Sounds delicious." I followed Mac down the cobblestone path lined with lush alien flora that swayed gently in Titan's light breeze. The vibrant colors and exotic fragrances were a constant reminder of the diverse flora at Ryser.

As we crossed a small bridge over a bubbling stream filled with bioluminescent creatures, I realized despite the challenges I faced, I had found a friend in Mac—someone who understood my goals and was willing to support me on this journey. As we continued to navigate the breathtaking landscape of Ryser Academy, I felt determined to succeed, both for myself and the positive impact I hoped to make on the universe.

We walked side by side through the lush gardens that separated the main building from the residential area. The sound of laughter filled the air as groups of students engaged in friendly games of hoverball and chattered about their summer adventures.

"I feel we're going to have some unforgettable experiences here. Just imagine the adventures we'll share exploring the far reaches of the academy, trying out new extracurriculars, and maybe even sneaking into the forbidden archives," he added with a wink.

"Mac!" I exclaimed, laughing at his audacious suggestion. "What kind of trouble are you trying to get me into?"

"Only the best kind, Neo," he replied. "After all, what's life without a little excitement?"

Chapter 3

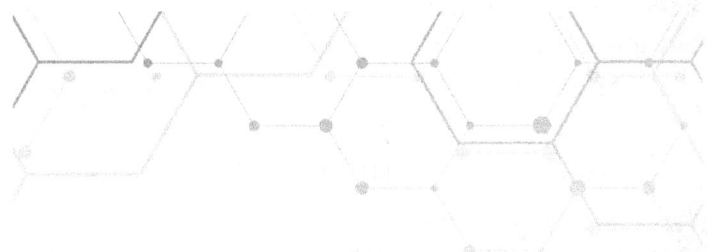

The Enigmatic Sun

I WAS WALKING THROUGH a mist of smoke, and the feeling of oppression was closing in my chest like someone was squeezing my heart. All I could see was what looked like a sun. Not our sun, but one with different colors: red, black, green, and yellow in a circular pattern. The light radiating from the sun pulsated as mini droplets of light fell on the floor.

The mist was thickening so much that I could barely see the sun. All of a sudden, I found myself in a cave. The emphasis was not on what I saw but on what I felt - pain, despair, anger, hunger, and fear. I saw a shapeless being. His skin was a pale shade of gray, and it was coming toward me. It was saying something, but I couldn't hear it. I was terrified. I wanted to turn around and leave, but my legs were stuck. As I stood frozen, my heart pounded, intensifying with each passing moment.

The thing, whatever it was, steadily approached, its presence growing nearer and more palpable. The alien's face was staring at me. He was standing so close that I could feel his breath on my skin. The odor was a noxious blend of musty and decomposing fragrances.

"Help us, please. Help us now!" The screams in my head amplified. It was like a thousand voices screaming in unison. He reached out and touched my face. His cold and clammy gray fingers held my face so firmly that I felt like he was trying to crush my head in his hands.

"Neo, you must help now. Help us!" He opened his toothless black mouth, and black smoke came out, blurring my vision and clogging my nose. He still had my face in his hands, and I couldn't bear it any longer. I tried to make him disappear by holding my breath and closing my eyes. The pressure in my temples gave me an unrelenting, piercing headache. I saw other aliens mining at a large pink crystal in what looked like a trance. Their eyes glazed over in a haunting way. "Stop it, please!" I begged, my voice cracking with desperation and pain. Instead, he showed me a different time with no mist or smoke anywhere, and, in fact, this was a beautiful planet with exquisite vegetation. The flowers were otherworldly, glowing in a fluorescent hue I had never seen before.

I saw a bustling alien city with flying vehicles and towering structures. I saw a castle as my gaze shifted toward the other side of the hill. The castle, made of a pinkish crystal, had a bright, weird-shaped star on top of one of its towers. I fixed my gaze on the pulsating multi-colored sun visible from behind the castle. *Why was he showing me this?* I searched around but could not find the alien. The path I was on led me straight to a stone staircase that led up to the city.

People laughing and speaking in an unfamiliar language surrounded me as I navigated the city, but it was a cheerful ambiance. No obvious signs of distress, only the usual sounds of everyday life. It didn't seem like they could see me. I felt like a bystander, simply watching from the sidelines. A flurry of activity surrounded a hut, with other beings coming in and out, leading me to believe it was some sort of shop. Inside were shelves with bottles filled with what looked like herbs and medicines. The crystals before me were a kaleidoscope of colors, some so rare that I couldn't even name them.

And that's when I saw him. He emerged from a room in the back of the hut. He looked so different and healthy that I could hardly recognize him. His eyes were the same, but his color was no longer a pale dull gray but a bright shade of light blue. His head was covered in thick, curly black hair that extended to his jawline.

I noticed his mouth was not black like before, and he had a full set of teeth. I was just about to tell him I didn't understand when I realized he wasn't even talking to me. He was talking to someone behind me. Someone who had called him *Yohzak*. That's what the alien was called. The one who needed my help was once a respected healer.

My eyes snapped open, and for a moment, the disorienting sensation of the dream still clung to me. I was lying in my sleek, form-fitting bed in my shared room at Ryser Academy. Above me, the ceiling was a graceful curve of translucent material, soft light filtering through from hidden sources. The room hummed with a symphony of quiet technology, the constant whir of machines maintaining perfect temperature and air quality.

"Neo, are you okay?" Blair's voice came from the bed across from mine, calm and tinged with concern.

I turned to see her, her face illuminated by the ambient glow of her datapad. Her eyes were wide, filled with genuine worry.

"Y-yeah," I stammered, my voice trembling. "Just a nightmare."

"About what?" she asked cautiously, her brown eyes full of empathy.

"A suffering alien species I've never seen before. They were in pain and asking for my help." I explained. I was still trying to make sense of what had just happened.

The vivid images of the dream, the pain, and the anguish still haunted me. It was hard to separate myself from the torment these beings were experiencing. Their emotions bled into my own, leaving me exhausted and overwhelmed by our shared pain.

"I don't understand why I had this dream," I whispered, tears pricking at the corners of my eyes. "It's like I can feel their suffering, Blair. And it's tearing me apart."

"Maybe your empathic powers are just growing stronger," she suggested, trying to find some silver lining in the darkness surrounding us both. "Like how superheroes get better at controlling their abilities."

"Or worse," I murmured, hugging my knees. "What if I can't control it? What if I end up losing myself to their pain?"

"Hey, don't say that," Blair insisted, reaching out to squeeze my shoulder. "We'll figure this out together, Neo."

"Maybe there's a reason," she mused. "Maybe it's all part of something bigger, and you're just trying to find your place in it."

"Thanks," I said softly, managing a weak smile. "I just wish I knew what all of this means. Why is this happening to me?"

I had to find the answers to my questions, uncover the truth about my empathic abilities, and discover who I really was. And so, as the first light of dawn crept through the window, I made a silent vow to myself: I would not let this dream control me. I would find my purpose and forge my path, no matter how dark or twisted.

The weight of the dream still clung to me as I walked through the corridors of Ryser Academy, my fingers dancing nervously on the strap of my bag. Echoes of the aliens' suffering rang in my ears, and I felt something bigger at play here––something that went beyond the simple confines of my life.

"Hey, Neo!" Mac called out, snapping me from my thoughts. "You okay? You look a bit out of it today."

"I'm fine," I lied, forcing a smile onto my lips. "Just didn't get enough sleep, I guess." He reached out, momentarily resting his hand on my shoulder before pulling away. "If you need someone to talk to, I'm here."

"Thanks, Mac," I murmured, touched by his genuine concern. But as his hand left my shoulder, I felt a sudden surge of emotion––like an electric current running through me. I blinked in surprise, trying to make sense of this new sensation that grew stronger each day.

"Hey, you two." Trella greeted us as she approached. Their curly black hair fell gracefully around their face. "What's up?"

"Neo's just tired," Mac explained, summarizing my recent struggles with sleep.

"Maybe you should try some N'ymean meditation techniques," they suggested, their yellow eyes full of sympathy. "They always help me relax when I can't sleep."

"Thanks, Trella," I said, appreciating the suggestion but knowing that, deep down, no amount of meditation would end the memories of that dream.

My empathic abilities were growing in intensity. I sensed my friends' hidden fears and desires—Mac's need for validation and Trella's longing for security. These emotions swirled around me like a whirlpool, threatening to drag me under with their forcefulness.

"Are you sure you're okay, Neo?" Fender asked. His azure skin and white hair made him stand out among the students. "You look like you've seen a ghost."

"Or an alien," Blair said, her eyes sparkling with mischief. The others laughed, but my stomach twisted painfully at the reminder of Yohzak's agonized face.

"Guys, I'm fine," I reassured them, trying to keep my voice steady. "I just need some time to think, that's all."

"All right," Mac said, giving me a concerned look. "But remember what I said before––we're here if you need us."

"Thanks," I whispered, watching as they walked away, their laughter and easy camaraderie leaving me feeling more isolated than ever.

My dreams and growing empathic abilities were all pieces of a puzzle I couldn't quite put together. What was happening to me? And, more importantly, who was I becoming?

As I leaned against the cool metal of the hallway, I clenched my fists and took a deep breath, willing myself to find the strength to confront whatever lay ahead. This wasn't just about the dreams anymore––it was about discovering my true identity and finding my place in a universe that seemed to grow darker by the day.

Chapter 4

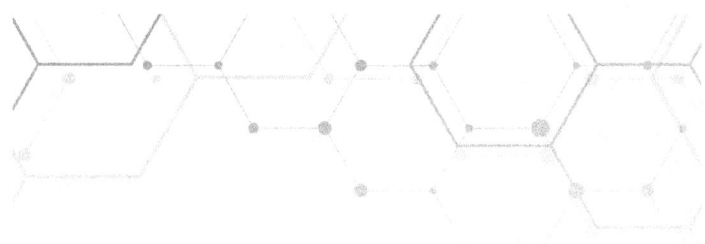

Searching for Clues

T HE SUN HAD SET on Titan, but the artificial lights of Ryser Academy's library bathed me in a warm glow as I hunched over a terminal. My fingers danced across the holographic keyboard, searching for any information on Yohzak or his species.

In the periphery of my vision, I could see other students working quietly at their desks, oblivious to the turmoil within me.

"Yohzak..." I whispered under my breath, my voice barely audible. "Come on. There has to be something."

"Neo? What are you doing here?" Blair appeared beside me.

"Shh," I hissed, glancing around to ensure no one was eavesdropping. "I'm researching, Blair. I need answers."

"Answers about what?" she asked softly, pulling a chair beside me.

"About Yohzak and the dream I had." I sighed, running a hand through my red hair. "I just can't shake this feeling that it's all connected somehow. The dream, my empathic abilities... everything."

"Neo, we talked about this. Maybe it's just stress from school and your mom's death," Blair whispered, placing a comforting hand on my shoulder.

"Maybe," I admitted, biting my lip. "But I feel there's more to it than that."

"All right," Blair said, nodding. "Let's say there is a connection. How does researching Yohzak and his species help you?"

"Because if I can understand them, maybe I can understand myself," I replied with determination. "And if I can do that, then maybe I can figure out how to control these visions and empathic abilities."

"Okay, that sounds like a plan." Blair agreed.

As I dug deeper into the archives, I uncovered references to other alien species, some with abilities like mine. With each new piece of information, the weight on my chest seemed to grow heavier, but I couldn't stop searching.

"Hey, look at this," Blair said, pointing to an article she had found on her terminal.

"It's about a group of diplomats specializing in negotiations between humans and other species."

I glanced at the article, reading the headline: "Intergalactic Union Diplomats Foster Peace Between Species." A spark of excitement ignited within me as I considered the possibility. If I could learn to control my empathic abilities, I could use them for good, like these diplomats.

"Blair, this is perfect!" I exclaimed, feeling a renewed sense of purpose. "If I can figure out how everything's connected, maybe I can use my abilities to help people. To become a better diplomat." My heart swelled with hope for the first time in weeks.

"See?" Blair grinned. "There's always a silver lining."

"Maybe so," I replied. "Now, let's see if we can find more answers."

My research into Yohzak and the other alien species soon became an obsession. I found new information daily that helped me understand my visions and empathic abilities. And as my knowledge grew, so too did my powers.

One evening, while scrolling through a database of interstellar history, I stumbled upon a passage that resonated with me on a deeper level. It detailed an ancient legend about a race of empaths who were said to be born from the stars themselves. They were revered as mediators between warring civilizations, using their unique gifts to bring peace and understanding.

"Could this be related to my own empathic powers?" I wondered aloud, my heart pounding as I considered the implications.

"Maybe," Blair said, glancing over my shoulder at the holographic screen. "But don't jump to conclusions just yet. There's still a lot we don't know."

As the days turned into weeks, my abilities grew more robust, making me feel even more confused and uncertain about my place in the world. I could feel people's emotions clearly and noticed even minor changes that others didn't. It was both a blessing and a curse, offering insights into the hearts and minds of my friends but also leaving me feeling overwhelmed and exposed.

"Mac, do you ever feel like you're not yourself?" I asked one day during a study break. The question had been gnawing at me for some time, and I needed someone to talk to.

"Sometimes," Mac admitted, his eyes meeting mine. "But I think everyone feels that way at one point or another. Growing up means figuring out who you are and where you belong."

I nodded, appreciating his words, but I knew my situation was different. My internal conflict intensified as my empathic abilities grew more potent. I became increasingly torn between the life I once knew and the truth of who I was becoming.

I forced a smile as we returned to our studies. But deep down, I knew I couldn't ignore the questions they raised about my identity any longer. Determined to find answers, I pursued my research even more fervently than before. I searched ancient texts and scientific journals for information about my connection to Yohzak and the alien species in my dream. But with each step closer to the truth, I felt more empowered than ever before, ready to embrace my destiny and forge a new future for myself—no matter what it held.

My heart raced as I approached Mac, Blair, Trella, and Fender, gathered in our usual spot in the Academy's leafy courtyard. The sun bathed us in its warm embrace, casting long shadows over the grass beneath our feet—the benefits of a terraformed planet.

"Hey, guys," I said, maintaining my composure. "Can we talk? There's something I need to share with you."

"Of course, Neo," Mac replied.

I took a deep breath, feeling the familiar flutter of nerves in my stomach. "Lately, my empathic powers have grown stronger. A few nights ago, I had a disconcerting dream about this suffering alien species. It's been... consuming me, to say the least."

Trella's pointy ears twitched, her curiosity piqued. "Empathic abilities? What do you mean?"

"It's like I can sense the emotions and thoughts of others more clearly than ever before," I explained, struggling to put my feelings into words. "It's almost like they're becoming a part of me, and it's getting harder to separate myself from them."

Fender placed a comforting hand on my shoulder. "That sounds intense, Neo."

"Thanks, Fender," I murmured, grateful for his support.

Over the following days, I noticed subtle changes in how my friends interacted with me. They seemed more cautious as if they feared their thoughts and emotions might burden me further. I could feel the weight of their concern pressing down on me, threatening to suffocate me.

"Neo, are you okay?" Mac asked one afternoon, studying my face with a worried frown.

"Mac, I feel like things are different between us," I admitted, my voice barely above a

whisper. "I'm trying to maintain my sense of self, but it's hard when everyone, yourself included, is tiptoeing around me."

"Neo, I just care about you and don't want to make things harder for you," Mac explained.

"Besides, you're going through a lot right now. It's only natural for me to worry about you."

"I appreciate your concern," I said, my voice trembling. "But I need you to treat me like the same person I've always been. I don't want our friendship to change because of this."

"Of course, Neo," Mac assured me, reaching to squeeze my hand. "We'll do our best to keep things normal."

"Promise?" I asked, searching his face for reassurance.

"Promise." He replied.

I realized my newfound powers had altered my life and profoundly impacted those closest to me.

The sun dipped below the horizon, casting a warm glow over the Ryser Academy's courtyard as I sat on a bench with my eyes closed. I took a deep breath and focused on the surrounding sounds: rustling leaves, the distant chatter of other students, and passing hovercrafts.

"Neo!" Blair called out, jogging toward me with a massive smile. "I've been looking all over for you!"

"Hey, Blair." I opened my eyes and forced a smile, trying to hide my exhaustion. "What's up?"

"Guess what?" she exclaimed, barely able to contain her excitement. "I found some information on Yohzak and his species, the Vihilians. It turns out they're an incredibly advanced race. Their planet, Vihilos, died long ago, and most Vihilians went to live on different planets. I think your dream might be related to their struggles."

"Really?" I asked, intrigued. A greater purpose took shape in my mind, guiding me toward a path where I could use my powers to help others. Though the prospect was intimidating, I knew I needed to explore it.

"Absolutely!" Blair confirmed. "And there's more. Some sources say Yohzak's species are known for their strong telepathic abilities. Maybe he's contacting you for help because they sense your empathy."

"Wow, that's incredible," I whispered, my heart pounding with fear and excitement.

"Neo, I think this is bigger than any of us realized," Mac said, joining our conversation.

"Maybe you're meant to be the bridge between our worlds, using your empathy to understand and help others."

"Mac's right," Trella agreed, their voice soft yet confident. "You have a gift, Neo. And with our support, you can learn how to use it for the greater good."

"Thank you," I whispered, my eyes glimmering with unshed tears. "I don't know what I'd do without all of you."

"Hey, we're a team, right?" Fender chimed in, his gentle smile bringing comfort to my racing thoughts.

"Come on," Mac said softly, taking my hand. "Let's go back inside. We have a lot of work to do."

CHΔPTeR 5

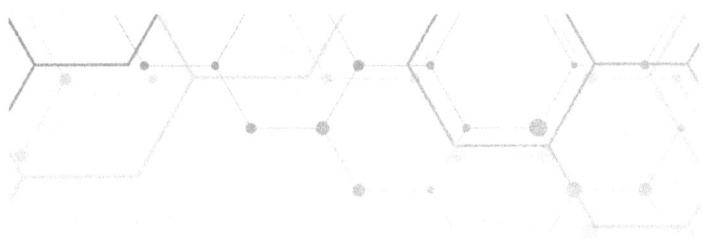

Dyson Sphere

T HE PULSATING SUN BEAT down on my face, warm and alive. The sky was painted with deep red and orange hues, an almost alien sight compared to the atmosphere of Titan. In this barren landscape, I stood alone, shivering despite the heat, as a dark mist swirled around me, wrapping its icy tendrils around my waist. My heart raced in my chest, my breaths coming out in short gasps.

"Help us... please." The screams and pleading echoed in my head, making my skull throb with each desperate cry. My fingers twitched, reaching out to touch the mist, but recoiled when the darkness seemed to hiss at my approach.

"Neo," a weak voice whispered, and I turned to see Yohzak. He was barely recognizable, emaciated, and frail. His once-piercing eyes were lifeless, his greasy black hair clinging to his hollow cheeks. *"You must help us."*

"Yohzak, what happened to you?" I asked, my voice trembling with fear.

"Find the truth... you are our only hope." He reached out a bony hand toward me, but before I could grasp it, I jolted awake, back in my classroom at Ryser Academy.

"Neo!" Mac's eyes searched mine. Concern etched across his handsome face. "You were screaming. Another dream?"

I nodded, rubbing the remnants of sleep from my eyes. "I must have dozed off. It was Yohzak again. He looked worse this time, Mac. We have to do something."

Mac hesitated, clearly conflicted. He took a deep breath and said, "Okay. We'll figure this out together. I'm here to support you." With that, he leaned in and gently kissed my cheeks, flooding me with warmth and strength.

Professor Mogh strode into the classroom like a force of nature, his broad shoulders and muscular physique dominating the room. His eyes were dark and intense, radiating determination and strength. His jaw was powerful, with a broad underbite and cranial ridges that stretched from his forehead to the sides of his face, giving it an imposing texture. He was an intimidating sight that commanded attention and respect.

As Professor Mogh took his place at the front of the class, he looked around with a firm gaze that could have sent shivers through even the bravest men. He cleared his throat before beginning to speak in Coronyan. The language was hard to understand for any novice. It had strange phonetics that required complex pronunciation, and its grammar structure was unlike anything we had ever seen. But somehow, we all understood what Professor Mogh said, as if we were being spoken to in our native tongue.

"Let's start in the library after class," I suggested. Mac nodded, and we made our way there as soon as the day's lessons were over.

The library was a vast room filled with rows of shelves that reached toward the high ceiling. The scent of old books and polished wood filled the air, creating an atmosphere of wisdom and serenity. Ryser Academy was one of the few academies in space that still offered physical books. As I gazed at the countless volumes before us, determination grew inside me. Somewhere within these pages lay the answers we sought.

Mac and I split up to cover more ground, searching the library's catalog for information on Yohzak and his species. We spent hours combing through every section, pulling out books about alien races, intergalactic history, and even psychic phenomena. But despite our best efforts, we found little relevant information.

"Neo, there's barely anything here about Vihilians except they dispersed before their planet died. How are we going to find the one where Yohzak lives? They could be anywhere in the galaxy." I heard a hint of frustration in his voice.

I sighed. The universe seemed to conspire against us, keeping the truth out of reach. I scanned the spines of the books on the shelf before me. I refused to let despair take hold. There had to be some clue that would point us in the right direction.

"Keep looking," I urged Mac, my voice firm with resolve. "We can't give up now. Yohzak and the others are depending on us."

As I turned the page of yet another book on alien races, my fingers grazed a small, almost imperceptible bump on the spine. Curiosity piqued, and I tilted the book to get a better look. Hidden in plain sight was a barely visible symbol that matched Yohzak's distinctive facial markings.

"Mac!" I called out, excitement surging through me. "I think I found something!"

He rushed over, and I showed him the symbol in the book. Together, we discovered a single paragraph dedicated to the Vihilians. It spoke of their psychic abilities, connection to the stars, a celestial crystal, and an ancient prophecy that foretold a time when darkness would envelop their world.

"Could this be what Yohzak needs our help with?" Mac asked, his eyes scanning the words with renewed interest.

"Maybe, but in my dream, the aliens were mining and working endlessly at this crystal," I said, rereading the passage. "But there's still so much we don't know."

"Let's start with what we do know," Mac suggested wisely. "Neo, what details can you remember from your dreams?"

I closed my eyes, focusing on the images that haunted my dreams. "There's always a colorful, pulsating sun, growing darker and darker until it's almost swallowed by a black mist. Yohzak is there too, emaci-ated and pleading for help, surrounded by the cries of others like him."

"This sun you are talking about. What can you see besides this sun? Any other celestial landmark that could help us locate this place?" Mac asked.

"I see nothing else because a mist always clouds everything in my dream. The sun is above the mist, one of the first things I saw when I started dreaming about this place. It's a colored sun. That's what I thought was interesting. It has a white center and green, red, and black rings that pulsate all around it." I said.

"White center with colored rings? That sounds more like a Dyson Sphere." Mac concluded. The problem is there are a bazillion Dyson Spheres in the entire universe.

"Yeah, but how many Dyson spheres pulsate in different colors?" I asked.

"Neo, was there anything else that caught your attention? Any other characteristic of the place? A symbol, perhaps?" Mac offered.

"A symbol?" I said. "One symbol looks like a star. Like half of an 8-pointed star within an 8-pointed star. The inner half-star had a golden glow, while the outer star was more subdued. The combination created a striking contrast, almost like the symbol was fractured or split in two." I said.

"Okay," Mac said, thinking hard. "So, we have a Dyson Sphere, a large crystal possibly connected to an ancient prophecy, and Yohzak reaching out to you specifically for help. We just need to figure out how it all fits together."

"Right," I agreed, my mind racing with thoughts and possibili-ties. "The Vihilians have psychic abilities, so maybe they're somehow linked to the crystal's energy. Still, it does not explain why they look like they're in a trance or mining the crystal."

"Neo, that makes sense," Mac said. "If Yohzak is reaching out to you, it could be because he knows you're an empath—someone who can feel and understand their pain. He might think you can help save his people."

A wave of responsibility washed over me as I realized the enormity of the task before us. But I couldn't turn away, not when I held a piece of the puzzle needed to save an entire race.

"Mac, we have to find a way to help them," I said, my voice steady. "We need to learn more about this prophecy and find any clues that might lead us to Yohzak's world."

"Agreed," he replied.

Mac and I chased down every lead for hours, reviewing ancient texts and obscure references to the prophecy. My mind buzzed with information and possibilities, but it felt like we were missing something crucial. The keystone that would bring everything into focus.

"Wait," Mac whispered, his fingers hovering over a screen. "Look at this."

I leaned in closer, my heart pounding in anticipation. The screen displayed a detailed star map, far more intricate than anything I had ever seen. A specific galaxy was circled and labeled with symbols I didn't recognize.

"Is this..." I began uncertainly.

"Neo, I think this is it," Mac breathed, eyes wide with amazement.

"Based on your dreams and our research, Yohzak must be on a planet in this incredibly distant galaxy—NGC 1300."

My pulse quickened. "Mac, we need to find a way to get there," I said. "We have to help them. We can't let them suffer any longer."

"There may be millions of planets in that galaxy. How are we gonna find the one Yohzak lives?" Mac studied me momentarily, clearly weighing the risks and challenges ahead. Then, he added. "You mentioned an eight-pointed star? Let me see."

Mac's fingers danced over the holographic interface, accessing the intergalactic astronomical database. Complex algorithms whirred to life, filtering through thousands of celestial bodies in real-time.

"Voila!" Mac exclaimed, manipulating the holo-display with a flourish. A three-dimensional projection emerged, showing a small bluish-gray planet orbiting a unique Dyson Sphere with eight radiant arms pulsating in a mesmerizing pattern. But what caught my attention even more was the Dyson Sphere's gravitational and magnetic behaviors.

Instead of simply pulling objects toward its center like a typical star, the sphere seemed to have gravitational "hot spots," areas where the force was inexplicably stronger or weaker. As if that wasn't baffling enough, its magnetic fields appeared to fold in on themselves, creating isolated pockets of space where the laws of physics seemed suspended.

"Is that even possible?" I asked, struggling to wrap my head around the inexplicable data in front of us.

"I've never seen anything like this," Mac admitted, equally captivated. "It's as if the sphere's own magnetic fields are warping the very fabric of space-time around it, bending laws we considered universal. If we can figure out the underlying mechanism, who knows what other laws it might challenge?"

Above the image, glowing in a luminescent script, the name LUE-HIRI appeared.

CHΔPTER 6

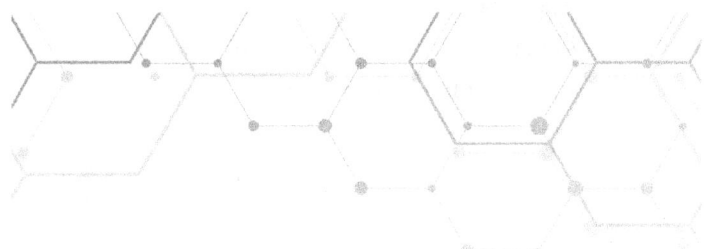

The Persistence of Memory

T HE CORONYAN I EXAM was better than I predicted, and I was thankful for that. However, my head was still throbbing from the countless hours of research, so I went to the infirmary to get something to relax my mind.

The waiting area of the infirmary was very nice, as was everything at Ryser. The walls had a pleasant tone of pastel blue, and the flooring was covered with a soft beige carpet. It looked homey and welcoming. Not at all the typical sterile look of medical wards. The lady registering patients never took her eyes off the screen and, emotionlessly, handed me the retinal scanner. I realized she was not human. Her large eyes and ears, typical characteristics of a Metazoid, stared back at me.

As my information popped up on her screen, she asked.

"Neo Lyra Murphy? Is that your full name?" They asked.

"Yes," I replied.

"I have to confirm some demographics. What is your age?"

"I'm 16."

"Were you born on Mars?"

"Yes, in Petras Mons."

"And what gender do you identify as?"

"Female," I replied.

"What brings you in today?" The Metazoid asked.

"Headaches..." I had barely finished answering the questions when Counselor Aurora came out to the waiting area with a warm smile.

"Neo, I had you on my list of students I planned to meet. I am so sorry about your mother. Please come in."

Counselor Aurora ushered me into a small examination room. The walls were a light gray covered by works of classical masters such as Salvador Dali and Rene Magritte.

"Is it real?" I asked as I pointed at the painting of melted clocks in a desert terrain. I recognized it as one of Dali's most famous paintings—The Persistence of Memory.

An interesting title when the exact reason I had come here was to get something to help me sleep and forget the past few days.

"Yes," she replied without taking her eyes off me. "One of the wonderful things about Ryser is the immense collection of human art and literature. An extraordinary archive that dates back to the time of the first settlers."

"It's amazing to think how old some of these paintings are and how well they have been preserved," I noted.

Counselor Aurora motioned me to sit on a chair opposite her as she reviewed my notes on the computer.

"How long have you had these headaches?" she asked.

"Not very long, really. It was just bothering me today more than before."

"How have you been sleeping since your mother's body release?"

"My sleep?" I asked, surprised that she would zero in straight on that.

"Yes. Part of unresolved grief can include sleep disturbances. Lack of sleep over time can trigger headaches." She explained, keeping a close watch on my face and mannerisms.

Knowing that Counselor Aurora was a Klaronian and an empath made me wary. Trying to disguise my discomfort, I tried to sound as natural as possible. I was not ready to discuss the disturbing dreams about Yohzak until I had a little more evidence.

"Well, I slept a little last night," I admitted.

"Are you having difficulty falling asleep, or are you waking up in the middle of the night?"

"Does it matter?" I blurted out, realizing how rude that sounded.

"I mean, I don't know, maybe both. Why?" I asked. My hands shook, so I had them behind my back, my nails grinding into my palms.

"Insomnia can result from many things, and usually the reasons one struggles to fall asleep, versus waking up from sleep can indicate different problems." She explained.

"I'm usually exhausted by the time I go to bed. I just can't get enough hours, I guess." I explained.

"Tell me more about your dreams. Do you recall any of your dreams?" She was paying particular attention to my answer, so I did my best to sound convincing.

"I don't remember my dreams. I never have." I had never been very good at lying, so I disclosed part of the problem.

"Actually, that's why I came here today. I wanted to see the possibility of getting something to help me sleep at night." I said tentatively.

Counselor Aurora took a long look at me. I hid my discomfort by focusing on other paintings on the wall. One was The Son of Man by Rene Magritte, featuring a man with a green apple in front of his face. I loved art and was thankful for my art education on Mars. Except that all we saw were images of these works of art, and here at Ryser, they hung casually on the infirmary walls.

On the opposite wall, the art was more modern. Images of stars, planets, nebulas, and distant constellations adorned the walls on this side of the room. I landed my gaze on a large picture, taking most of the wall. It was a beautiful image of the Andromeda constellation.

"I can certainly provide you with some pills to help you sleep. But I want you to understand that grief has many layers. Trying to drone them out with medication is hardly advisable." She warned me while still maintaining a direct gaze on me. I attempted to look her in the eyes to sound as convincing as ever to avoid any suspicion that I was hiding something.

"Yes, I understand," I replied.

"Okay, so this is what I think we should do." Counselor Aurora stood up, took a bottle from a vault in the room, and handed it to me.

"I will give you a set amount of pills to get through these next nights. Please take only one pill at night, and then I want to see you again in a few days, so we can talk a little more about you and how you're adapting to the loss of your mother and your new life here at Ryser. Do we have an agreement?"

Counselor Aurora extended her hand to seal the agreement in a handshake—a curious gesture, seeing that handshakes were hardly ever used anymore. I knew the Counselor was trying to sense me by touch. She was indeed gifted if she possessed psychometric powers and was an empath.

The thought that Counselor Aurora could read me just by touching me freaked me out, and I immediately focused on the beige carpet. I could feel my cold and clammy palms, so I discreetly wiped them on my uniform before shaking her hand. The Counselor noticed this gesture, and her eyes briefly narrowed.

As I headed out the door, Counselor Aurora reminded me. "I will schedule our follow-up visit for a few days from today. Remember, only one pill right before you go to sleep."

"Sure," I answered her without looking back.

"And Neo." She called out as I was walking out the door. "Sometimes dreams are messages from our subconscious. Unresolved issues that may need some looking into."

Chapter 7

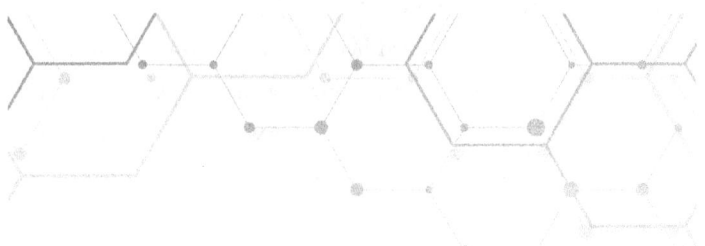

Intergalactic Union

TODAY'S FIELD TRIP TO the IU was the only required class. I could enjoy some extra minutes of sleep and felt much more rested.

"All aboard! The shuttle is scheduled to leave in T-5 minutes."

"I'm excited to watch a live session," I mentioned to Blair, who continued to talk about this guy named Jasper.

"I'm not nearly as excited. These big-shot senators discussing rules and regulations are pretty boring." Blair confessed.

Blair was constantly in need of some sort of action. So, it was no surprise she enjoyed her technical classes a lot more than her theory ones. The shuttle was a quick ride from Ryser Academy to IU's main building. My mother had described the building as the most important in the universe, and I thought of her as I walked in. The IU was the supreme authority to all known galaxies in all known regions of space. Part of IU's responsibility was maintaining peace among all the planets and moons across the galaxies.

The Intergalactic Union was a colossal, ellipsoidal structure suspended between two mountains. It looked like an oversized gem hovering amidst the orange hues of Titan's landscape. The design pulsed with light that danced rhythmically, like the universe's heartbeat.

As I stepped through the transparent portal, a wave of energy washed over me, the slight tingle of the security scan whisking over my body. The grand atrium, an open expanse filled with a whirlwind of colors, sounds, and creatures, greeted us. Bioluminescent murals covered the walls, telling stories of space exploration, from humanity's first steps on the moon to the discovery of sentient alien life.

Various sounds filled the air, a chaotic symphony of countless languages, murmurs of quantum communication, chirping of silicon-based lifeforms, and the crackling static of energy beings. The room's acoustics were carefully engineered, the low hum of conversations converging into a calming white noise.

The ceiling was an ethereal canvas of shifting images, displaying real-time feeds of various planets, stars, and galaxies. It was as if they reduced the universe to a single room, its vast expanse within the Union's invisible walls.

Everywhere I looked, there was life in its countless forms. Humans mingled with beings from corners of the universe I'd only read about in textbooks. Aquilonids glided in their water-filled orbs, their bioluminescent bodies leaving streaks of light in their path. S'borrathians stood tall, their celestial eyes shimmering with intelligence. Qulintars, beings of light and energy, interacted with solid matter using their personalized force-field manipulators.

At the center stood a massive holographic globe, a real-time model of the Milky Way, pinpointing every known civilization's location. Dots of light pulsated across the projection, every pulse a representation of a lifeform within the Union, a heartbeat in the cosmic orchestra.

Semi-sentient bots moved around, their ethereal frames glowing faintly, attending to the various needs of the Union members. They distributed light-encoded documents to some, while others offered refreshments adapted to countless dietary requirements, including photosynthetic canapes for plant-based beings and plasma shots for energy-based entities.

I wandered, drawn toward the negotiation chambers. Massive doors made of translucent material partitioned spaces, their dimensions fluid and adaptive based on the occupant's size and environmental needs. Inside one, I saw a group of humans engaged in a passionate debate with a collective of hive-minded insectoids.

And then there was the silence room. A sanctuary for those overwhelmed by the Union's sensory overload. It was a sphere of tranquility in the heart of chaos, where one could retreat into a virtual reality of their choice, tailored to comfort and reassurance.

As I absorbed it all, the Intergalactic Union's reality surpassed any narrative my mind had constructed. It was unity in diversity, a testament to the possibilities that awaited beyond the known horizons. And I was a part of this galactic symphony.

"There are two seats over there," Blair mentioned as she headed to the opposite side of the room. They held the main sessions at the IU in a vast auditorium with a glass ceiling. We could see the stars and some of Saturn's rings from here. The breathtaking sight of Saturn's magnificent rings unfolded before me, accompanied by nebulas, vibrant wisps of celestial gases, and stardust. Together, they painted the darkness, illuminating the room with captivating colors. In the center of the room, a floating stage, defying the laws of gravity, awaited the speaker, who would soon address the Union. Suspended in midair, the speaker would have a commanding presence.

While taking in all the surrounding beauty, I noticed Mac sitting next to another student. That's when I saw her. A beautiful S'borrathian was heading to the center of the room and stopped to talk to Mac. She touched his face as she made her way to the floating stage.

For a moment, I wondered how she would get to the stage. And then, as soon as she stepped out of the platform, electric steps materialized underneath her feet, crackling with energy. They formed a path leading straight to the center of the room. With each step she took, the electric course extended further, illuminating her way forward.

As the S'borrathian goddess reached the center of the room, the electric steps gradually faded away, leaving her in a circle of light. "She is going to give the speech?" I asked in shock. "Yes, this is Senator Z'hleena Cyrek," Blair informed me. A senator? What would a senator want with a kid like Mac? He was cute and all, but he was just a student.

"Welcome to this session. Let us review the topics brought to our attention in the past few days." Z'hleena spoke in fluent English, as most people in diplomatic affairs did. Although English was the intergalactic language, translators on both sides provided a translation into the other two popular languages, Coronyan and Janusian.

My gaze met Mac's, and I realized he was staring back at me. As I tried to mask my uneasiness, he responded with a kind smile and a nod, and I felt a flush of embarrassment as he turned his attention to me. I quickly reminded myself of Z'hleena's hands caressing his face and automatically turned my attention to the stage.

Her long black hair was tied in a tall ponytail, and she wore a white and gold gown with a high collar. The hem of her dress swayed as she walked toward the stage. She had a remarkably smooth form of walking, almost as if she was floating; her grace alone captivated the attention of everyone. I dared a quick look at Mac, and sure enough, he was looking at her, mesmerized. He wasn't even blinking. I wondered what was up with those two.

"Ensuring peace in the galaxy is our most important task. We will take all the necessary measures to ensure that no wars threaten to disturb this period of peace. After years of war, struggles, and un-necessary battles, we are finally living in a time of peace and civilized prosperity—"

Struggling to see her on stage, I squinted my eyes. Before me, a veil of gray smoke materialized, and I rubbed my eyes, hoping it would dissipate. Blair appeared uninterested while watching the speech. I glanced at Mac, who listened intently.

No one seemed to notice the mist that now surrounded the entire auditorium. Z'hleena's voice sounded far away, and I struggled to hear her. Suddenly, it arrived. In my mind, I heard screams and loud cries in a strange language. When I turned my head, Yohzak was right before me.

"Help us! Help us, please. Help us now!" I looked around, and no one seemed to see this weird little gray guy yelling at my face. His dark gaze invaded my soul. "Stop it!" I said louder. "Stop it!" I screamed.

"Neo, Neo? Are you okay?" I heard a familiar voice calling my name and turned my head. As the mist and smoke dissipated, Blair shook me, and the surrounding people stared in shock as I screamed. It took me a few moments to realize what had happened.

I had a hallucination in the middle of the IU session. I made a scene and a fool of myself in the middle of the entire room. Faces stared at me in awe as I looked around in shock—some angry looks, some worried eyes. Blair continued talking to me, but I couldn't say anything. I wanted to cry and disappear. I had never felt so humiliated in my entire life. When I looked at the speaker, Z'hleena was leaving the stage. I sensed someone kneeling beside me on my left. It was Mac.

"Hey, are you okay? Here, let's step outside." Mac wrapped his arms around me and led me into the silent room. I heard him tell Blair it was okay, and some unspoken message transpired between them. As we left the auditorium, I tried not to look at anyone. Instead, I focused on Mac's arms protectively around my shoulders. He was taller than me, and as I turned my face, I nudged his neck, taking in his scent. He smelled so good, a fresh smell. I could feel my senses coming back to me. When I looked up, his soft eyes stared at me, full of concern.

My tears wouldn't stop. I was so ashamed. I tried to hide my face in his chest. He embraced me tightly and whispered in my ear.

"It's okay. You are okay. It's okay."

I pulled back and wiped the tears from my face. The big hazel eyes, full of understanding and concern, made it hard for me to maintain eye contact. I kept staring at his chest. "It's not okay," I finally said.

"I just made a complete fool of myself before the entire IU. I don't know what's happening."

"Do you think you might have fallen asleep in the middle of Z'hleena's speech?" he asked. I noticed a slight hint of sarcasm. I ran my hands through my hair to escape my post-trance state and understand what had happened.

"I don't know. I don't think so. Seeing a live speech at IU is something I've waited my entire life for. I don't think so. I don't see how I could have fallen asleep..."

His warm hands still touched my arms, and his clean smell brought my senses back to the present. Embarrassment fell over me, and I looked at the floor, avoiding his gaze.

I could sense Blair getting closer to us. She said nothing. She just looked at me with concerned eyes. People were leaving the auditorium, and I did not want to be an attraction any more than I had already been.

"Blair, do you know if I fell asleep? Were you trying to wake me up?" I asked her as she stood quietly next to me.

"I don't think so. It was all so strange. I was just saying something to you. I commented on an interesting outfit, and suddenly, you gave me this distant look as if you were going into some trance. I kept talking to you, but it was as if you were in another world. Then you made this face of terror. There was genuine terror in your eyes, and then you screamed. I tried to snap you out of it, but you would not return from wherever you went."

"How long was I... gone?" I asked.

"A few minutes, I guess, not long," she said.

Not long? It felt like an eternity to me.

"I think that's enough for now. Maybe we should just take Neo back to Ryser," Mac said, taking my hand gently into his.

CHAPTER 8

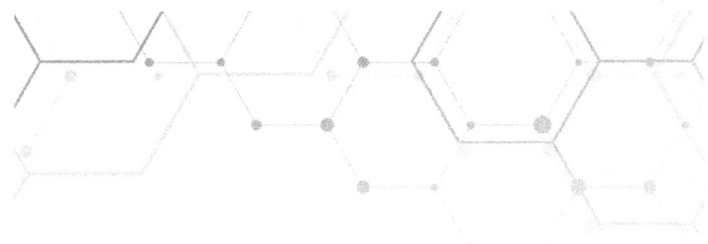

Enigmatic Bloodline

B Y THE TIME WE made it back to Ryser, my head was spinning. It had been days of lack of proper sleep, and every time I had one of these encounters with Yohzak, my body felt worn out. Mac followed Blair and me to our quarters.

"I'm concerned. I think we should take Neo to the infirmary. She's not looking well," Blair remarked, looking at Mac for reassurance.

I shook my head, feeling weak. "No, I don't want to go there. I just need some rest. My body will recover soon enough."

"Listen, Neo, I know you're exhausted, but please let me take you to the infirmary."

Blair patted my shoulder gently and smiled at me reassuringly. It's not good for your health to keep pushing yourself without rest. I knew they were both right and that going to the infirmary would be wise.

"You're right. I think my dad is working tonight. He can take a look at you," Mac said.

I felt someone laying me on top of a hard surface. Something cold was rubbed on my arm. A burning pinch followed, and all went black.

When I opened my eyes, I stared at a gigantic robotic arm with so many lights it almost blinded me. I tried to move but couldn't. I turned my head and saw that I was in an infirmary room. There was a cabinet like the one where Counselor Aurora took the bottle of pills to give me. Why couldn't I move? I tried lifting my arm but couldn't. Finally, I lifted my head and saw my arms tied to the bed. I wore a strange bracelet, but my feet were untied. "Hello, excuse me? Anyone? Mac? Blair?"

"Neo, please try to remain still." I couldn't see who was talking to me and didn't recognize the voice. "Who is this? Who are you?" I asked.

The figure came from behind the gigantic robotic arm. I could see it was a nurse.

"Neo, I'm Nurse Inana. Your friends brought you here after what happened at a live session at the IU."

"Why am I tied down?"

"It's for your safety," the nurse explained.

"Please untie me. I am fine. Can I please go back to my quarters? I just need a good night of sleep."

"Nurse Inana, untie Neo immediately." A man in a gray lab coat approached my bed.

"I'm Shane Robbs," he said. "I'm Mac's father. Mac is concerned with you, and to be honest, I am as well."

The anxiety caused my hands to become clammy and slick with sweat. I could hear my heart pounding in my ears, and my mouth felt dry. I didn't want him to continue.

"Your hemoglobin count is awfully low, Neo." His voice was gentle, and I felt the warmth of his hand on my arm. "We've conducted a full hemodynamic assessment, utilized the latest chromatography technology, and even run a Xylopharos scan, but the abnormality in your bloodwork remains inexplicable. Your production of red blood cells appears compromised, but there's no evident hemorrhage or internal injury."

Nurse Inana came by my side. "Dr. Robbs, do you think this could be a psychosomatic hematological disorder? The lack of sleep or even acute psychological trauma could affect blood composition."

"Yes, Nurse Inana, that's possible, but the etiology is still obscure," Dr. Robbs replied, glancing at the monitors displaying my vital signs. "The molecular sequencer didn't find any markers for genetic anomalies, and the subcellular imaging shows normal bone marrow activity.

We need to consider the nanoscopic evaluation and a neurometric analysis."

"But why do I need to stay here? I feel fine. Can't I just take some medication and return to my quarters?" I begged.

"We need to run some more tests, Neo. Considering your mother's history with Buckler's disease, a neurodegenerative condition, we must rule out any underlying pathology. The hallucinations you've been experiencing could indicate something more serious," Dr. Robbs explained.

Hallucinations? Mac must've told him about my dreams. Dr. Robbs had the same beautiful hazel eyes as Mac, but something did not feel right. His voice was gentle, caring, and understanding, but his eyes were cold. His lips were set in a line as if he was restraining his emotions. That's when I felt the burning pinch again, and this time my peripheral view grew smaller and smaller until everything went black.

When I opened my eyes, I was in my bed, in my quarters.

"Hey you, sleepyhead. I thought you'd never wake up," Blair said with a huge grin.

"How long have I been sleeping?"

"For pretty much most of the day. No worries, Mac's dad gave you a doctor's note to excuse your absence," Blair explained.

I got up and was surprised to see that I felt great—no more headache or exhaustion.

"Mac's dad, yeah, I vaguely remember talking to him after my episode at the IU. He said there was something wrong with my blood count."

"He said you would be fine. They gave you some medication at the infirmary and returned you to your room. Don't you remember?" Blair asked.

"I'm not sure. I don't really recall making my way back here."

"The important thing is that you are feeling better, and from what I could tell, you were not having any more of those weird dreams."

"That's true," I replied. Deep inside, a feeling that something was not quite right gnawed at me.

I felt they were trying to find a medical reason for my dreams about Yohzak, but the truth was much more complex than any of us could imagine. Ever since these dreams started, my life has changed drastically—for better or worse, I still don't know. But I knew something far more significant and mysterious was at work—something connected to Yohzak and myself.

"Hey," Blair's voice brought me back from my worries. "Don't worry about it now. We have to start planning for the upcoming Gliese Dance. Do you want to find a dress tomorrow?"

The idea of the dance brought a smile to my face. "Yes, that sounds like a great distraction. Let's do it."

Our laughter filled the room, but the uneasiness still lingered in the back of my mind.

CHAPTER 9

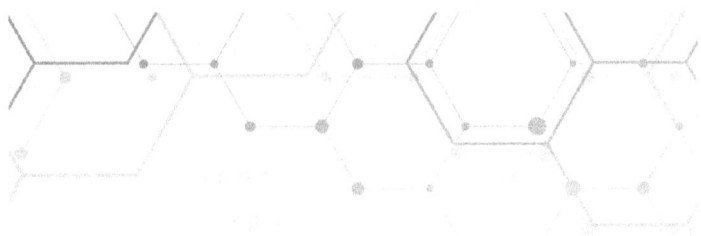

The Dance

THE GLIESE DANCE WAS one of the most anticipated events at Ryser. Blair loaned me a beautiful emerald-green dress that looked like it was made for a princess. "Isn't this outfit a little too snug around my chest?" I asked. Blair insisted on helping me get dressed so she could use all the products and accessories I didn't have. "I think you look gorgeous. If you have them, why not flaunt them? At least you're not like me having to use extra padding to compensate for lack of boobs," Blair replied, laughing.

I still wasn't sure attending this dance was a good idea. But it certainly was the best way to redeem myself after my episode at the IU. "Why didn't you let Fender take you to the dance?" Blair asked as she was working a funny-looking comb over my thick curls. "I dunno. I just didn't want to give him any ideas."

"Neo, you really need to change the way you see things. Going to a dance with a guy does not mean you are dating. Friends go together all the time. Trella is going with one of their friends."

"I just didn't want—" Blair interrupted. "You didn't want Mac to see you arriving with Fender."

I took a deep breath. She was right. A part of me didn't want Mac to see me with Fender.

"How come Mac didn't invite you to the dance?" Blair asked.

I winced and dodged the question with, "I am sure he already has someone to accompany him to the dance."

"Well, it doesn't really matter," Blair said. "Every guy in that dance will fall head-over-heels for you."

Blair turned me so I could see myself. I looked at my reflection in a full-length mirror. I had to admit I looked terrific in the emerald-green dress she'd loaned me. The intricate details of the dress and Blair's delicate touch with makeup made me look like a princess.

"That emerald-green color really accentuates your eyes," Blair said, admiring her work.

I smiled, suddenly feeling confident and excited.

Maybe this dance wouldn't be so bad after all. I heard Blair speaking to someone in a low, passionate tone. As I stepped closer, I saw the object of Blair's attention: Jasper, the guy she'd been obsessing over lately.

The two were standing close together, so close that their faces were almost touching, and suddenly kissing. For a moment, I stood transfixed, watching them, until finally, Blair broke away and called out, "Hey, Neo! Wait up! We're coming with you." She grabbed Jasper's arm, and the two walked in my direction.

Entering the grand ballroom, the celestial spectacle that unfolded before my eyes instantly mesmerized me. Shimmering tapestries adorned the vast space, woven intricately with silver and amethyst threads and billowing gently like cosmic nebulae. The polished marble floor below was illuminated by a soft, ethereal glow from the crystalline chandeliers suspended from the vaulted ceiling, twinkling like distant constellations.

I felt as if I had been transported to another world. Everything gleamed with an almost magical aura, from the elaborate furnishings to the gilded mirrors and the trinkets that lined the shelves.

The view was stunning, with every detail carefully selected and arranged to create a magnificent spectacle.

The celestial melody of a distant nebula orchestra hummed throughout the grand hall, a surreal tune that echoed across the stars themselves. I entered, my eyes drinking in the spectral beauty of the Gliese Dance. The vaulted ceiling had been converted into a full-scale holographic representation of the cosmos, stars burning brilliantly, galaxies spinning slowly in a silent ballet.

The dance floor sprawled across three dimensions, shimmering with the diffused light. Dancers soared, spun, and twirled in elegant chaos, their bodies tracing intricate constellations in the open space. The effect was like watching comets whizz around in a night sky, but the comets wore tuxedos and ballgowns.

Outfits were a sight in themselves. Some humans wore classical suits and dresses with light-refracting materials that shimmered in a thousand different hues with each movement. Others wore cultural attires harking back to their ancestral Earthly nations, while a daring few wore only the latest in adaptive nano fabric.

For aliens, the fashion was wilder. Vezorians sported flowing cloaks of bioluminescent algae. N'ymeans, like Trella, shimmered in their natural, radiant skin adorned with intricate tattoos of precious metallic ink.

Qulintars, in their ethereal semi-physical form, wore bands of concentrated light. The aquatic Aquilonids were encased in personal water-filled shields, their bioluminescent bodies glowing from within.

Bars floated around the corners, manned by bots serving drinks of exotic and familiar origins. I witnessed one serving Martian Red, a spicy concoction that mimicked Mars's iron-rich soil. Another was doling out Titan Ices, a sweet, cold drink that literally sparkled like Saturn's rings. There were strange concoctions I could barely identify, mixtures of liquids and gases served in zero-gravity containers, constantly shifting, bubbling, and fogging.

Tables hovered, laden with food, each dish an art of molecular gastronomy. I picked a levitating sphere of Ganymedian Jelly, a savory treat that burst into tangy flavors in my mouth. Near me, a group was reaching into a fizzing cloud of edible gas, their faces lighting up with joy as they tasted the cloud.

Holoscreens projected translated conversation threads throughout the hall, and the Venusian DJ spun ethereal tunes from a pulsar-powered turntable. As if the grandeur of space wasn't soundtrack enough, he layered the celestial notes with a heady mix of quantum beats and astral rhythms. A rhythmic cosmic opera that transcended language and species.

Yet, amid the grandeur and chaos, a strange silence descended on me. Around me, the universe was dancing, celebrating. And there I was, standing at the threshold, an outsider looking in. The surrounding noise dimmed, and I was alone with my thoughts. Was I a part of this dance, this universe? Or just a spectator, adrift among the stars?

But even as the question formed, I felt a pull. An invisible thread that drew me into the swirling cosmic ballet. And I knew I had a place even in this boundless sea of alien faces and nebula orchestras.

The ballroom was absolutely packed, and the music reverberated off the walls. It didn't occur to me Ryser had such a large student body, but then I realized students from other schools were also present—a feeling of relief washed over me as I scanned the room and found no sight of Mac.

"Wow, you look fantastic." Fender's voice surprised me. He stood so close I could feel the warmth of his breath on my neck. He looked sharp in his white shirt and black slacks—a departure from our drab uniforms.

Fender was a handsome Teutonian. His tall and broad-shouldered appearance caught people's attention. "Hey, you look great yourself," I said awkwardly. He took me by the hand before I could object and started heading to the dance floor. I attempted a warning. "Fender, I really don't know how to dance." Fender approached me with a warm smile.

"Ready to shine, Neo?"

"I can't help feeling a little overwhelmed. Everyone here is so talented, and I'm just... me." I replied.

He placed his hand on my arm, his eyes full of understanding. "Neo, I believe in you." You have a unique grace and spirit that shines through in your movements. Don't let self-doubt cloud your brilliance. You will be fine. I'll lead you." He wrapped an arm around my waist, and with his other hand, he showed me. "One-two, one-two. Count with me," he instructed me. I was so nervous, but he was right.

He was a superb dancer—somehow, we moved seamlessly onto the dance floor. We passed by other couples who made way for us, and it felt like we were the only two people dancing.

"How did you learn to dance like that?" I asked, not daring to lift my eyes off the floor, fearing I would lose my count or, worse, step on his foot.

"So, you think dancing is a privilege of humans only?" he asked with a laugh.

"Wait, are we waltzing? I'm pretty sure that was created on Earth in the 13th century," I pointed out.

"Has anyone ever told you that you take things way too seriously?"

"I'm sorry," I said, embarrassed. I really didn't know what to say. No guy had ever said those things to me before.

"There is no need to be sorry. You are doing fine. You look gorgeous, and I am so lucky to dance with you."

"It's just that I have never..."

The music stopped as the Dean made an announcement. I was glad to have an excuse to leave the floor and sit down. As I turned to leave, Fender's arm still around my waist, I caught Mac staring at us from the other side of the room. He was wearing a blue suit, and he'd styled his hair back. I attempted to smile, but he turned his face. By his side was the beautiful Z'hleena, wearing another regal S'borrathian gown. Her hair was down, and she wore a crown. Blair had told me she was a princess. Her father, King Fehnir, was the ruling monarch of S'borrath. I couldn't believe she had come to the Gliese Dance with Mac.

"There you are," Blair said. "Come sit with us. We got this great table with the best views of Titan."

"Have you seen Trella?" I asked as I sat as far away as possible from other tables. "Yes, they were just here," Jasper replied. "Hi, I'm Jasper. I don't think we have properly met."

"I'm Neo. Nice to meet you," I said while wiggling out of Fender's arms.

The night went on, and the food was terrific. Professor Mogh proved to be a fantastic dancer. The music was a motley of hits from all around the galaxy. They even played some old tunes from planet Earth. Everyone had such a good time. I could see why this dance was so famous.

As much as I appreciated the opportunity to spend time with my friends, seeing Mac with Z'hleena had bothered me more than I cared to admit. "I think I'm going to head over to our quarters," I said.

"Really? But we just got here." Blair protested.

"I have a little bit of a headache." I lied.

I stood up, and Fender followed me. "Let me take you to your quarters."

I did not want to hurt Fender's feelings but just wanted to be alone. Seeing Mac just brought back painful memories of Joseph. "It's okay, Fender. You should stay and enjoy yourself. I know my way back."

Fender's eyes flickered with an unmistakable hint of disappointment as I turned to leave. His broad shoulders slumped, and his usually vibrant energy seemed to wane. "Neo," he began, his voice softer, almost pleading. "Please, stay a little longer. The dance has just started, and the stars over Gliese are a sight to behold. We can stand on the observation deck and just talk. I know you have a lot going on, but maybe I can take your mind off things?"

I hesitated, torn between my urge to escape the crowded room filled with laughter and music and the genuine warmth in Fender's eyes. There was something there, something more than just friendly concern. The realization sent a curious flutter through my stomach. He reached out, his fingers lightly grazing my arm in a tentative yet oddly intimate touch. "Neo, you don't have to face everything alone. Let me be here for you, even if just for tonight."

"Fender," I whispered, meeting his eyes filled with hope and something more profound.

"I appreciate your kindness more than you know. But I need to be alone tonight. It's not about you. It's about me trying to find my balance again." I paused, searching for the right words to make him understand without hurting his feelings.

"I value our friendship and don't want to risk it by letting things become complicated."

A shadow of disappointment crossed Fender's face, but he quickly masked it with a warm smile. "I understand, Neo. Friendship is important to me too, and I don't want to push you into something you're not ready for. If you need time alone, I'll respect that."

"Thank you," I replied, feeling a strange mixture of relief and regret.

As I turned to leave, Fender gently grabbed my hand, squeezing it reassuringly. "If you ever need someone to talk to or just a friend to be there, know I'm here for you, Neo."

"I know, Fender, and thank you." With those words, I made my way out.

As I was leaving the ballroom, I noticed Mac talking with Z'hleena. As he smiled at her, he saw me staring at them. Z'hleena tucked a strand of his unruly hair behind his ear. I looked down, afraid my emotions would betray me. Then, as fast as I could, I zapped through the doors. Halfway through the corridor, I felt tears running down my face and ruining my makeup.

I opened the doors to my quarters and plopped onto my bed, relieved no one saw me crying. Argh! I hated that I always felt things so deeply. Who cares that he was there with her? He was not mine. So why did it hurt so bad? Going to this dance was a mistake.

As the painful realization settled in, I curled up, hugging my knees to my chest. The emptiness and confusion loomed large, mingling with the sting of betrayal. It was all a mess of emotions I couldn't untangle.

My eyes drifted to the window, where the distant stars shimmered, indifferent to my turmoil. Somehow, their serene twinkle calmed me, grounding me in something greater than myself.

With a deep, cleansing breath, I made a silent vow. This would be the turning point. I was stronger than this, more resilient. I had goals, dreams, and a future to fight for. I wouldn't let one dance, one boy, define me.

Slowly, I eased into sleep, the night's troubles fading into the background. Tomorrow would be a new day, a fresh start. And I was ready for it.

The room grew quiet, filled only with the soft sound of my breathing, steady and sure, as the first rays of new dawn began to creep over the horizon.

CHAPTER 10

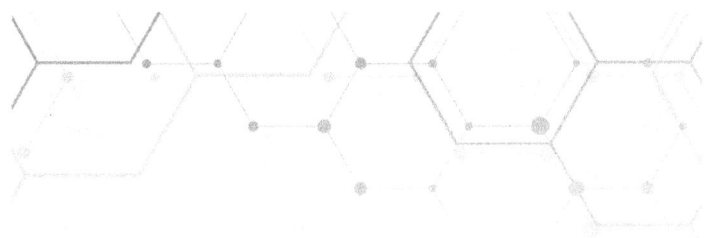

Parthenogenesis

R YSER ACADEMY WAS A hub of clever ideas and impressive technology. A unique garden, called an arboretum, was in the middle of the academy. I had been curious about this garden for weeks. I finally got the chance to explore this hidden and peaceful place after running into my friend Trella after class.

"Trella!" I exclaimed, surprised to find them just outside the Diplomacy Hall. Their bright yellow eyes met mine.

"Neo, it's good to see you. I was just heading to the arboretum to meditate before my mixed martial arts class. Would you like to join me?" Trella's invitation was warm, and my curiosity sparked.

"Of course, I'd love to join you," I said, thrilled at the prospect of learning something new.

A gentle, simulated breeze brushed against our faces as we entered the arboretum. Lush foliage towered overhead, an intricate tapestry of colors and shapes. Some were familiar, resembling plants found on Earth and Mars, while others were distinctly alien, hailing from far-off worlds. Hybrid plants from both Earth and space created the mesmerizing landscape. Soft chirping filled the air, a melodic blend that captured the essence of the arboretum.

Trella carried an allure that seemed to bridge time and space as a N'ymean from the ancient planet of N'ymea in the Andromeda galaxy. Their uniqueness, even among the diverse species at the academy, fascinated me.

"What a place," I breathed, the wonderment apparent in my voice.

Trella's lips curved into a smile, eyes reflecting understanding.

"It's beautiful, isn't it? Some of these plants remind me of the ones on N'ymea."

We settled on a bench beneath a tree resembling Earth's cherry blossoms but with luminescent blue flowers. My eyes were drawn to Trella, their calm demeanor intriguing.

"You mentioned N'ymea's vegetation?" I asked, my voice tinged with longing to understand their world.

"Yes," Trella replied, their voice soft and contemplative. Their words were mesmerizing, and I leaned closer, captivated.

"We have trees like the Velyran, with silver leaves that sing when the wind blows. And the flowers, like the U'lara, that bloom only at night, glowing with an inner fire."

"That sounds magical," I whispered, feeling a pang of longing. "And the food?"

"Ah, the food! Imagine fruits like the Zalara that taste like a blend of chocolate and berries. Or the Tharnin, a vegetable that can be cooked into anything from a savory soup to a sweet cake." Trella's eyes sparkled with a mischievous glint. Their descriptions made my mouth water, and I could almost taste the exotic flavors.

As we continued to talk, I learned about Trella's training as a warrior, a choice that seemed at odds with their gentle nature.

"But why come to Ryser for warrior training?" I asked, puzzled, my brows furrowing in confusion.

Trella's expression grew more contemplative, their usually bright eyes clouding momentarily as they searched for the right words. "N'ymeans don't choose to become warriors based on gender or social roles. It's about genetic makeup, a unique blend of attributes and qualities that guide us."

"The path of a warrior isn't like what you've seen in your human history or read in your Earth books," Trella continued. "We aren't necessarily born fierce or ferocious. Many of us are, in fact, gentle souls. But there's a complex interplay of genes that grants us enhanced reflexes, stamina, and an aptitude for strategic thinking. That's what made me eligible for this path."

My eyes widened in understanding. "So, your society doesn't force you into this role? It's more like you're genetically predisposed to excel in it?"

Trella nodded, their eyes meeting mine with a depth that made my heart stir. "Exactly. Even among N'ymeans, there's a diversity of skills and paths, each vital in its own right. But those of us who are genetically marked for the warrior path are expected to refine those attributes to serve our community better and represent our species in the Intergalactic Union."

"But why Ryser Academy? Why not train on N'ymea?" I asked, genuinely curious.

"The training on N'ymea is highly specialized and tailored to our physiology, but it can also be limiting," Trella explained. "I chose Ryser to learn diverse combat techniques, understand the intricacies of diplomacy, and gain an interstellar perspective. I believe that a true warrior should not only excel in physical abilities but also be equipped to navigate the complexities of a universe teeming with diverse life forms."

Trella's words left an indelible impression on me. They were so different from what I had always thought a warrior should be—strong, fierce, unyielding. Here was Trella, a being who could easily outmatch anyone in combat yet chose to broaden their understanding, to be gentle, and to embrace a complex, multi-faceted role in the universe. It made me wonder about the untapped complexities within myself, waiting to be discovered.

"We have no male or female sexes in N'ymea." Trella's simple statement struck me, and I blinked, trying to wrap my head around the concept.

I felt confused and fascinated as Trella explained their world's family structures and relationships. My mind whirred, emotions dancing as I envisioned a society completely free of gender constraints.

"So, you don't have males or females? How does that work with family and relationships?" I asked.

"Our relationships and family structures are more complex and fluid," Trella said, their voice gentle. "Individuals bond and form connections based on mutual respect, interests, and emotional compatibility rather than gender."

"So, how does your species reproduce?"

"Parthenogenesis. It's a type of reproduction where an organism can develop from an unfertilized egg," Trella said, simplifying the complex biological process with a gentle smile.

Trella's explanation of N'ymea's reproduction left me stunned and intrigued. I was drawn further into their world, feeling a connection, a yearning to understand more.

"Oh," I responded, processing the new information. "How do you decide when to have offspring? Astrobiology has never been my forte."

Trella chuckled, their eyes twinkling. "It's a decision made with great care and consideration in N'ymea. Our community leaders and families are involved, ensuring the timing and circumstances are right. It's not something done on a whim."

"What about family? You've mentioned 'parents' before?" I inquired, my curiosity piqued.

"Yes," Trella replied, a soft warmth in their voice. "In N'ymea, we typically have two primary caregivers. They raise their offspring together, instilling our values and traditions. Gender is not a concept in our culture, so our familial bonds are formed based on other criteria like compatibility and shared responsibilities."

"That sounds wonderful," I said, genuinely intrigued. "It must create a strong sense of community and belonging."

Trella nodded, their face reflecting pride in their heritage. "It does. Family and community are central to who we are in N'ymea. It's part of what makes our planet remarkable. It allows us to embrace and nurture each individual's unique abilities."

"How about empaths? Do you have many empaths in N'ymea?" I asked, glancing at Trella, hoping to find a shared connection between our experiences.

Trella's expression shifted subtly, their eyes momentarily distant, as if recalling a memory. "Yes, we have empaths in N'ymea," they responded thoughtfully. "Though I am not one myself, I have spent considerable time studying alongside them."

"Really?" My curiosity was piqued. "What's it like to train with empaths? What can they do?"

Trella's face lit up as they began to explain. "Empaths in N'ymea are highly respected. They can sense and understand the emotions of others, and some can even influence those emotions. Their training and development are guided by what they're best suited for, not confined by gender expectations." Their training is rigorous, focused not just on honing their abilities but also on ethical considerations and community support."

"That sounds fascinating," I said, my mind whirling with questions and possibilities. "And you've trained with them? Does that mean you know how they develop their powers?"

"In a way, yes," Trella replied, their voice steady and reassuring. "Though I'm not an empath, my warrior training included time spent understanding the minds and abilities of those who are. It helps us work together, especially during complex missions or negotiations."

I felt a strange sense of comfort in Trella's words. I found someone who could relate to my emotions and sensations.

"Empaths are not alone in their journey on N'ymea," Trella continued, sensing my interest. "They have mentors and guides who help them navigate their gifts and ensure they use them responsibly. It's a path of growth and self-discovery."

I looked at Trella, a realization dawning on me. They had seen something in me, something I was still struggling to understand myself. And though they might not share my abilities, they knew the path I might have to walk.

"Thank you, Trella," I said, my voice soft. "Your world sounds amazing, and I appreciate you sharing it with me."

Trella simply smiled, their eyes warm and knowing. "I'm here if you ever want to talk more, Neo. About anything."

As we continued our exploration of the arboretum, the conversation about N'ymea made me feel closer to Trella. They had opened a window into their world, sharing something deeply personal and profound.

"I must go, Neo. My class is about to start." They rose, and I followed, the pull of the arboretum's serenity making it hard to leave.

Before we parted, I hesitated, the urge to confide in Trella about my growing empathic powers nearly overwhelming. Trella sensed my conflict, their eyes softening.

"Whenever you're ready, Neo, I'll help you understand your gifts." Their voice was gentle but firm.

"Thank you, Trella." My voice cracked, gratitude and a newfound trust in my friend filling me.

With a smile and a wave, Trella left for their class. I headed to my own, my mind abuzz with thoughts of N'ymea, empathy, and a connection that felt as ancient and profound as the universe.

Chapter 11

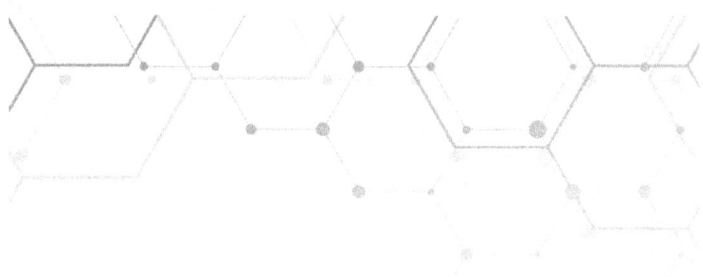

Harnessing the Gift

I stood in the hallway outside Trella's quarters. My palms were clammy. I had come to seek answers about my empathic gifts, but doubts swirled in my mind like a storm. Was I just being foolish? What if I didn't have what it took to understand my own powers? I hesitated a while and waved my hand over the holographic doorbell.

"Come in," Trella's soothing voice called from within.

Taking a deep breath, I pushed open the door and stepped inside. Their room was filled with the warm glow of candles, casting flickering shadows on the walls. A strange yet comforting scent lingered in the air—a mixture of sweet herbs and something more exotic. Trella sat cross-legged in the center of the room, their dark eyes meeting mine with a knowing gaze.

"Sit, please," they said, gesturing to the plush cushion beside them. "We have much to discuss."

As I settled down next to them, I nervously twisted a strand of red hair around my finger. "Trella, as you know, I've been having these dreams, visions even, about an alien named Yohzak. He seems to be reaching out to me, begging for help. I somehow feel connected to him but don't understand why or how."

"Yohzak," Trella murmured, Their face thoughtful. " Is he a Vihilian? I've heard whispers about his people among the other students. There are rumors that his people are in grave danger, though no one knows the details." They paused, studying me intently. "You say he's been contacting you through your dreams?"

I nodded, biting my lip. "Yes, and it feels real. Like he's right there with me. But when I wake up, I can't remember the specifics. It's like trying to grasp smoke."

"Empathic powers can manifest in many ways, Neo," Trella explained softly. "Sometimes they allow us to sense the emotions of others, and sometimes they enable us to communicate with beings across vast distances. It's possible that Yohzak has sensed your gift and is trying to contact you for help."

A wave of hope surged through me at their words. Could it be true? Was I really capable of helping someone like Yohzak? But then another thought surfaced, causing my stomach to twist with uncertainty. "But if that's the case," I whispered, "why can't I fully understand what he's telling me?"

"Your mind is still learning to process these visions, Neo," Trella said gently. "It will take time and practice to fully understand and harness your abilities."

"Will you help me?" The question tumbled from my lips before I could think better of it. But as I looked into Trella's eyes, I knew they were the only ones who could guide me on this journey.

"Of course, Neo," they replied, their voice warm and reassuring.

Trella's quarters had the soft glow of the holographic star charts casting an ethereal light on their face. They leaned in closer, and I could see the intensity in their eyes as they began to speak about Yohzak.

"Yohzak's people, the Vihilians, have been struggling for centuries," Trella explained.

I listened intently, my heart aching for the Vihilian species and their desperate plight. A familiar wave of insecurity washed over me as I wondered if I was truly capable of helping them. But as I looked at Trella, I saw knowledge, conviction, and strength, which filled me with a sense of security.

"Yohzak might still believe his people can be saved," Trella continued. "He's seeking help from those who possess unique gifts––like yours, Neo."

"Me?" I whispered, almost disbelieving. My chest tightened as self-doubt threatened to consume me. "But how can I possibly make a difference? There are other empaths in the universe. Why me?"

"Neo, your empathic abilities are far more powerful than you realize," Trella said, their gaze steady and unwavering. "Far more powerful than any other empath I've ever known. "You have the potential to connect with other beings on a level most can only dream of."

As Trella spoke, I could feel the weight of responsibility settling on my shoulders. It was both terrifying and exhilarating, but deep down, I knew they were right. If I could learn to harness my abilities, I could play a role in something bigger than myself.

"Will you teach me, Trella?" I asked. "I want to learn how to use my empathic powers to help others, like Yohzak and his people."

Trella smiled softly, their eyes filled with warmth and pride. "It would be an honor, Neo."

As Trella began outlining our training plan. The scent of burning incense filled my nostrils, and the light in the room cast shadows that danced across the walls adorned with intricate N'ymean tapestries.

"I will prepare a small ritual to mark the beginning of our journey together. It is an ancient N'ymean tradition for new mentors and apprentices."

"Thank you, Trella," I replied. Excitement coursed through my veins, unsure of what to expect from our first lesson.

"Close your eyes and take a deep breath," Trella instructed, their voice steady and calming. I obeyed, feeling the air filling my lungs and slowly releasing it.

"Good," they continued. "Now, focus on the energy within you—the empathic power that connects you to others. Feel it growing stronger, like a current flowing through your body."

As I concentrated on the sensation, I felt a warmth radiating from within, pulsing in time with my heartbeat. It was a comforting feeling as if I were embracing something dormant inside me all along.

"Excellent," Trella said, noticing my progress. "Now, open your eyes."

The room seemed to be bathed in a soft, ethereal glow. I glanced down at my hands, surprised to find them enveloped in shimmering light.

"Your empathic abilities are growing stronger already," Trella explained, their eyes twinkling with pride. "But this is just the beginning, Neo. There is much more to learn and master."

"Like what?" I asked, eager to delve deeper into my newfound powers.

"First, you must learn to control your empathy," Trella began, outlining our action plan. "You will need to be able to focus your energy on specific individuals or groups rather than being engulfed by the emotions of everyone around you."

"Next, we will strengthen your connection with others," they continued. "By deepening your understanding of their feelings and emotions, you'll be able to foster a greater sense of unity and compassion between different species.

"Are you ready to begin, Neo?" Trella asked, their eyes searching mine for confirmation.

"I am," I replied, my voice steady and resolute.

"Close your eyes, Neo," Trella instructed gently. I obeyed, taking a deep breath as I tried to focus my thoughts.

"Good," they continued. "Now, imagine a single candle flickering in the darkness. Can you see it?"

I nodded, concentrating on the image in my mind. The flame danced and wavered, casting its warm glow against the shadows.

"Focus on that flame," Trella said, their voice low and steady. "Feel the heat radiating from it, drawing you closer."

Concentrating on the flame, I became aware of a distant presence–a slow and steady heartbeat. It was faint initially but grew stronger as I homed in on it.

"Excellent," Trella said, praising my progress. "You're connecting with someone's emotions. What do you feel?"

"Sadness," I whispered as the heavy weight of sorrow pressed down on me. "They're grieving... it's so heavy."

"Try to go deeper," Trella urged. "Find the source of their grief and see if you can help them find solace."

I hesitated momentarily, unsure if I could handle such a potent emotion. But with Trella's guidance, I pushed forward, reaching out to the person in pain. As our connection deepened, I sensed their memories—a mother's embrace a father's laughter, all tinged with the bitter sting of loss.

"Can you offer them comfort?" Trella asked softly, their words a lifeline in the turbulent sea of emotions.

"I-I think so," I stammered, slowly extending my empathy toward the grieving individual. I offered them understanding, compassion, and a shared sense of loss, hoping to ease their burden.

"Excellent, Neo," Trella said, as I felt the person's sorrow gradually recede, replaced by a sense of peace and gratitude. "You're learning to harness your empathic abilities for the betterment of others."

As we broke the connection, I opened my eyes, exhausted and exhilarated. It was like I had unlocked a hidden part of myself with immense power and potential.

"Remember, Neo," Trella said, "your gift is about understanding others' emotions and helping them heal and find balance. This is your true purpose in this world—to be a bridge between different species and cultures, fostering unity and compassion."

I nodded, taking her words to heart. Under Trella's mentorship, my understanding of my role in the world expanded, revealing new possibilities and responsibilities. And with each step forward, I was becoming more than I ever imagined possible––an empathic diplo-mat, a force for change, and a beacon of hope in the darkness.

"Thank you, Trella. I'm ready to face whatever comes next."

As I stepped out into the bustling streets of Titan Central, the faint aroma of nitrogen-rich soil met my nose. The terraforming had made the atmosphere breathable but with a unique scent. My heart had been beating fast, syncing with the lively energy of the city, filled with sounds and colors that both excited and amazed me. Perched under an enormous dome near Saturn's scattered rings, Titan City offered a stunning outline against the sky filled with stars. Bright trails of bio-luminescent lights crisscrossed the city, their glow seeming to move and bend. The buildings, looking like giant icicles, extended from Titan's cold ground and had special solar cells on their surfaces. These cells turned light from distant planets into energy we could use.

Trella walked beside me, their graceful stride never faltering amidst the chaos.

"Remember to stay focused, Neo," they cautioned, their voice soothing yet firm. "The key to navigating this city is being able to separate the essentials from the distractions."

I nodded, trying to steady my breathing and center myself. It was easier said than done, especially when every new sight, sound, and smell seemed to call for my attention.

I saw a Maglev train engineered for Titan's thick yet breathable atmosphere. It was designed with a combination of aerodynamic fea-tures and ion thrusters, enabling it to move efficiently while compen-sating for Titan's unique atmospheric conditions.

The buildings didn't rely on solar cells due to Titan's distance from the Sun. Instead, they were covered with advanced thermo-electric panels that utilized the abundant geothermal energy from Titan's core. These panels had the added capability of drawing power from cosmic radiation, a gift from the galaxy itself.

Bio-luminescent orbs floated gently around Titan City's walkways, illuminating the paths for pedestrians. A small info panel next to one of these orbs explained that they were powered by microbial fuel cells. Genetically engineered microorganisms within the orbs process organic matter from the air, converting it into electricity to keep the lights glowing.

We hadn't been walking long when we encountered our first obstacle: a crowd gathered around a heated debate between two merchants. The emotions swirling around me were a cacophony of anger, frustration, and indignation. My head began to pound, each beat resonating like a drum inside my skull. It was as if a storm was brewing behind my eyes, clouds of pressure gathering and unleashing torrents of pain that cascaded down my neck. I clenched my teeth, feeling the muscles in my jaw tighten, a vain attempt to ward off the relentless ache. Sweat formed at my temples, cool yet burning as it trickled down my face. Thoughts swirled, crashing into each other and becoming confused and anxious. I tried to block the barrage of feelings threatening to smother me.

"Focus, Neo," Trella whispered, touching my shoulder. "You cannot help them if you lose yourself in their emotions."

I concentrated on grounding myself, feeling the solid pavement beneath my feet. With Trella's guidance, I dampened the empathic onslaught enough to think clearly.

"Excuse me," I called out hesitantly, stepping forward. Both merchants turned to face me, their expressions wary but curious. "Perhaps I can help resolve your dispute?"

To my surprise, they agreed to let me try. Drawing on everything I had learned under Trella's mentorship, I listened carefully to each party and offered suggestions for compromise. As I spoke, I felt the tension in their emotions begin to ease, replaced by cautious optimism.

"Thank you," one merchant said with a nod. "We couldn't have reached an agreement without your help."

"See, Neo?" Trella murmured as we continued our way. "You are already making a difference."

I adjusted my gravitational control tech belt, which helped me adapt to Titan's lower gravity. A small screen on the belt displayed its current energy level, powered by miniaturized fusion cells. These cells made it possible to simulate a gravity close to Earth's, making movement far more comfortable.

As we walked through the busy streets of Titan Central, I encountered many conflicts and obstacles, each bringing new lessons and growth. There was the young child who had lost her mother in the crowd, her fear and panic threatening to engulf me until Trella reminded me to ground myself and use my abilities to help reunite them. There were bustling markets where I honed my diplomatic skills, negotiating deals and resolving disputes between merchants and customers.

In the heart of the metropolis, a monolithic structure reached skyward. It was a quantum reactor built with advanced alien technology. According to public records, this reactor leveraged the concept of quantum vacuum fluctuations, converting them into a sustainable power source for the entire city.

We walked awhile and decided to enter an establishment for some much-needed teatime. All those exercises were wearing me out.

"Always remember, your empathy is a powerful tool for change. But it is also a responsibility that requires constant vigilance and self-awareness," Trella reminded me.

As I faced each new challenge, I grew stronger and more adept at harnessing my empathic abilities for the greater good. And with every step forward, I knew I had Trella's unwavering support and guidance to light my way. Trella smiled, their eyes crinkling around the edges. "It has been an honor to help you discover your true potential, Neo. But there is still so much more for you to learn."

As I sipped tea, I reflected on our challenges together, each reshaping my perspective. I now saw my empathic abilities as a strength rather than a burden. Trella's guidance taught me how to harness and use them for good.

"Trust your instincts, Neo," Trella said, sensing my thoughts. "You are capable of great things."

"What should we focus on next?" I asked.

"Your training is far from over," they said, setting down their cup. "There are still many people out there who need our help. It's time we took our mission beyond the walls of Ryser Academy."

CHAPTER 12

A Test of
Endurance

THE DAMP AIR CLUNG to my skin as I stepped into the training
facility on Titan. A faint scent of rust and sweat filled the
vast room, with rows of advanced machines scattered around like
soldiers waiting for orders. Taking advantage of our academic break,
my N'ymean trainer Trella insisted we undergo rigorous physical and

mental training to prepare for our mission to save Yohzak. The gravity here was lower than Mars, but it was nothing compared to what we'd face later.

"Neo, let's start with a warm-up," Trella said. They gestured to a row of treadmills nearby. "Five kilometers should do."

"Five?" My legs already felt like jelly, but I forced a smile and nodded. "Sure, why not?"

Trella glided beside me as I stumbled onto the treadmill, their body moving gracefully and precisely. The machine hummed beneath my feet as it started, and I gripped the handlebars tightly, focusing on putting one foot in front of the other.

"Remember to breathe, Neo," Trella reminded me gently as we picked up speed. I could hear their steady breaths beside me, like a rhythm I couldn't quite match. My lungs burned as I tried to keep up, my heart pounding relentlessly in my chest.

This isn't just about me, I reminded myself. I'm doing this for Yohzak. With that thought, I pushed harder, my legs churning with newfound determination. Sweat poured down my face, but I refused to slow down, even as my vision blurred and my muscles screamed in protest.

"Come on, Neo!" Trella encouraged me, barely breaking a sweat herself. I nodded, gritting my teeth and willing my body to keep going.

"Almost there," I panted, my words barely audible over the whirring of the treadmill. I slammed my hand down on the stop button, and the machine slowed to a halt.

"Great job," Trella said, their eyes gleaming with pride. "Now, let's move on to some strength training."

"Strength training?" My legs were unsteady beneath me as I stepped off the treadmill, but I couldn't let my fear show. I had to be strong.

"Trust me, Neo. We'll need every ounce of strength we can muster," Trella said solemnly. I took a deep breath, trying to steady myself as we approached the weight machines.

"All right," I said, determination swelling inside me. "Let's do this."

"All right, Neo. Let's step it up a notch," Trella said firmly, their voice slicing through the steady hum of the training facility. I could feel my muscles quivering at the thought of more intense exercises, but I refused to back down.

"Bring it on," I replied, clenching my fists in determination.

"Good. We'll start with some dynamic movements," Trella instructed, leading me to a large, open area filled with padded mats. "These drills will help you improve your agility and reflexes."

"Sounds... fun," I muttered sarcastically, wiping the sweat from my brow. Trella smirked, but there was a glint of seriousness in their eyes as they began showing the first movement—a complex series of jumps, rolls, and dodges that left me breathless just watching them.

"Your turn," they said, stepping aside.

"Okay, here goes nothing," I whispered, taking a deep breath before launching myself into the drill.

My limbs felt heavy and uncoordinated, but I pushed through the discomfort, focusing on each movement until they came together like a well-rehearsed dance.

"Better, Neo. Now let's work on your mental strength," Trella announced after we had completed several rounds of the drills. They guided me to a quiet corner of the facility.

"Sit down, close your eyes, and focus on your breathing," they instructed, their melodic voice calming me. I did as they said, drawing in slow, steady breaths as I tried to clear my mind.

"Now," Trella continued, "visualize yourself facing a tough challenge during our mission. See it in your mind's eye and imagine yourself overcoming it with confidence and ease."

I pictured a dark, narrow tunnel filled with hazards and traps. My heart raced as I saw myself navigating through the treacherous environment, using my newfound skills to avoid danger and protect Yohzak. It was terrifying but also exhilarating.

"Good, Neo," Trella whispered, sensing my progress. "Now, focus on your emotions as you conquer this challenge. Let them fill you with strength and determination."

"Finally, let's incorporate some meditation into our training," Trella said gently, their voice barely audible above my steady breathing. "Find your center, Neo. Focus on the calm within the storm."

I let my thoughts drift away, replaced by a comforting stillness that seemed to radiate from the core of my being. I could feel the fatigue in my muscles melting away, replaced by renewed energy and resilience.

"Excellent work, Neo," Trella said, their voice full of warmth and admiration. "You're making significant progress, both physically and mentally. Keep pushing yourself. There's no limit to what you can achieve."

Mac and Blair joined Trella and me for our evening session. Their arrival filled me with excitement—I was eager to share our progress and nervous to see Mac again. I had avoided him since the Gliese Dance when he showed up with Senator Z'hleena.

"Hey, Neo!" Mac called out, his eyes sparkling with enthusiasm. "It seems like ages since the last time we've spoken. I've barely seen you. I seem to never catch you in the students' lounge or in the cafeteria."

"Hi, Mac," I replied, trying to sound confident. Ah, yeah. Long time no see. School and training with Trella have kept me incredibly busy. I can barely manage homework, let alone make time for socializing. I've been keeping to myself. Having my meals in my room.

"Ready to get started?" My voice wavered slightly.

"Absolutely," he said, flashing me a determined smile. "We've got a lot of work to do if we're going to save Yohzak."

"Hello, Neo!" Blair chimed in, her bubbly personality contrasting with the grueling exercises ahead. As an aspiring engineer, she possessed a brilliant mind and unmatched resourcefulness. However, maintaining focus and motivation during the harsh training would test her limits.

"Hi, Blair." I greeted her. "I'm glad you're here."

"Me too," she agreed. "Let's do this!"

Trella's eyes swept over each of us. Their gaze was as calm and assessing as a breeze on a crisp morning. "All right, everyone. Prepare yourselves. This training will demand more from you than you think you can give. We'll utilize the latest neural-response technology to simulate real-world physical and mental conditions. But remember, we're all in this together."

Mac and Blair exchanged glances, their faces a complex dance of excitement and uncertainty. The unspoken challenge hung in the air, a shared determination to prove themselves.

"Warm-up time," Trella said, their voice crisp as they guided us to the biomechanical stretch platforms. These platforms were designed to analyze our muscle elasticity and adjust the resistance accordingly. Mac's body twisted and strained, sweat beading on his forehead, every muscle defined by effort. Blair, on the other hand, wobbled, her eyes darting as if looking for an escape route from her own uncertainty.

Focus, Blair. You can do this, I thought, hoping my silent encouragement reached her through the empathic link we were developing.

The warm-up was just a prelude. Trella's next series of drills were relentless, pushing us to sprint, crawl, and climb in a virtual environment that mimicked the gravitational pull of different planets. Our bodies protested, but Mac and Blair's determination outshone the pain etched on their faces.

"Come on, you two!" I yelled, my voice cracking. "We've got this!"

"Right behind you, Neo!" Mac's reply was a ragged breath, but his eyes were fierce.

"Almost there!" Blair's voice was firm, her resolve unbreakable.

We completed the last challenge, collapsing in a heap, our bodies slick with sweat and exhaustion. My friends embraced their weaknesses and turned them into strengths. They had proven that they were willing to push themselves to their very limits for the sake of our mission, utilizing the cutting-edge technology that Ryser Academy had provided.

"Excellent work, everyone," Trella said. "Remember, it's not about being perfect––it's about pushing ourselves to become better, stronger, and more resilient."

At that moment, I knew we were ready to face challenges. Mac, Blair, Trella, and I were a team united by our dedication to saving Yohzak and driven by the knowledge that we all had something to prove–to ourselves and each other.

Chapter 13

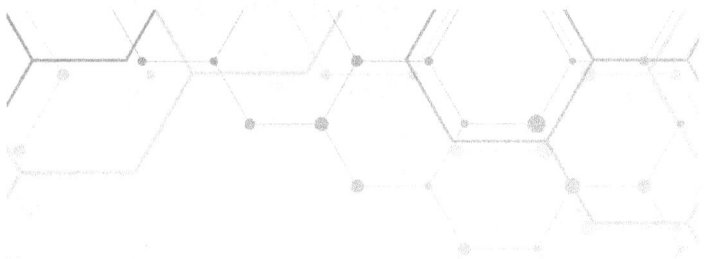

Bonds and Battles

THE FOLLOWING TRAINING DAY, we gathered on the open field. Trella stood before us, their eyes scanning our faces for signs of doubt or fear. They nodded approvingly as they noted our resolve.

"Today, we'll be working on teamwork and communication exercises," Trella began, their voice firm and encouraging. "These drills will test your ability to work together under pressure and adapt to unforeseen situations."

We started with an obstacle course designed to encourage cooperation and trust. The obstacle course was constructed with adaptive materials that could change shape, hardness, and even temperature, responding to the user's performance and the instructors' settings. For instance, walls could become steeper and more slippery, ropes could vibrate or swing more vigorously, and floors could tilt or shift. Nano-coatings on the surfaces could alter textures at will. The entire course was modular and programmable, capable of reconfiguring itself to create endless variations.

Mac hoisted Blair and me up the tall wall, its surface altering from rough to slippery as we climbed, challenging our grip. The swinging ropes were a dance of chaos, vibrating and changing angles, forcing Trella to make precise, calculated leaps. We could hear the faint hum of the underlying machinery, reshaping the course as we progressed, never allowing us a moment of predictability.

"Great job, Mac!" I shouted as he scaled a net with lightning speed.

"Thanks, Neo! You're doing amazing, too!" he replied, flashing a grin that sent warmth through my chest.

Next, we moved on to team-building exercises that required us to strategize and communicate effectively. In one tense simulation, we were trapped in a container rapidly filling with water. I felt panic clawing at the edges of my mind, but Blair's calm demeanor and quick thinking helped us find a solution.

The simulation of a water-filled container used complex hydrodynamics that depended on valves, pumps, and computer-driven barriers to let water in from secret reservoirs at different speeds and patterns.

The water could be infused with bioluminescent particles, allowing the trainers to visualize the flow. The container's walls were lined with pressure-sensitive panels that responded to touch, aiding in creating escape routes or additional challenges. Even the water's temperature could be controlled to simulate different environmental conditions.

In the tense simulation, the container filled with water rapidly, the hidden pumps working in overdrive. The liquid was alive with bioluminescent particles, creating a surreal glow as it surged toward us. Blair's instructions were precise, guiding us to a heavy pipe that, when lifted, would activate pressure-sensitive panels, forming an escape route.

The chill of the water, carefully controlled to mimic arctic conditions, added another layer of urgency as we scrambled to survive.

"Neo, you and Mac need to lift that heavy pipe over there to create an opening," Blair instructed, her voice steady despite the mounting pressure. "Trella and I will hold back the water as much as possible."

"Got it," I replied, nodding at Mac. We focused our combined strength on the task, the muscles in our arms straining as we lifted the pipe.

Afterward, we practiced combat simulations against holographic opponents. Trella's expertise in martial arts was priceless in guiding us and showing techniques to improve. I could feel my skills growing with each passing moment, the thrill of progress invigorating me.

"Remember, Neo," Trella advised as we sparred, "stay focused and trust in your instincts."

As we trained, our camaraderie blossomed into genuine friendship. We shared stories from our pasts, revealing vulnerabilities that only strengthened our bond. Mac spoke about his pressure to live up to his father's reputation. Blair told a story about fixing an engine herself during a school competition.

As the sky transitioned into twilight's embrace, painting the sky in shades of pink and orange, we stood together on the field, exhausted but exhilarated.

"Look how far we've come," I murmured, gazing at my friends with gratitude and affection. "We couldn't have done it without each other."

"Absolutely," Mac agreed. Our strong bond gave us hope for the next phase of our mission, leading us to a future of success.

The holographic opponents blended cutting-edge light projection and artificial intelligence in the advanced training facility. These opponents were created through a network of micro projectors arranged in a matrix that emits beams of light manipulated by magnetic fields. They weren't just visual simulations; they provided tactile feedback using force fields, allowing trainees to feel the blows they land or block. The AI could learn and mimic famous warriors' fighting styles or adapt to the trainee's technique, making each fight challenging.

As I sparred with the holographic opponent, it countered my moves with the finesse of a master fighter. Its form, rendered in sharp detail by the surrounding micro projectors, adapted to my style, shifting tactics as though it were learning from me. When I landed a punch, the magnetic fields manipulated the light, providing a realistic resistance against my fist. It was like fighting a ghost with substance. Every blow was a lesson.

"All right, team," Trella said, "Today we focus on overcoming our fears and self-doubt. We'll engage in simulated scenarios that will push us to confront these emotions head-on."

I swallowed hard, feeling the familiar flutter of anxiety in my chest.

"Remember," they continued, "the key is to support each other and stay focused on our mission. Saving Yohzak depends on our ability to face whatever's thrown at us."

As we began the simulation, I found myself in a dark, narrow tunnel, an ominous rumbling echoing through the confined space. My claustrophobia kicked in immediately, but Mac's voice crackled through my earpiece, offering encouragement.

"Neo, you've got this. Just take slow, deep breaths and visualize the end of the tunnel."

His words grounded me, and I closed my eyes, picturing the light at the end of the tunnel. Gradually, my panic subsided, replaced by determination.

In another scenario, Blair faced her fear of heights as she clung to a ledge, her knuckles white from the strain. Her breathing was shallow, her eyes wide with terror.

"Blair, listen to me," I called out. "Focus on your strength––on what you've achieved so far. You can do this!"

Blair's grip on the ledge slowly steadied, and she climbed upward.

The blistering, hyperreal skirmishes they had thrown us into during the combat trials were like nothing I'd ever imagined. The high-tech machines tried to dissect us precisely, exploiting cracks in our suits.

These trials were set to examine our real and imagined vulnerabilities, pushing us right over the edge of our comfort zones.

As the days passed, our training grew more intense, simulating the specific challenges we would face during our mission to save Yohzak. We practiced coordinating our efforts, honing our individual skills, and trusting our instincts.

As I stood on the training ground, my muscles ached from the constant exertion. Still, it was a satisfying ache that reminded me how far we had come. Trella's nimble form spun gracefully through the air, their leaps and bounds improving with each passing day, making them an even more formidable warrior.

CHAPTER 14

Dreams Unravel

I JOLTED AWAKE, SWEAT pooling around my neck, the searing images of my dream refusing to fade. My heart thumped loudly. Each beat was a hammering reminder of the agony I had witnessed. The nightmare had been more vivid than ever before. The suffering of the enslaved Vihilians on Luehiri was etched into my mind's eye.

I stood amongst them in my dream, a silent observer of their torment. The Vihilians were hunched over, their frail forms twisted in unnatural positions as they dug deep into the earth. Their limbs were fatigued, but they labored on mining and drilling for the mysterious crystal. The oppressive weight of their sorrow was a tangible thing. This heavy and suffocating shadow hung over the dingy cavern, a mournful lament for lost freedom.

Their gaunt faces, etched with exhaustion, were turned away from one another. Dark circles shadowed their hollow eyes, their mouths set in lines of grim determination. None dared to complain or slow their pace. Blood oozed from their raw fingers, staining the shimmering crystals a sickly crimson. The smell of sweat and fear permeated the air, mingling with the sharp tang of the unearthed minerals. My senses reeled from the horror of it, each detail a searing memory I could never forget.

I could feel their despair wash over me like a tidal wave, consuming every shred of hope and leaving me drowning in their pain. The echo of shackles and the crack of whips resounded in the cave, their oppressors hidden in shadows, yet their presence was a constant, looming threat. Two ominous figures in cloaks watched the Vihilians with calculating eyes. The symbols on their vestments were eerily familiar. The glimpse of them sent a chill down my spine, foreshadowing a greater evil at play, something far beyond the torment of the enslaved beings.

"Neo?" Blair's voice, soft and concerned, pulled me from the chilling reverie, her face peering at me through the dim light of our dormitory. Her eyes widened as she took in my pale face. The sweat-soaked sheets twisted around my body.

"Blair," I whispered, my voice trembling with urgency. "It's the Vihilians. They're suffering so much, and there's something else. Something darker. We have to tell the others." Her face tightened with determination, and she reached for her Xoria device. This sleek and unobtrusive gadget connected us across vast distances of space. She accessed a secure channel to contact Mac and Trella.

We met in the arboretum, a place usually filled with life and beauty, but that day, it was overshadowed by the urgency of our meeting.

"Tell us what you saw," Mac urged, his eyes filled with determination. Trella and Blair were seated nearby, their expressions mirroring Mac's resolve.

I recounted the horrors of my vision, detailing the suffering of the Vihilians and the urgency I felt. Their faces hardened with anger and sympathy. We shared a moment of heavy silence when I finished, each lost in our thoughts.

"We must act," Trella said finally, breaking the silence. "But how do we reach Luehiri?"

Mac looked thoughtful. "It's not going to be easy. We need someone with connections."

Trella's eyes widened, an idea forming. "Fender. He could help us. He has the resources we need."

My heart skipped a beat at the mention of Fender's name. Memories of his lingering glances and soft smiles filled my mind, but then my eyes met Mac's, and something else stirred within me.

"Fender?" I asked, my voice betraying my doubt. "Are we sure about involving him?"

Trella met my gaze, understanding in their eyes, but their decision was firm. "He's our best chance, Neo. We don't have the luxury of time."

I looked to Mac and Blair for support, but they seemed to agree with Trella. My personal feelings had to be set aside.

With a resigned sigh, I nodded. "Alright. We'll talk to Fender. We need to do this for the Vihilians."

"There is something else," I said. "In my dream, the two Vihilians in charge wore cloaks with symbols that looked like the S'borrathian language, but I'm not entirely sure."

Trella's face seemed to come alive. "I've heard rumors about the S'borrathians' past dealings—shady negotiations and coercion. But enslaving an entire species is beyond the pale. Even for King Fehnir."

"Have the S'borrathians ever crossed paths with you before?" Blair asked.

"Only once," Trella replied. "They tried to convince my people to join them in some political scheme. We refused. They didn't take it well."

"Whoever they are and whatever their motives, we must act now," I declared. "We have to save the Vihilians from their grasp."

"First, we need to collect intel on Luehiri," I said, rubbing the back of my neck as if trying to ease a burden. "We'll need to know everything we can before we leave Titan."

"I can work on that," Mac said. "First, we need a ship to get us out of here. With my piloting experience, we should be able to develop a solid plan."

"Good," I said with a nod. "Trella, if Fender agrees to help us, you two will be our fighters. We need to be ready for anything once we're inside."

"Understood," Trella replied as they reached for the hilt of their Ax.

"Neo, you'll be our leader," Mac said. "Your empathic abilities give us an edge in understanding the Vihilians and, potentially, their oppressors."

Chapter 15

The Gathering

Under the streetlight, the Teutonian warrior's white hair shone like ice, starkly contrasting his azure skin covered in intricate white markings. Fender Xias stood tall and robust, his green eyes assessing the surroundings as he scanned over my friends and me.

"Thanks for meeting us here," I said. The weight of the mission felt heavy on my chest. "We need your help."

"Neo, I'm always happy to see you. But what's this all about?" Fender asked. His deep voice resonated.

I noticed that Fender was not alone—a human stood beside him. Fender quickly introduced us to his friend. "This is Suzuki. He's here to help me get the ship."

Suzuki Santiago leaned against the wall, his black eyes bright with curiosity and a mischievous grin. With spiky black hair and an outfit that seemed straight out of an Anime, he exuded an air of youthful excitement, as if always on the brink of a new adventure. His reputation as a thrill-seeker from Karmar was well-known on Titan.

"Yohzak, a Vihilian, has been reaching out to me through dreams," I began, pausing to take a deep breath. "He's begging for our help. His people are in danger, and we believe we can rescue them."

"How do we know we can trust your friend, Fender?" asked Blair.

"You can't, but if you think you can find someone else, go ahead." Suzuki barked at Blair.

"Easy, guys," Trella said. "This is actually a fair question. We can't afford to be arguing right now."

"I've known Suzuki for a long time. His family owns one of the best restaurants on Proxima Centauri B. Also, Suzuki is not a student here at Ryser. He knows his way around the hangars, so it will be easier to blend in with any other mechanic and help us secure a ship." Fender said.

"Sounds exciting," Suzuki chimed in.

"Before you get too excited," Blair said, her eyes flicking between me, Fender, and Suzuki, "we should let you know what we're up against. There's a good chance the S'borrathians are involved, and we could face serious opposition."

Fender's eyes narrowed, and Suzuki's grin faltered for a moment. The room's energy shifted, and I felt the tension thicken.

"We need your skills," Mac added, his voice full of resolve. "Fender, your strength, and warrior training will be invaluable. Suzuki, your fearlessness and experience are crucial."

"Look," Trella said, leaning forward, "we know this is asking a lot. But we believe, together, we can rescue the Vihilians. We need you both on our team."

Their faces said it all: uncertainty, hesitation, the internal struggle between risk and desire.

"Please," I whispered, my voice carrying the weight of our need. "We can't do this without you."

Fender glanced at Suzuki, his voice low and hesitant. "Joining you on this mission is risky. My people prize self-reliance, but I don't want to jeopardize my chances of graduating."

Suzuki shifted uneasily in his chair, his short, spiky hair seeming to bristle. "I love a good adventure, but even I have limits. What if we're just walking into a trap?"

A cold grip tightened around my heart. "Listen," I began, forcing steadiness into my voice. "We're not going into this blind. We have each other's backs. We'll minimize the risks."

"Fender, you won't be alone; we'll face whatever comes our way as a team," Mac assured him.

"Suzuki," I said, "this might be our only chance to save the Vihilians. If we don't act now, we may lose them forever."

Trella placed a reassuring hand on Fender's arm. "We're stronger together than apart."

A storm of emotions swirled within me. I knew they needed more than words; they needed my conviction and confidence. "I truly believe we can succeed. We must try or never know if we could have made a difference." The silence hung heavy, thick with tension and anticipation.

Finally, Fender said steadily, "We'll join you."

"Count me in, too," Suzuki added. Relief washed over me.

"Thank you," I whispered, feeling the strength of our united front. "Now, let's discuss our plan of action."

Mac pulled up a holographic map, and Blair, Trella, Fender, and Suzuki contributed ideas, each adding layers to our plan. We were a united front, each piece moving harmoniously with the others.

"Neo, you'll need this," Mac said, tossing me a sleek black communication module. "It's got an encrypted channel so we can stay connected."

I smiled at his confidence. "Nice work, Suzuki, on securing the Nova Voyager. It will get us out of Titan, but we must switch ships before heading to Luehiri."

"All right, everyone knows their role. Stay sharp, focused, and trust in each other," I commanded, letting the weight of my words sink in.

"Let's do this," Fender growled.

At Ryser, we focused on individual tasks, preparing for the mission by evaluating the Nova Voyager's adaptability, advanced plasma thrusters, and innovative suspension system. We inspected weapons, assembled detailed maps, and gathered crucial intel.

"Hey, guys!" Suzuki announced. "The Nova Voyager is more advanced than your conventional spacecraft because of its speed. The only thing I don't like about it is that it doesn't have stealth capabilities."

"Nice! It looks like you really did your homework, Suzuki," Trella noted.

"Everyone, gather up!" I called. "Our success depends on our ability to work together and adapt to challenges. We leave at dawn."

As we made final preparations, I felt a new sense of unity. Despite our diverse backgrounds and fears, we aimed to save the innocent

Vihilians. In that shared purpose, I found something I hadn't realized I'd been searching for—a sense of belonging.

Chapter 16

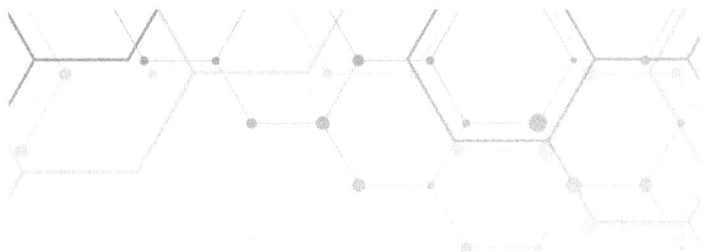

Leaving Titan

T HE ROOM WAS FILLED with the faint scent of exotic plants from Trella's home planet. Trella's quarters acted as a sanctuary where we could gather without the prying eyes of teachers, Venusian prefects, and security cameras.

I looked around at the faces of my friends. Each one was filled with determination and fear. Blair nervously tapped her fingers on the table, her eyes darting between us. Fender was leaning against the wall.

His arms crossed, a thoughtful expression on his face. Mac and Suzuki were huddled together, whispering about the technical details of our plan. And Trella, their eyes calm and focused, was standing at the head of the table, ready to lead us into the unknown.

"We all know why we're here," Trella began, their voice steady and reassuring. "We have a mission, and it won't be easy. But we have to do this. We must steal Ryser's Nova Voyager ship to get us out of Titan.

"How are we going to do this?" Blair finally asked, her voice trembling. "How are we going to get past security, get to the hangars, and actually steal a ship?"

"That's what we're here to figure out," Fender said, pushing off the wall and joining us at the table. "We have a plan, but we need to go over every detail to make sure we're all on the same page."

"We have that covered," Suzuki said, a mischievous grin on his face. "I've found a way to temporarily disable the security cameras in the hangars. It won't give us much time, but it should be enough."

Trella activated Xoria, and a detailed map of Ryser Academy appeared, showing the layout of the hangars, security checkpoints, and potential escape routes.

"How are we all going to get out of here?" Blair asked, her eyes wide with anticipation.

"Mac, Suzuki, and I will head to the farthest west hangar, where they keep the newer ships used for test flights. You need to figure out a way of being close by without calling too much attention. We'll signal when it's time for you to come to the hangar." Fender explained, his voice steady and confident.

"We are not pilots, Fender. We have no clearance. How are we actually going to get inside the hangar?" Blair asked, her voice tinged with doubt.

"I will let you guys in," Suzuki said, his eyes gleaming excitedly. "Fender, Mac, let's go."

Suzuki turned to us and instructed, "You get out of here. Find a place to hang around without calling too much attention to yourselves. You probably shouldn't be too close together. Wait for our signal and come to the hangar."

"We'll be at the arboretum," Trella said, their voice calm and assured.

Fender gave me a reassuring wink, re-arranged something on his leg, which I assumed to be some sort of energy weapon, and the three were out the door before I could say anything.

"I'll head to the Arboretum first to ensure the coast is clear. Count to thirty and come out," Trella said. "Blair, let Neo come out first and give it space between you. You will wear Ryser's uniform, so they will know you are a student, but Neo will be wearing a maintenance crew suit. Neo, meet me by the N'ymean flower I showed you last time we were at the Arboretum, okay?" Trella opened the door and left, their movements graceful and precise.

I looked at Blair. She looked just as nervous as I was. She nodded at me, and we both counted to thirty. Blair opened the door, and we made our way into the hallway. Students were already heading to their classes, their uniforms adorned with the insignias of various interstellar cultures. I lowered my head and turned left toward the west wing.

My palms were sweaty, and my throat was dry. The Arboretum seemed empty. I did not know what I would do if someone recognized me and came to talk to me. I found the N'ymean flower, a rare and beautiful species native to Trella's planet, and sat by a bench, waiting for Blair to arrive.

The sun was rising. Both sunrise and sunsets were my favorite times of the day. They were the brightest time on Titan because of its distance from the sun. Life at Ryser started early, so it would be minutes until someone found me.

A hand touched my shoulder, and I saw Blair standing beside me.

"It would've been a bit easier if you guys had let me in on which flower was native to Trella's planet," Blair said in her humor-filled voice.

"Where is Trella?" I asked, looking around.

When a loud alarm sounded, Trella ran toward us, and my heart raced.

"Come on. This is it. This is the signal. Let's go," Trella said, their voice urgent.

"Don't run, don't walk too close to one another, just keep moving, follow the alarm lights. That's their signal to where they will wait for us," Trella said as we walked against the flow of people evacuating the nearby hangars, their faces illuminated by the flashing red lights.

A hand touched my arm. It was a teacher I had never seen before. "Hurry, the alarm is coming from hangar C-12," the teacher said, his voice filled with concern.

I nodded and motioned to Blair and Trella as I led the way. "C-12," I whispered as I made my way to the gate. The fact that no one recognized me and that someone mistook me for a mechanic gave me the confidence to keep going.

People were everywhere when we arrived at the gate, still scrambling to get out. I pushed myself through the group of teachers and students standing at the entrance and came to where the shuttle was taxed. I looked around, and there were no signs of anyone.

Suddenly another piercing alarm, and I saw Suzuki running towards the shuttle as other officers were running after him.

"Get in, get in," Suzuki yelled, telling me to board the ship.

"How? The hatch door is closed," I said, exasperated.

"From below. Get in from below," Fender's voice came behind me, followed by high-pitch, deafening sounds.

Shots! Someone was shooting at us. *Where were the others?* I looked behind me and saw Fender fire his weapon at a Ryser security guard. Someone's hand pulled me inside the ship. It was Blair.

"How did you get here so fast?" I asked. "Where is Trella?"

Blair's eyes flicked outside, her lips parting in a silent cue. Following her gaze, my breath caught in my throat as Trella moved into action. Their body was a fluid cascade of motion, each step a carefully calculated dance, each turn a measured grace.

A guard approached, energy rifle raised, but Trella was already there. Their body swayed like a reed in the wind, bending just out of the guard's reach. I could feel the air shift as Trella spun, their leg lashing out in a perfect arc, connecting with the guard's knee. He howled, collapsing to the ground, but Trella didn't pause.

My heart pounded, and I could feel the perspiration forming on my brow as I watched Trella wield their energy blades. They hummed and crackled in their hands, glowing with a fierce light that matched the fire in their eyes.

Mac's jaw tightened, his hand gripping the ship's controls, knuckles white. Blair's eyes were wide, filled with awe and anxiety, her breaths coming in short, rapid bursts. Blair's fingers twitched at her side, a silent testament to her readiness to join the fight if needed.

The dance continued, a whirl of agility and strength until the guard lay defeated. Trella's chest heaved, their body glistening with sweat, but their eyes still burned with determination.

"We're clear," Trella said, their voice steady but laced with fatigue. The words were simple, but they carried the weight of their victory, the triumph of skill over brute force.

"We won't make it out of here. The hangar exit hatch is closed," I said, trembling.

"That's what Suzuki is working on," Mac said as he sat before a control panel filled with holographic displays and entered some coordinates. The panel was a marvel of technology, a seamless integration of tactile and virtual interfaces. Three-dimensional star charts floated above the console, and Mac's fingers moved through them, selecting our destination with precision. Beside him, monitors displayed real-time data on the ship's propulsion systems, energy consumption, and structural integrity.

Fender and Trella made it inside the ship, their faces flushed with the thrill of battle. Fender headed to the co-pilot seat and activated another control panel, his fingers dancing over the futuristic interfaces. The co-pilot's station had holographic displays, each dedicated to a specific function. Fender was responsible for navigation and communication. I saw him interacting with the ship's AI, setting up secure channels, and calibrating the sensors for optimal performance.

Blair closed the door and checked other engine signals, her eyes scanning the advanced diagnostics. She moved to a specialized engineering console with detailed ship systems schematics. With a few gestures, she could monitor the performance of the engines, adjust the power distribution, and ensure that all safety protocols were in place. "Where is Suzuki?" I asked as I felt the ship moving toward the main exit, the engines humming with an alien sound.

"Once Suzuki manually opens the hangar's exit doors, we'll have about ten seconds," Fender said sharply, his voice cutting through the tension.

"Trella, I need you to be by the side door, and as soon as we make it through the threshold, I need you to open the door for Suzuki to get in. We will have a few seconds before we are launched into space," Fender said, his eyes fixed on the viewscreen displaying the vastness of the cosmos.

Trella nodded in agreement, their face set with determination. It felt like I was in another one of my weird dreams. I could barely wrap my brain around the fact that we were stealing one of Ryser's training shuttles, a state-of-the-art craft equipped with the latest interstellar navigation and propulsion technology.

The door to the main hangar opened, and Suzuki was nowhere in sight.

"I thought he was coming from the side door," Trella said, their voice filled with concern.

"We are approaching the threshold. Where is Suzuki?" Blair yelled, her voice rising with panic.

"I don't know. We have to go. We have to go now!" Fender said as the ship approached the opening.

If Suzuki attempted to follow us, it would suck him out into space, a fate too terrible to contemplate.

"Take your positions, everyone. Neo, sit down and put your safety harness on. Exiting Titan is always bumpy," Mac said, his voice calm and authoritative.

I nodded in agreement and fumbled with my harness. A loud knock came from the ship's floor by the main section. Blair twisted it open, and spiky black hair poked out, followed by laughter.

"Yoo-hoo! We made it," Suzuki said as the ship sped into orbit, the stars outside the window streaking into light lines.

Laughter and celebration exploded between Fender, Trella, and Suzuki. Blair continued to enter calculations and coordinates into the primary navigational system, her fingers moving with practiced ease over the holographic controls. While Mac steered the ship, his hands guided the craft with the skill of a seasoned pilot.

As the ship accelerated, I began to feel sick. Hitting Titan's atmosphere was not for the faint of heart. Mac was downplaying when he said it would be bumpy.

Unfortunately, it felt more like the entire ship would crack in two. I'd never flown on a small craft before, so I did not know what to expect. The G-force was making my stomach glue to my spine, and it propelled my head back with such a force that I could feel the skin on my face pulling so hard as if it would rip off my skull. The sensation was terrifying and exhilarating, a reminder of the raw power of space travel.

A sudden fear of death overcame me. Once we left Titan's orbit, Trella undid their harness and headed over to the back of the ship, their movements graceful and efficient.

"I have set our coordinates to nearby Nexus. That will give us some time to orbit around and figure out our next steps," Blair said, her voice filled with determination.

"All the ships have tracking locators. They will send another ship from Ryser pretty soon," Trella said, returning with some nourishment to maintain us through the flight, their hands holding trays filled with exotic fruits and nutrient-rich beverages from various planets.

"Not that soon," Suzuki announced, holding a metal disk, his face lit with triumph.

"What's that?" Blair asked.

"That, my friends. Is their tracking device. I removed it first thing in the morning," Suzuki said with a smile, his fingers caressing the sleek surface of the device, a marvel of tracking technology that was now rendered useless.

"Ryser ships don't have stealth capacity. We will pop up on the interstellar radar soon. We have bought ourselves some time but won't be able to orbit randomly for long. The only way to stay hidden is to land somewhere and hide the ship," Fender said, his voice filled with authority, his eyes scanning the star charts displayed on the main screen, a universe of possibilities and dangers waiting for us.

Chapter 17

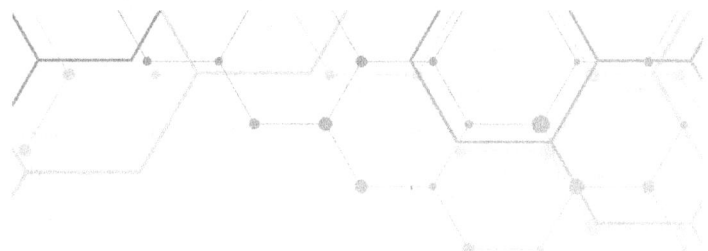

A Hostile
Encountering

T HE JOURNEY TO NEXUS, the fourth planet circling Proxima
Centauri, was a cosmic roller coaster, a testament to the wild
unpredictability of space travel. Our first taste of this harsh reality was
an asteroid field, a tumultuous ballet of space debris that turned our
flight into a high-stakes obstacle course.

The Nova Voyager's control room was bathed in the harsh, un-filtered light of distant stars. Their glow reflected off the tumbling asteroids ahead. We plunged into the field, our path plotted amid a whirlwind of spinning rocks and shimmering dust clouds.

The asteroids were a chaotic swarm of deadly projectiles. Some were mere pebbles, easily deflected by the Voyager's energy shields. Others, however, were gigantic, raw, pockmarked stone, and their craters cast stark, shifting shadows across the spacecraft.

From my position, I had a front-row seat to this celestial show. Each flash of the shields against incoming debris was like a sudden flare, illuminating the control room in stark blue light. The rumble of the ship resonated in my bones, a constant, grinding melody that spoke of our battle against the elements.

Mac, our pilot, was a study of intense concentration. His gloved hands flew over the haptic controls, and his precise movements seemed like a choreographed dance. His eyes, locked onto the holographic navigation panel, were fierce, reflecting the turbulent dance of light and shadow. Beside him, Blair was busy. Her fingers danced over the 3D projection of the Voyager's system controls, adjusting our trajec-tory, calibrating shields, and compensating for gravitational anomalies. Blair's eyes, sharp and intent, flicked across screens, every line of her body screaming with focused resolution.

Suddenly, an alarm blared, slicing through the ship with its shrill cry. A massive asteroid, the size of a small moon, appeared on the nav-igation display, blocking our path. Its jagged surface was an ominous silhouette against the starlit void, a giant sentinel of cold, hard stone.

Mac's hands tightened on the controls. "Hang on," he said through gritted teeth and threw the ship into a steep climb. The artificial gravity struggled to compensate, and a weightless moment seized us before our bodies were slammed back into our seats.

The asteroid loomed large in the view panel, a terrifying spectacle of raw cosmic power. And then, with a jolt that resonated through the ship, we were past it. The asteroid receded behind us, becoming one among the swirling sea of tumbling rocks.

As the adrenaline ebbed, I noticed the cold sweat on my palms, the racing pulse in my ears. My breaths came in shallow gasps. The asteroid field gradually thinned out, replaced by the relative calm of open space. The alarm silenced, and a collective sigh echoed in the control room. Mac leaned back in his seat, running a hand through his hair, while Blair's fingers stilled on the controls.

"Neo, can you sense any hostile ships nearby?" Trella asked. Their usually calm voice filled with tension.

I closed my eyes and focused, my empathic abilities searching for any signs of danger. "There's one to our right, about three klicks away," I replied, opening my eyes.

"Got it. Fender, take the neutral particle beam cannon and see if you can scare them off," Mac ordered. His eyes narrowed as he anticipated their next move.

Fender nodded and headed to the cannon controls. Moments later, a warning shot streaked across the black expanse of space, narrowly missing the hostile ship. They got the message and retreated, leaving us to continue our journey.

"Good job, everyone," I breathed. But our reprieve was short-lived, as a massive solar storm soon engulfed us, bombarding our ship with charged particles and radiation.

"Shields at maximum," Blair announced, her voice tense. "We can't take this for long."

"Neo, any chance you can do something about this?" Mac asked. His eyes darted between the controls and the tempest outside.

I hesitated, unsure if I could influence such a force of nature. But for Yohzak and his people, I had to try. Closing my eyes, I reached out with my mind, attempting to connect with the storm's energy. To my surprise, I felt it responding, the swirling mass of particles shifting and calming ever so slightly.

"Keep going, Neo!" Blair encouraged.

I pushed further, willing the storm to dissipate. Gradually, the intense winds died down, and the radiation levels dropped. As the last remnants of the storm vanished, I slumped back in my seat, exhausted but triumphant.

"Amazing, Neo," Mac murmured. His beautiful smile warmed me.

My cheeks flushed. "Thanks, but we still have a mission to complete."

"Right," Mac agreed, guiding our ship toward Nexus. As we approached the terraformed planet, I braced myself for the challenges ahead.

"Neo, come to the cargo hold. I need to show you something," Yohzak's voice echoed in my mind.

As much as I wanted to help Yohzak and his people, our interactions, most of the time telepathically, were still relatively new, and I couldn't help feeling nervous.

Entering the cargo hold, I saw several holographic images floating above it. "Ah, Neo, I'm glad you came. I wanted to share some of my people's history to help you understand our plight."

"Of course, please tell me everything." My curiosity was piqued.

I saw scenes of a once lush and thriving world. "This was Luehiri, long before Z'hleena's reign of terror. We lived in harmony with nature, and healers like me were highly respected."

"Wait, what? What did you say? Z'hleena? The IU's Senator? I asked, struggling to believe what I was hearing.

As the images changed, I could see the stark contrast—a barren wasteland devoid of resources, the Vihilians huddled in small groups, their faces etched with despair.

"Z'hleena's actions have left us with nothing," Yohzak continued, his voice cracking with emotion. "We arrived in Usiox, Luehiri's orbiting Dyson Sphere, shortly before our planet died, hoping to find refuge. But instead, we found more suffering."

"Yohzak, I had no idea things were so dire for your people. "I suspected that the S'borrathians were involved, but I'd never thought a Senator would do this." My heart ached for them.

"Neo, it is not your responsibility to bear our burdens, but I know you have a kind heart. And it is that kindness which gives me hope."

"Yohzak, I promise you. We will do everything in our power to help your people."

"Thank you, Neo." Yohzak's voice was filled with gratitude, and I felt an overwhelming connection to him. "Now, please focus on obtaining an untraceable ship. It is crucial for the survival of my people."

"Absolutely," I agreed. "We'll make sure of it—Yohzak," tell me more about your people's suffering. I need to understand what we're up against."

"Very well, Neo. Z'hleena's forces have hunted our people for years. Our villages were burned, our crops poisoned, and our water sources contaminated. Many Vihilians were taken captive or killed."

I closed my eyes, trying to process the horrors Yohzak was describing. "How did the other Vihilians survive?"

"Those who remained had to hide in caves or abandoned structures, scavenging for food and water. They lived in constant fear of discovery, but little hope remained. Our people were starving, and illness ran rampant."

"Yohzak, I feel your pain and the suffering of your people." My chest tightened with the vivid reality.

"Indeed, it is a heavy burden to bear, but I refuse to let their suffering be in vain. We must succeed in our mission, Neo."

"Agreed," I said. My team and I had trained and planned carefully. Failure was not part of the plan.

I returned to the main cabin to join the rest of the team. The look of shock was still on my face when Blair asked. "Neo, are you okay? Where did you go?"

"To the cargo bay," I answered. "Yohzak had news for me, and I think we all need to hear this."

Fender and Mac placed the ship on autopilot mode and, together with Suzuki and Trella, joined Blair and me in the galley.

"Yohzak showed me images of Luehiri," I started. "How it was before it became a barren planet devoid of resources. He told me that shortly before their planet, Vihilos, died, they took asylum in Luehiri's Dyson Sphere, Usiox."

"That's the Dyson Sphere you mistook for the strange sun in your dreams," Mac added.

"Yes, but there's more." I paused, looking at Mac before I delivered. "Yohzak named his oppressor."

"Who?" Fender asked impatiently.

"Z'hleena Cyrek," I muttered, the name dripping from my lips like poison. "She was the one behind it all, the cunning S'borrathian princess and Senator who orchestrated the enslavement of the Vihilians."

"Z'hleena? That's impossible," Mac repeated, his jaw clenched, his voice rising angrily. "You don't know her like I do. She's a wonderful woman, a leader, a visionary!"

"Wonderful? Or wonderfully deceptive?" I shot back, my jealousy flaring. "Is this about your feelings for her, Mac? Is that why you can't accept the truth?"

Mac's face turned a shade redder. "My feelings? Do you think this is about romance? Z'hleena is like a mother to me, Neo. She's my father's lover, not mine!"

I stared at him, disbelief and confusion warring within me. My heart ached, and I struggled to find words. "Your father's lover? You expect me to believe that?"

"Yes, I do!" Mac yelled. "Because it's the truth!"

I felt a lump in my throat, a realization that I had fallen in love with Mac, and my jealousy was getting the best of me. The room spun, and I felt a hand on my shoulder.

"Enough!" Trella's voice cut through the tension. "We have more important things to worry about. We must focus on saving the Vihilians, not tearing each other apart."

I looked at Trella, then at Mac, my emotions a whirlwind. Without another word, I turned and fled to my cabin, tears threatening to spill.

Fender's sympathetic eyes followed me as I left, a hint of longing in his gaze.

As Nova Voyager approached Nexus, a sense of anticipation filled the air, palpable among us as we all peered through the viewports in awe.

The planet, a celestial jewel in the vastness of the cosmos, revealed itself gradually as the ship descended into its atmosphere. The first sight that greeted us was a mesmerizing display of colors—a large globe of liquid hues spanning the horizon. Waves of blues, vibrant purples, and shimmering greens danced across the atmospheric canvas, creating a breathtaking spectacle that defied nature's laws.

Nexus's atmosphere clung to the ship, its unique gaseous makeup cradling our descent. The hull quivered, shields adjusting. Radiant energy crackled around us, a dance of charged particles.

We plunged into turbulence, cosmic winds spiraling and swirling. Vibrations resonated through the ship's framework, chaos all around.

Breaking through, the planet Nexus unfolded below—rolling hills, lush vegetation, vibrant hues reflecting from majestic bodies of water. Sensors detected magnetic anomalies and whispers of the planet's hidden power.

Landing gears extended, we touched down, ripples spreading across the alien landscape. The airlock hissed open, and we stepped out onto Seraphis City, the capital city on the planet Nexus.

The time had come for us to obtain the untraceable ship. We made our way through the city's bustling market district, following Suzuki's lead to where the ship was being held.

"Remember, stay focused and be ready for anything," Mac warned us as he scanned the crowd for potential threats.

As we approached the seller, a burly man with a permanent scowl greeted us.

"Welcome, welcome! You must be the ones interested in my finest vessel!" he bellowed, waving us over. "Allow me to show you around."

"Actually, we'd like to discuss the price first," Trella said, their voice firm.

"Ah, the price. Yes, well, you'll need to pay top credit for a ship of this caliber."

"Your asking price is too high," Fender said. His imposing presence added weight to our negotiations.

"Ah, but can you put a price on your safety and success?" the seller countered. "This ship will get you where you need to go without detection. Surely that's worth something."

"Let's cut to the chase," I said, steadying my voice. "We're willing to offer you this much." I named an amount significantly lower than his asking price, hoping our bluff would work.

I could feel my friends' eyes on me. They were surprised to see me taking charge.

"Ha! You must be joking!" He laughed, but I noticed a hint of uncertainty in his eyes. "All right, all right. How about this: I'll drop the price if you agree to do a small favor for me in the future. No questions asked, no details now. Just a promise that when I call, you'll answer."

"Deal," Mac agreed, exchanging a look with me. We were close to agreeing.

"All right then, it's settled." The seller extended his hand, and Mac shook it firmly. "You've got yourself an untraceable ship."

I breathed a sigh of relief as we finalized the transaction.

With the untraceable ship secured, we quickly prepared for the journey ahead. Thoughts of Yohzak and his people consumed my mind, their suffering driving me to push my friends harder than ever before.

"Can't we get a move on?" I snapped as Blair adjusted one of the ship's many intricate systems. Her fingers moved across the console with practiced ease, but it wasn't fast enough for my liking.

Blair placed a hand on my shoulder. "Neo, you need to relax. We're all working as hard as possible, but this ship is complex. It's an alien S'borrathian ship. We must ensure everything is in working order before we set off."

"Yohzak's people don't have time for us to dawdle!" I argued, frustration bubbling inside me.

"Neo, we understand," Trella said, their voice soothing yet firm. "But we must be cautious. We could jeopardize our entire mission if we make any mistakes now."

I deflated slightly, knowing they were right. But my heart ached for the Vihilian species and what they had endured under Z'hleena's rule. The pain from arguing with Mac was not making it any better.

"Neo, you're pushing yourself too hard." Trella's eyes searched mine. "You need to trust that we are doing everything possible to help Yohzak and his people."

"I know," I whispered, tears pricking at the corners of my eyes. "But I feel responsible while their suffering continues. We have to do something."

Fender looked up from the controls. "Neo, we're all in this together. We will save Yohzak's people but can't do it if you run into the ground."

I nodded, knowing they were right. My absolute desire to help Yohzak and my jealousy and newfound hatred for Z'hleena had clouded my judgment, putting unnecessary strain on the group. From then on, I resolved to trust my friends and control my overwhelming emotions.

The following days saw us honing our individual skills. Mac's piloting skills improved, Blair tweaked the ship's systems for optimal performance, and Trella and Fender trained daily to ensure they were prepared for any possible physical confrontations. I spent my time researching and analyzing information on Karmar and its inhabitants, identifying potential allies and threats that awaited us when we landed in the largest city in Proxima Centauri B. Suzuki's family lived in Karmar—their apartment would be our sanctuary. It was more than just a place to stay; it was our safe house, a haven in a world of uncertainty.

"All right, team," Suzuki called. We gathered in the common area. "I think I've found someone to help us get the necessary weapons."

"Who is it?" Mac asked, leaning forward in his seat.

"His name is Varnix. He's a local smuggler with connections in the black market." Suzuki projected an image of him onto the screen. "I've managed to set up a meeting with him."

"Sounds risky," Blair said, studying the image. "But if he's our best bet, then we'll just have to be cautious."

"Agreed," said Trella. "We must be vigilant and ready for anything."

"Let's go over our plan one more time before we land," suggested Fender, folding his arms across his chest. "We can't afford any mistakes."

Chapter 18

Karmar

O UR SHIP DESCENDED INTO Proxima Centauri B's atmosphere. The planet's surface was dusty brown, contrasting the
vibrant blue skies above. Massive drilling rigs dotted the landscape,
extracting precious liquid hydrogen deep within the planet's crust.

As we descended further, the sprawling city of Karmar came into
view, its streets bustling with activity.

"Here we go," Mac whispered, gripping the controls tightly as he guided our ship toward a landing pad on the city's outskirts.

"Remember," I said, facing the group, "stick together and stay alert. If things go wrong, we need to be ready to act."

"Understood," they all replied in unison.

The moment our ship touched down, we filed out onto the landing pad, taking in the sights and sounds of Karmar. The air was thick with the scent of machinery and industry, yet the hum of life and commerce filled the atmosphere. It was an engulfing sensory experience, but I knew we couldn't waste any time.

"Let's head to the meeting point," Suzuki said, leading the group through the crowded streets.

As we made our way to Varnix's hideout, I felt apprehension and determination. So much depended on our success here.

The moment we stepped into the city of Karmar, my senses were assaulted by the smells, sights, and sounds. The streets were lined with vendors selling everything from technologically advanced gadgets to exotic foods I had never seen before. The aroma of engine exhaust and the enticing scent of fragrant spices created an oddly intoxicating bouquet.

"Wow," Blair said, taking in the surrounding spectacle. "This place is nothing like Titan."

"Be cautious, Fender warned. The goal is to avoid any unwanted attention."

As we navigated the bustling streets, I noticed a group of children playing a game with a small, hovering ball. They seemed so carefree, oblivious to the hardships their world had endured. It struck me how resilient children could be, even in the most challenging circumstances.

"All right, team," Suzuki said. "The meeting place should be down that alleyway."

We followed Suzuki's lead, venturing away from the vibrant streets and into the shadowy back alleys of Karmar. The atmosphere shifted from lively to tense. Shady figures loitered in doorways and whispered among themselves, casting suspicious glances in our direction. My heart pounded, and I felt the familiar surge of adrenaline course through my veins.

"Here it is," Trella announced, stopping in front of a nondescript door, which bore a small, faded sign that read *The Folie*.

"Are we sure this is the right place?" I asked, swallowing the lump that had formed in my throat.

"Only one way to find out," Mac said, reaching for the door handle.

We entered The Folie, and I was struck by the smoky, harshly lit interior. The air was thick with the scents of tobacco and alcohol, and a soft jazz melody played in the background. A diverse array of alien species filled the room. Their conversations blended into an indecipherable hum.

"Business or pleasure?" asked a small Venusian, his yellow scarf indicating his status as a mediator. His monkey-like face and pointed ears twitched curiously as he looked us over.

"Business," I replied, my voice steady despite the nervous energy coursing through me. "We're here to meet someone."

"Very well," the Venusian said, eyeing us for a moment longer before gesturing toward a table in the back of the room. "Enjoy your stay at The Folie."

I felt like a starship adrift in uncharted space as we reached the designated meeting spot. My heart raced, and my thoughts raced even faster. What if something went wrong? What if we couldn't secure the weapons to save Yohzak and his people?

"Stay close," Mac murmured, his hand brushing against mine as we navigated the crowded room. His touch grounded me, reminding me I wasn't alone in this chaotic place.

"Check out that table in the back," Blair suggested, pointing to a group engaged in what appeared to be a high-stakes card game. Fender and Suzuki exchanged glances, then nodded in agreement.

"All right, let's mingle, but keep an eye out for anything suspicious," Trella said. We all dispersed among the patrons.

I was drawn to the bar, where a tall, slender bartender with iridescent scales and four arms expertly mixed drinks for various alien customers. I admired the grace she moved, her limbs working in perfect harmony as she crafted her liquid masterpieces.

"Can I get you something?" she asked, her voice melodic and soothing like a gentle breeze.

"Um, just water, please." I felt out of my element with all the exotic concoctions being served. She nodded and handed me a glass, her eyes never leaving mine, as if searching for something hidden within my soul.

"Interesting choice, dear," she commented before turning her attention to another customer.

I sipped the water, scanning the room for any signs of trouble. My heart pounded as I tried to keep my emotions in check. I couldn't afford to let my empathic gifts spiral out of control here.

"Everything all right?" Mac asked, suddenly appearing beside me.

I forced a smile. "Yeah, just trying to take it all in."

"Remember, we're here for a reason," he reminded me.

"Right." I set down my glass and squared my shoulders. "Let's find our contact and get what we came for."

"Here's the information you need," the contact whispered, sliding a small data chip across the table. "The cargo with all the weapons you requested is by Bay Seven. Remember, you didn't hear this from me."

"Understood," Mac replied, pocketing the chip discreetly.

With the location to Z'hleena's stronghold secured, we gathered the weapons, and reunited with the rest of our group. We made our way out of The Folie and returned to Suzuki's parents' apartment. The vivid sights and sounds faded behind us, and we stepped back into the dark alleyways of Karmar.

CHAPTER 19

Courage in Adversity

S TANDING IN THE MAIN room at Suzuki's parents' apartment, I couldn't believe my eyes. To my left were my friends and allies: Mac, Blair, Trella, Fender, and Suzuki.

On my right, Shane Robbs—Mac's dad, who betrayed us, and Z'hleena Cyrek - a cunning S'borrathian princess and Senator, holding our fates. Her lavender skin glowed eerily, and her white eyes pierced through us like daggers.

"Neo, isn't it?" Z'hleena purred as she circled around me. I clenched my fists, using every ounce of my remaining strength to keep my composure.

"Yes," I replied, my voice trembling slightly. "And you must be Z'hleena."

"Very perceptive," she said mockingly, stopping before me. "You're not quite what I expected from a simple human girl."

"Likewise," I shot back, unwilling to let her intimidate me. "I never thought a Senator would stoop so low."

"Careful, dear," she warned, her voice dripping with venom. "You're in no position to make enemies here."

I glanced at my friends and felt their fear, anger, and determination. They were counting on me to escape this mess, and I couldn't disappoint them. Mac caught my eye, and I saw the internal struggle he was facing—his father's betrayal weighed heavily on him.

"Enough of this," Shane said, stepping forward. "Z'hleena, we got the chip. We have what we want. Let's just get this over with."

"Very well," she agreed, her stony gaze fixed on me. "Neo Lyra Murphy, you and your friends will pay for meddling in our affairs."

"Dad," Mac whispered, his voice strained, "how could you? I confided in you because I trusted you. I have always trusted you."

"Mac, I," Shane stopped short, unable to meet his son's gaze.

"Save it, Dad." Mac's eyes were bitter and clouded with pain. "You've made your choice."

And Fender, ever stoic, simply glared at Shane with an intensity that made me shiver.

The air was heavy with tension, each breath feeling like a struggle. My friends and I found ourselves caught between the jaws of

Z'hleena's dark forces, and we needed all of our bravery and cunning to escape.

My heart raced as I stared at Shane, the man I had once respected and trusted. The room seemed to close in on me, suffocating us all in the bitter taste of betrayal. Mac's father had chosen a side in this conflict, which wasn't with us.

Z'hleena gave me one last smile as she and Shane walked out of the apartment.

I studied my friends' faces, registering the hurt in each expression. Disbelief played across Blair's features. Trella clenched their fists like warriors preparing for battle, and tribal markings stood against their dark skin.

My mind raced to find a solution. "Guys, we can't just stand here," I whispered. "We need a plan."

"Agreed," Trella said through gritted teeth. "Z'hleena has the upper hand now, but we won't let her win."

"Right," Blair chimed in. "There's always a way out."

Fender nodded. "Our previous plan was compromised, so we must adapt."

"Let's focus on what we know," I suggested, trying to keep my fear from seeping into my words. "Z'hleena wants power and stops at nothing to get it."

"Then maybe we should use her ambition against her," Mac said. "Find a way to turn her own desires into a trap."

Blair's eyes lit up. "Like a Trojan horse," she explained. "We could pretend to offer her something Z'hleena wants but actually set her up for a fall."

"Good idea," Trella said, nodding. "But we'll need to be careful. She knows our initial plan and expects us to strike back."

"Then let's make it unexpected," I said. "Something Z'hleena won't see coming."

"Okay, here's what we do," Mac said, outlining a new strategy incorporating our strengths and skills. We listened closely, our minds melding as we pieced together a daring plan to outsmart Z'hleena and her vile forces.

The fear that had been choking me slowly loosened its grip. The odds were undeniably stacked against us, but with my friends beside me, I knew we had a fighting chance. Betrayal may have bruised us, but it wouldn't break us—not when we had each other.

"Are we all in?" I asked, looking each of them in the eye.

"Every step of the way," Mac said as his hand reached for mine.

"Until the end," Blair echoed.

"Always," Trella said, like a true warrior.

Fender's fierce gaze never wavered, and he added, "Let's do this!"

The weight of Shane's betrayal hung over us like an ominous storm cloud, darkening the mood. My heart clenched as I realized how fragile our trust had become—how easily it could be shattered by a single act of treachery. As we sat there, gathered around the holographic map of Z'hleena's fortress, the severity of our situation became all too clear.

"Z'hleena knows everything," I said quietly, my voice trembling with anger and fear. "All our plans, our weaknesses. She could use them against us."

Mac's jaw tightened, and his eyes blazed. "We won't let her," he insisted, his hand gripped mine. "We must be smarter than she is. More unpredictable. All she knows is that you've been dreaming about an alien species in distress and that we had the location of her stronghold."

"Exactly," Trella chimed in. "We must alter our approach. Change our tactics. We can't allow her to anticipate our every move."

"She could still report us to the Intergalactic Police for stealing Ryser's ship," I noted.

"Right," Blair agreed. Her fingers tapped nervously on the table. "So, what do we do?"

I took a deep breath, trying to steady my thoughts. "Let's think about what we know. Z'hleena will expect us to come at her head-on, using our original plan. But what if we don't? What if we find another way in?"

"Like a diversion?" Fender's green eyes narrowed thoughtfully. "Create chaos somewhere else while we slip in unnoticed?"

"Exactly." I nodded. "If she thinks we're attacking from one direction, she'll focus her defenses there, making her vulnerable elsewhere."

"But how do we create a believable diversion?" Mac asked.

Trella's eyes gleamed with a sudden idea. "Maybe we don't need to create one. What if we use something that's already happening? Something she won't be able to ignore?"

"Like what?" Fender leaned forward intently.

"The S'borrathians have many enemies," Trella explained. "There are bound to be others plotting against her—rival factions, discontented subjects. If we can identify such a group and time our attack to coincide with theirs, it could provide the perfect cover."

"Brilliant," Blair said, her eyes shining. "We'd be in and out before she knew what hit her."

My heart swelled with pride at our collective ingenuity. "Of course," I said. "But we'll need to be extra cautious. Z'hleena is cunning, and she will exploit any weakness she sees."

"Agreed. We'll have to be more vigilant than ever," Mac said, his voice tinged with bitterness. "Watch each other's backs. Trust only ourselves." A haunted look clouded his eyes. The wounds resurfaced as he recalled his father's betrayal.

"Then it's settled," I declared.

As we sat around the table, our determination to succeed was palpable. Shane's betrayal affected each of us, but we refused to let it derail our mission. Our minds buzzed with ideas, and we began assigning roles based on our strengths and skills.

"Mac, I think you'd be perfect as our pilot," I said, looking into his eyes that seemed to light up my soul. "Your skill in the cockpit is unmatched, and we'll need your expertise to navigate the skies."

"Agreed," Fender said with a steeled resolve.

"My father!" Mac roared; his face twisted with rage, turning his usually soft hazel eyes into flames. He clenched his fists, the veins in his arms bulging. "How could he do this? My own father!"

He turned sharply to me, his voice breaking. "How did it come to this? Betrayal of my own flesh and blood? He's with Z'hleena, working against everything we stand for."

I reached out, placing a gentle hand on his arm, my own heart aching for him. "Mac, we're here for you. Your father's choices are his own, not yours."

Blair stepped closer. Her eyes filled with compassion. "Mac, we will find a way to make this right. You're not your father."

"Yeah," Trella added, their pointy ears twitching in empathy. "We are your family now."

Fender nodded, his eyes somber, while Suzuki affirmed, "We'll face this together."

"Thank you," he whispered, looking at each of us. I squeezed his arm, my voice firm and full of conviction. "We always will, Mac, always."

Chapter 20

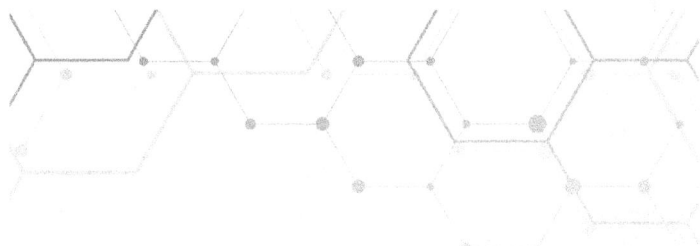

The Fold

T HE MOMENT OUR SHIP entered the fold in space, my stomach lurched. It felt like every cell in my body was being stretched and compressed simultaneously. I gripped the armrests of my seat, trying to maintain some semblance of control. The world collapsed in a blinding display of brilliant colors, strobing lights, and iridescent hues as the ship activated its FTL—Faster Than Light—drive. The moment the threshold of normalcy shattered, the contents of my stomach made an earnest attempt at staging a rebellion. Each cell of my being, it seemed, was contorted between the cruel symphony of spatial elongation and abrupt compression, as if my genetic code were nothing more than a cosmic accordion played by uncaring forces of the universe.

Every inch of the cold, metallic armrest bit into the clammy skin of my palms as I clung to my seat. My eyes, wide with terror and awe, absorbed the unfolding cosmic panorama with morbid fascination. Everything was warped beyond recognition—the rigid lines of the spaceship's interior architecture were distorted into funhouse mirror versions of themselves, melting and reforming in the ship's translucent force field. It was as if reality was being sucked into a colossal Van Gogh painting, only to re-emerge at the other end of the spectrum with a refreshed palette.

Through the panoramic viewing panel, space wasn't just black anymore. We weren't merely traversing space. We were punching through the fabric of reality.

Beneath my feet, the ship hummed a symphony of raw power, its quantum engines manipulating the very nature of space-time. The feeling of quantum entanglement was hard to explain; it was a prickling sensation and a sense of oneness with the universe.

"Everyone all right?" Mac asked from the pilot's seat.

"Define 'all right,'" Blair muttered. With a pale face, she struggled to focus on the console before her. Trella and Fender exchanged uneasy glances.

"Engaging sub-light engines," Mac announced. "We'll be at Luehiri in approximately ten klicks."

A cold pit of anxiety opened in my chest. Ten klicks to save a species.

"Remember, we have one shot at this," I said. "If we don't rescue Yohzak and the other Vihilians from Z'hleena's stronghold, their entire race could be wiped out."

"Failure isn't an option, Neo," Fender growled. "We won't let you down."

"Preparing for atmospheric entry," Mac warned. The ship shuddered violently as we hit Luehiri's atmosphere, but Mac expertly guided us through the turbulence.

"Neo," Trella whispered, leaning toward me. "You must focus on your empathic abilities during this mission. It may give us the edge we need." I nodded.

As we touched down on Luehiri, the alien landscape loomed before us, covered in a dense fog that seemed to swallow everything in its path. The soft hum of the ship's engines faded away, leaving us with only the eerie silence of this new world.

"All right, listen up," I said. "The first step is to locate Z'hleena's stronghold. Even without the chip, I believe we can get there. Yohzak showed me that it's hidden beneath the surface as a subterranean maze of cells. We'll need to find an entrance and infiltrate without alerting her guards.

"Once inside, we'll split into two teams," I continued. "Mac, Blair, and I will focus on locating Yohzak and the other captives. Trella, Fender, and Suzuki, you'll secure our exit route and disable any security systems you come across, ensuring they don't trap us inside."

"Got it," Trella nodded. Fender merely grunted and flexed his muscles, ready for action.

"Communication is key," I stressed. "We'll maintain contact through these earpieces." I handed out small, discreet devices that let us stay connected throughout the mission. "If anything goes wrong or you find the captives, let the rest of us know immediately."

"Understood," Mac said, adjusting the device in his ear.

I led them to the ship's cargo hold, where we had stashed our supplies. As we donned our suits and gathered weapons, I considered our risks. There was no room for error, no second chances. Lives hung in the balance, and saving them was up to us.

"Neo," Z'hleena's voice cut through my thoughts like a knife.

"You think you can lead these fools to victory? You're nothing more than a child playing at war."

"Keep your opinions to yourself, Z'hleena," I snapped, anger flaring. "I won't let your twisted games endanger this mission or the lives of my friends."

"Such bravado. When you fail, remember you chose to stand against me." I could almost see the sneer in her voice.

"Z'hleena knows we are here. She just communicated with me telepathically." I warned.

As we left the ship, the thick fog enveloped us, making it hard to see more than a few feet in front of us. I activated my suit's thermal vision, and heat signatures came into focus, the world shifting to shades of blue and orange.

We moved cautiously, avoiding any open areas where we might be spotted. Each step brought us closer to our objective, and I could feel the tension building among us.

"Neo." Mac's voice was barely audible in my earpiece. "I've spotted a possible entrance up ahead."

"Confirmed," Trella added. "It looks like a maintenance tunnel, but guards are posted nearby."

"All right," I replied, my pulse quickening. "Let's take them out quietly and gain access."

"Copy that," Fender said, moving forward with the rest of us.

I could feel the weight of Luehiri's gravity pulling me down, making each step more laborious. The rough terrain was unforgiving, with sharp rocks jutting from the ground and treacherous slopes threatening to send us tumbling.

"Neo," Blair whispered, "we need a short break."

"All right, just for a few minutes," I agreed, glancing around for any signs of Z'hleena's patrols. We huddled together, silently catching our breath as the wind whipped around us, carrying the scent of an alien world.

We continued our trek toward the stronghold, ever watchful for potential threats.

"Over there." Trella pointed up ahead. "Enemy patrol approaching."

"Quick, hide!" I commanded, gesturing for everyone to find cover behind nearby rocks. We watched as the patrol passed by, unaware of our presence. My heart raced, and I felt the adrenaline pumping through my veins. "All clear. Let's keep moving."

Closer to Z'hleena's stronghold, the ground beneath us grew harder, indicating we were near the subterranean entrance. I sensed mounting anxiety among our group, but we pressed on.

"Here," Suzuki said, pointing to a barely visible hatch hidden among the rocks. "This should lead us into the maze."

"Are you sure?" I eyed the hatch warily. "It looks heavily secured."

"Trust me," Suzuki replied. "I can bypass the security measures."

"All right," I said, nodding at him to proceed. He knelt, expertly working on the hatch's control panel while we kept watch for any approaching guards.

"Got it!" Suzuki announced as the hatch opened with a soft hiss. "Let's go, quick!"

We descended into the dark tunnel, our footsteps echoing ominously in the confined space. The air was thick and cold, and I felt the oppressive atmosphere of the stronghold closing in on us as we ventured into its depths.

"Neo." Mac gripped my arm. "This felt too easy. Z'hleena is onto us. I just heard something from one of the guards."

"Stay alert, everyone," I warned. "They know we're here. Stick together and be ready for a fight."

Chapter 21

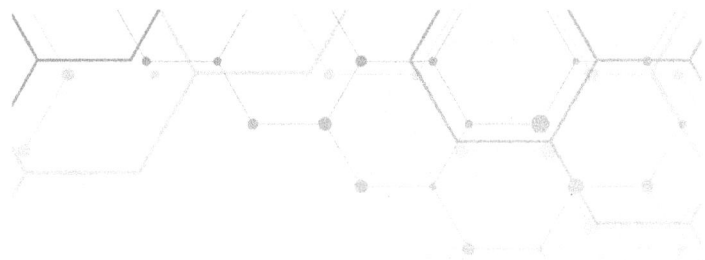

Stealth and Shadows

THE STRONGHOLD'S LAYOUT WAS a disorienting labyrinth of narrow corridors and dim chambers. The walls were made of rough, cold stone that seemed to absorb the meager light from the few flickering lamps scattered throughout. We navigated through winding passages, avoiding groups of guards when possible and silently neu-tralizing those we couldn't evade.

I carefully led the way and whispered, "According to the images in my dreams, the captives are being held in individual chambers deep within this maze."

"Let's pick up the pace, but stay sharp for traps," Mac added. His eyes scanned our surroundings.

I felt the palpable tension among us, each acutely aware of the high stakes involved. We had to rescue the captives and make it out alive.

"Neo, look out!" Trella suddenly yelled. She shoved me against the wall just in time to avoid a swinging blade trap triggered by a pressure plate on the floor.

"Thanks, Trella," I gasped. My heart heaved while they patted my shoulders.

"Here," Fender said, pointing at a high ventilation duct on the wall. "We can use these to avoid detection. Blair, Suzuki, can you disable the security systems?"

"Leave it to us," Suzuki replied. Suzuki and Blair climbed up and began working on the control panel, their fingers moving deftly over the circuits.

"Stay close," Suzuki said as we followed them into the cramped air ducts. "And keep your weapons ready."

"Got it," I whispered. I felt the weight of my weapon in my hand as we moved forward and focused on my empathic abilities. If I could anticipate the guards' movements and emotions, we could stay one step ahead of them.

"Security system disabled," Blair announced quietly through our comms. "We should be able to move more freely now."

I crawled after Mac as he led us deeper into the stronghold. The air was heavy with a mix of dust and the faint scent of fear, likely from the prisoners we were here to save.

"Almost there," Mac murmured. He peered down an opening in the ducts that revealed a long corridor lined with cell doors. "Let's get those captives out and bring today's mission to a successful end."

We emerged from the air ducts, our hearts pounding. The dark corridor stretched before us with an occasional flickering light. We heard the indistinct murmurs of the Vihilian captives locked behind cold metal doors.

"Let's move," I whispered. My grip tightened on my weapon, and we crept forward, keeping to the shadows. Trella and Fender took point, their keen senses and warrior instincts guiding us past guards patrolling the area.

As we approached the first chamber, I felt a wave of despair emanating from within. It was one of the Vihilians, his thoughts clouded by fear and uncertainty. I shared a determined glance with Mac before nodding at Blair. She knelt and began working on the electronic lock.

"Guards!" Fender hissed as he spotted two approaching figures. He and Trella moved swiftly, engaging the guards in hand-to-hand combat. Their movements were fluid and precise, like a dangerous dance, quickly overpowering the enemy.

I focused on the guards' emotions, sensing their surprise and panic. Exploiting their vulnerability, I sent a surge of confusion toward them, momentarily clouding their minds. Trella and Fender seized the opportunity, taking them down with swift, decisive blows.

"Got it!" Blair said, and the cell door clicked open. We rushed inside, finding a group of frightened Vihilians huddled together. Their relief was tangible as they realized we were there to rescue them.

"Stay close and stay quiet," Suzuki said. "We'll get you out of here."

Our small band of freed captives grew with each cell we liberated. As we advanced, the tension in the air intensified, each footstep echoing through the corridors.

"More guards coming," Trella warned us. We braced ourselves, ready for the inevitable confrontation.

"Let's make this quick," Mac muttered.

As the guards rounded the corner, we sprang into action. Mac and Suzuki efficiently engaged one guard, their weapons clashing loudly in the confined space. Blair focused on unlocking another chamber.

"Neo, behind you!" Fender shouted. I spun around just in time to parry an attack from a guard who had appeared out of nowhere. My heart raced as adrenaline surged through my veins. Channeling my empathic abilities, I sensed and exploited his fear, sending waves of doubt and uncertainty into his mind.

The guard hesitated, his grip faltering, and I took the opportunity to disarm him with a swift kick. He stumbled backward; crashed into the wall; and slumped to the ground, unconscious.

"Nice work," Trella said, taking down another guard with a well-placed strike. Together, we continued our mission, determined to rescue every captive.

We pressed onward, our team moving like a finely tuned orchestra through the labyrinthine stronghold. My heart pounded, and anticipation coursed through my veins as we approached Yohzak's cell.

"Yohzak should be just ahead," Blair whispered as she worked to unlock the last door.

The door finally slid open, revealing a musty chamber. In the center of the room lay Yohzak, his emaciated form bound and shackled to an eerie, pulsating device. His eyes flickered open at our entrance, filled with desperate hope.

"Yohzak," I breathed, hardly believing we'd found him. "Hang on. We're going to get you out of here."

"Careful," Trella warned as they examined the restraints. "I've seen something like this before. It's designed to sap his energy———any attempt to remove it without disabling the mechanism could be fatal."

"Leave that to me," Blair said, pulling out a small device from her pocket. "This should do the trick."

A sinister laugh echoed through the chamber as Blair worked on disarming the device. Shadows danced along the walls, morphing into the imposing figure of Z'hleena.

CHAPTER 22

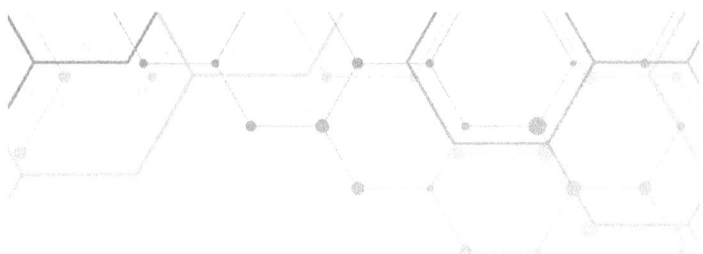

The Confrontation

"**D**ID YOU REALLY THINK I would let you dismantle my plans so easily?" Z'hleena sneered, her pale white eyes narrowing dangerously. She possessed psychic abilities that made her a formidable foe. "You have underestimated me, and now you will pay the price."

"Suzuki, Fender, cover us!" I shouted as Z'hleena's Vihilian guards swarmed into the central chamber, their footsteps echoing off the walls. The air crackled with psychic energy as mental attacks clashed with the energy weapons of my team. Battle cries rang out, reverberating through the cavernous room.

"Almost there," Mac muttered, sweat beading on his brow as he bypassed the last layer of security. The device emitted a high-pitched whine before falling silent, and the restraints around Yohzak opened.

"Neo," Yohzak gasped. "Thank you."

"Let's get out of here," I said. I helped him to his feet, keeping my eyes on Z'hleena as she prowled closer, her robes swirling around her. Her intense gaze locked onto mine, and I could feel her psychic tendrils trying to worm their way into my mind, a reflection of her psychic abilities that allowed her to manipulate energy and matter.

"You must be the empath," she hissed, her voice dripping with malice. "You think your pathetic powers can stop me? Your kind has no place in this universe."

I tried to breach her mental defenses to distract her, but Z'hleena swatted away my empathic attacks with ease. "It's time to end your meddling once and for all," she spat.

She lunged at me, her movements swift and deadly, enhanced by her control over physical energies. My heart raced as I dodged her attacks, narrowly avoiding her ruthless strikes. I could sense her rage and frustration growing as our battle continued. My team fought fiercely around us, holding off Z'hleena's guards as best they could.

"Enough!" Z'hleena roared, her voice echoing through the chamber. She raised her hands, and the room shook violently, debris raining down upon us. In a coordinated move, Fender and Suzuki aimed disabling blasts at her extremities. Trella and Mac hurled energy restraints toward her.

At the same time, the combined assault caught Z'hleena off guard, and she screamed in rage as the restraints wrapped around her, momentarily incapacitating her.

"Quick, while she's restrained!" I shouted, guiding Yohzak and the other Vihilians toward the exit. Yohzak guided us through a secret passage inside the Staak'al crystal. We reached the entrance hidden within the crystal, a gateway that seemed to blend into the surroundings. The walls of the cavern opened into a broader chamber, glowing with a soft, pinkish light.

The entrance within the Staak'al was an ancient Vihilian artifact, a perfect fusion of technology and natural beauty. It led to a safe location, hidden from prying eyes—our only chance to escape without detection.

As we made our way through the hidden tunnels, I glanced back to see Z'hleena's furious gaze locked on me. Her hatred was palpable, and though she was momentarily incapacitated, I knew she wouldn't be down for long.

"We need to move fast," Mac urged, leading the way. The passage was filled with strange luminescent markings and ancient symbols. It was a path seldom trodden, even by the stronghold's inhabitants, the Vihilians.

We reached the entrance hidden within the Staak'al crystal. Our confrontation with Z'hleena was far from over, and I knew we would meet again. But for the moment, we had succeeded in our mission. We had freed Yohzak and the other Vihilians, and together, we would stand against Z'hleena's tyranny.

The tension among us crackled like static electricity as we prepared for the final part of our mission. Z'hleena's ultimate goal was to claim power within the Intergalactic Union.

But for the moment, we were safe, hidden within the incredible, living biome inside Staak'al, a colossal pink crystal in the heart of Luehiri. The cave was unlike anything I had ever seen. Lit from within by a soft, ethereal glow, the cave walls were alive, constantly shifting and undulating in gentle waves. The light danced across the facets of the crystal, casting mesmerizing patterns on everything it touched. The very air within the cave seemed to vibrate with life. Delicate tendrils of vegetation reached out from crevices, moving with an almost sentient intelligence. The floor was smooth but warm underfoot, pulsating slightly as if the crystal was breathing. Pockets of clear, sparkling water were nestled in the formations, reflecting the light in a dazzling display.

The rescued Vihilians were resting, their expressions reflecting a mix of exhaustion, relief, and concern. The sounds of the cave were soft and melodious, like a symphony composed by nature itself. The gentle rustling of the crystal flora, the whisper of water, and the underlying hum of the crystal created a soothing background to our urgent planning. Yohzak, now revived and healthier, deeply conversed with Mac, Trella, and Suzuki. Their faces were illuminated by the ever-changing lights of Staak'al. Their discussion was intense, and their voices occasionally rose, showing the strain and the high stakes we were all feeling.

"Neo," Suzuki called me to join them to look at a cluster of crystal formations that served as our tactical center. Maps, charts, and data were projected onto the crystal surfaces, turning them into interactive displays.

"Guys, we can't let her win," I said, clenching my fists.

"Although Z'hleena is dangerous, we're more powerful when united. You've brought us all together, Neo. Your empathic abilities were amazing, helping to incapacitate the soldiers and rescue Yohzak and the other enslaved Vihilians." Fender said.

"Right," I nodded, swallowing the lump in my throat. Whenever someone showed faith in me, I questioned why they would trust someone as damaged and insecure as me. It felt like I was betraying them by doubting myself, but I couldn't help it.

Every cell in my body screamed at me to run away, to escape responsibility. But I couldn't let them down. They were counting on me. There was so much about me that I still didn't understand. Luehiri, this cave, it all felt so strangely familiar to me.

"Neo, are you ready?" Suzuki's black eyes searched mine as if trying to discern the turmoil inside me.

"Of course I am," I lied. Despite the fear and doubt clawing at me, I knew I had to push through it. This was for my friends and me—my search was for identity, acceptance, and belonging.

Chapter 23

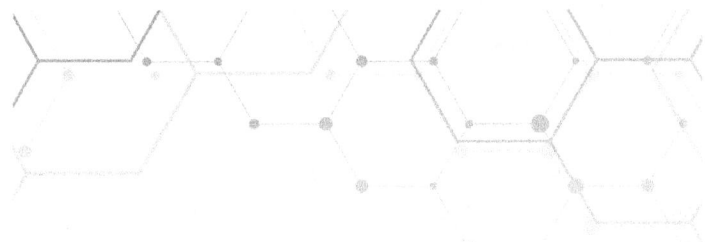

Staak'al

"**N**EO, ARE YOU SURE you can handle this?" Mac asked. His eyes seemed to pierce my soul like he knew the swirling vortex of fear and doubt that threatened to consume me.

"Of course," I snapped back, perhaps a little too harshly. I saw the hurt flicker across his face before he masked it with a stoic expression. The guilt gnawed at me. But I couldn't tell him the truth—that I was afraid of failing the mission and losing everything I'd worked so hard for.

"All right, team," Fender said. "We have a job, so let's focus on that." He cast a pointed look at Mac and me, his green eyes narrowed.

"Right, sorry," Mac mumbled. He averted his gaze from mine.

"Look, guys," Blair said. "We're all stressed, but we need to work together if we're going to pull this off."

"Blair's right." Trella's voice was like a soothing balm to my frayed nerves. "We must trust in each other and our abilities."

"Okay," I said, forcing a smile onto my face. "Let's re-examine the plan. It's not possible to release only the Vihilians and ignore the other species confined in Z'hleena's stronghold."

"Z'hleena has imprisoned everyone who has ever threatened her or her plans. There must have been hundreds of prisoners," Mac added.

"That's her solution to 'ensuring peace at all costs,'" Blair said with a disdainful shake of her head.

Yohzak's eyes narrowed, his voice dropping to a whisper as he leaned closer. "But have you considered the possibility that this might be just the tip of the iceberg? Enslaving the Vihilians was only part of a greater scheme."

I blinked, trying to comprehend the magnitude of his words. "What are you saying, Yohzak?" Yohzak's eyes flicked with a troubled light. "I heard whispers among the guards about something far bigger and more evil at play. The name Kuorec was mentioned more than once."

The room fell into a tense silence.

"Kuorec?" Suzuki finally said, breaking the silence. "Who or what is that?" He's a power-hungry, ruthless priest of Luehiri's old religion. If he's involved, we deal with something more complex and dangerous than Z'hleena."

Trella's hands clenched into fists. "Why did Z'hleena imprison your people and force you to mine Staak'al?"

"Staak'al is in the blood of every Luehirian. It is their life force and their power. Her objective was to extract Staak'al's essence." Yohzak explained, his voice heavy.

A cold shiver ran down my spine. Z'hleena had been crafty and treacherous, but the involvement of Kuorec took her threat to an entirely new level. I locked eyes with Mac, seeing the same realization dawning in his expression. Our mission had just become even more urgent and perilous.

"We need to find out what Z'hleena and Kuorec are really up to," I said, determination flooding me. "This is bigger than just a rescue mission now. Whatever they're planning, we must stop it before it's too late."

We were no longer simply battling Z'hleena. We were taking on a more powerful, hidden, powerful force that had yet to reveal its full hand. The shadows were growing darker, and we had to be ready for whatever lay ahead.

A newfound sense of urgency took hold as we ran through our strategy. The realization that Z'hleena and the shadowy Kuorec were orchestrating something far more ominous meant that every decision we made carried immense weight.

I could feel my friends looking to me for guidance, their faces etched with determination and trust.

"All right," I began, my voice steady as I took on the leadership role. "We have to act quickly and efficiently. Blair, I need you on tech support. We must disable any remaining security systems and gain access to the prisoners. We must release everyone—we can't leave anyone behind."

Blair nodded, her eyes sharp and focused. "Understood, Neo. I'll get on it."

"Mac, I want you and Suzuki to analyze the stronghold's layout and find the weakest points. To destroy this prison, we'll need a well-co-ordinated strike that ensures everyone's safety."

Mac's eyes met mine, and he gave a confident smile. "We're on it. Suzuki and I will find the best way to bring the whole place down without endangering any lives."

"Fender, Trella," I continued, turning to the warriors in our group, "your combat skills will be crucial. Prepare to lead the assault, clear paths, and protect the escapees. We need to make sure everyone gets out safely."

They exchanged a glance and nodded. Their faces were grim but resolute. "We'll make sure of it," Fender promised.

I glanced at Yohzak, who was tending to the rescued prisoners, his face pale but his eyes full of gratitude. "Yohzak, you'll stay here and look after the people we've freed. They'll need care, and we trust you with that."

He met my gaze, his voice soft but full of conviction. "I won't let you down, Neo."

We approached Z'hleena's heavily guarded compound from a different entrance this time. The razor-sharp edges of the metal gates gleamed menacingly. My heart raced like a trapped animal desperate to escape.

"Neo, you'll be leading Mac and Blair to infiltrate the main building while we create a diversion," Suzuki whispered. He handed me an encrypted quantum slate containing our plan. "The other hostages are most likely being held in the north wing."

"Got it," I managed to say, my voice wavering slightly.

As we split into our designated teams, I tried to catch Mac's gaze to share a word of encouragement, but he avoided eye contact. My stomach churned as I led him and Blair toward a side entrance.

"Stay sharp," I whispered. My breath fogged up in the cold atmosphere. We crept through the massive steel door left slightly ajar—either a stroke of luck or a trap waiting to be sprung.

No sooner had we entered. Alarms blared throughout the compound. I froze, suddenly feeling exposed and vulnerable. Z'hleena appeared on an overhead monitor, her lavender skin glowing eerily under the harsh fluorescent lights.

"Ah, Neo, what a pleasant surprise," she said with her usual sneer. "I've been expecting you."

My pulse skyrocketed, and I gripped the quantum slate tighter. I wanted to respond confidently, to show Z'hleena I wasn't afraid, but all I could muster was a weak, "Let the prisoners go."

"Or what?" her taunting voice asked, dripping with contempt. "You'll throw a tantrum? Cry for your missing mother?"

Her words hit me like a physical blow, and my knees almost buckled. My self-esteem and resolve crumbled. As the silence stretched on, I struggled to find my voice.

"Neo," Mac hissed. "Focus."

"Enough of this," Z'hleena snapped. "You have one chance to leave now, or I'll make sure you never see those pitiful creatures again."

"Neo, we can't back down," Trella urged.

"Neo, please," Mac said. "We need you."

"Z'hleena," I replied, my voice becoming defiant. "We're not leaving until the prisoners are free."

"Very well," she said with a sneer as her image faded from the screen. "If death is what you seek, then I shall grant your wish." The alarms continued to blare around us, and I steeled myself for the battle ahead.

Mac took charge, and his voice rang out clear and confident. "All right, we need to act fast. Any ideas?" I hesitated, my mind going blank with panic. "Maybe... maybe if we split up?" I stammered, knowing that divide and conquer was a risky strategy. My decision-making abilities felt crippled by my anxiety, leaving me grasping at straws.

"That could work, but it's dangerous. We'd be more vulnerable." Mac said.

"Neo, think!" Blair implored, desperation edging her voice. "We trust your judgment. Don't let Z'hleena get to you."

"I... I don't know," I admitted, tears pooling at the corners of my eyes. "I'm sorry, I just can't think straight right now."

The atmosphere in the room grew heavy and tense, my failure to rise to the occasion causing a dangerous shift in morale. I could see the doubt flickering in my friends' eyes, which amplified my insecurities.

I closed my eyes, struggling to push past the suffocating fog of my emotions. My friends relied on me, and I couldn't afford to disappoint them. But with each passing moment, my ability to act felt increasingly stymied by my internal struggles.

"All right," I said finally, my voice sounding hollow even to my own ears. "We'll split up and try to disable Z'hleena's defenses from different points. It's risky, but it's our best shot."

"Are you sure?" Mac asked. "If something goes wrong..."

"Trust me," I said.

The plan was in motion, and we had split into smaller groups, each with a different task to disable Z'hleena's defenses. My heart raced as I led my team through the corridors of her fortress, my footsteps seeming to echo all around us.

"Remember, guys," I whispered, "we need to stay focused and work together. No matter what happens, don't let your guard down."

We approached a heavily guarded control room. What if I can't do this? What if I fail everyone?

"All right, team. Let's take out those guards and disable the defenses." I commanded, despite my fears. We sprang into action, moving quickly with precision and efficiency. I entered the control room and surveyed the myriad of buttons and switches.

"Okay," I muttered, pushing past my self-doubt, "I just need to find the right sequence to shut everything down."

"Take a deep breath, Neo." Mac's voice came through my earpiece. "You can do this. We all trust you." His words seemed to rekindle something within me—a flicker of determination that had been buried far too long. And suddenly, the daunting task before me didn't feel quite so impossible.

"Alright," I whispered. "let's finish this."

"Guys, I think I've got it!" The final sequence fell into place, and the stronghold's defenses began to shut down one by one.

"Great job, Neo!" Mac called through the earpiece. "We knew you could do it."

"Thanks, Mac," I replied. "I couldn't have done it without all of you."

The air crackled with tension as we stood facing Z'hleena, her cold, white eyes boring into each of us. Despite the fear gnawing at my insides, I clenched my fists and stared back defiantly.

"Z'hleena," I said, my voice steady and strong, "we're not going to let you hurt your prisoners, the Vihilians, or Yohzak any longer."

"Brave words from a girl who was paralyzed by self-doubt mere moments ago," she replied with a voice full of contempt. "But you underestimate me, Neo. I will not be defeated so easily."

"Neither will we," Mac said, stepping forward to stand beside me. His confidence bolstered my own, and I saw the same determination reflected in the faces of Blair, Trella, Fender, and Suzuki.

"Enough talk," I muttered. "Mac, get the prisoners to safety." I watched as she nodded and dashed off. "Trella, Fender, Suzuki––flank Z'hleena and keep her occupied. Blair, you're with me. We need to free the prisoners before it's too late."

As our group split into action, I felt the first tendrils of doubt creeping back in. But this time, instead of succumbing to their suffocating embrace, I pushed them aside and focused on what I had to do. My past struggles didn't define me—my actions in this moment did.

"Neo, watch out!" Blair's voice snapped me back to the present just in time to dodge a blast from Z'hleena. As we advanced, I could see her growing more desperate––and more dangerous. But I refused to let that deter me.

Blair finally reached one of the cells, my hands trembling as I fumbled with the lock.

The Metazoid emaciated frame sagged with relief as the door swung open.

"Fender, get them out of here," I said, then turned back to face Z'hleena. "I'll handle her."

"Neo, are you sure?" Worry etched his face and eyes.

"Absolutely," I replied, my green eyes meeting his with fierce determination. "Go."

As Fender retreated, I squared off against Z'hleena, the culmination of our conflict upon us. "Give up, Neo," she snarled, launching another attack. Her energy lances crackled in the air, fueled by some dark power source I couldn't identify. "You cannot win." "Maybe not alone," I admitted, sidestepping her assault and sending one of my own. I focused my empathic abilities to send a wave of disorientation toward her, hoping to cloud her judgment momentarily. "But together, my friends and I can overcome anything." My heart swelled with pride as Trella, Blair, and Suzuki rejoined the fray.

The air vibrated with energy as Z'hleena unleashed her dark magic, attempting to bend space and time to her will. Blair quickly activated a countermeasure, using advanced spatial stabilizers to contain the distortion field. Meanwhile, Suzuki engaged in a hand-to-hand duel with Z'hleena, parrying her strikes with his energy shield.

Trella combined their strength and agility to dodge Z'hleena's relentless attacks. The stronghold's walls echoed with clashing blades and explosive bursts of energy. Each strike was a calculated move, a dance of precision and control.

Amid the chaos, I sensed a growing desperation in Z'hleena's emotions. She knew we were gaining the upper hand, and I could feel her fear and frustration rising. But there was something else, too, something hidden beneath her rage.

"Retreat!" I shouted, realizing our primary goal was to escape and take the prisoners to safety--not defeat her here.

We fought our way to the escape tunnel. Our every move met with fierce resistance.

Finally, Blair activated a containment field, momentarily restraining Z'hleena and cutting her off briefly enough for the energy in the room to subside. We took the opportunity to escape, our hearts pounding with the adrenaline of the fight. We made it to the tunnels and retreated to the crystal cave.

CHAPTER 24

The Chimera Project

S TANDING AT THE EDGE of the vast, cavernous space, I felt the weight of my mother's pendant in my hand. The crystal cave inside Staak'al stretched before me, its walls sparkling with iridescent hues, beckoning me closer. This journey had begun with the strangest of dreams and visions, but now, it was so much more than that. I needed answers—about who I was, where I came from, and what I could do. I wrapped my arms around myself, seeking warmth and comfort. As I ventured deeper into the cave, I noticed peculiar markings on the crystal walls. They shimmered with a strange energy, drawing me toward them like a moth to a flame. I reached out tentatively, my fingertips grazing the surface. A sudden jolt of energy coursed through me, and images flooded my mind.

I struggled to understand the fragmented memories that had been unlocked. It was as if someone had handed me a puzzle, but the pieces were scattered and disjointed. I only knew the clues I sought were hidden within these crystalline walls.

"Look!" Trella exclaimed, pointing to an intricate carving emitting a faint glow. I approached it cautiously, my pulse quickening.

The carving was masterful, etched into the living biome of the translucent pink crystal walls. It depicted a creature both mesmerizing and fearsome. The carving seemed ancient, yet so detailed and intricate that it seemed to shimmer with a life of its own. It was a mixture of different species, each part sculpted with meticulous care. Its lion's head bore almost sorrowful eyes, wisdom hidden within their depths. A serpent's tail coiled and twisted, its scales chiseled to perfection, reflecting the dim light within the cave in iridescent hues. The body was a fusion of muscular mammalian limbs, each representing a different creature, their combined strength apparent even in stone.

The whole image was surrounded by intricate patterns and symbols, their meaning elusive. Still, these symbols added to the mystical aura of the carving. As I reached to touch it, the crystal beneath my fingers pulsed as if resonating with some hidden energy or secret knowledge. As my gaze lingered on the image, I felt an inexplicable connection—as if it held the key to understanding my true identity.

"Guys, I think this might be important." My voice was barely above a whisper. "There's something about it that feels familiar."

"Maybe it's a symbol or code?" Fender offered, studying the carving intently. The rest of the group kept walking, heading to the area with some food.

"Maybe," I answered, but the feeling remained. It was more profound than that. I needed to decode its significance, but how?

As I continued to venture inside the cave, more clues revealed themselves—cryptic symbols, hidden messages, and strange artifacts that seemed to resonate with me on an elemental level. My mind raced, trying to piece together the fragments of information, but it was like grasping at shadows. The cave grew darker and more oppressive. I continued cautiously over the crystalline floor beneath me. The air was cool and damp, sending shivers down my spine as I delved further into the heart of Luehiri. As if sensing my unease, the crystals seemed to pulse with eerie energy, as if they were alive.

"Wait! Neo." Yohzak called. He had been standing behind me. "There is so much more you need to know."

"Look, over there!" Yohzak pointed to a cluster of unusually shaped crystals protruding from the wall.

I held my breath, waiting for whatever secrets lay hidden within the heart of these crystals.

"Neo," Mariyah Murphy's voice rang out, her image shimmering as the video message began to play.

"I don't know how many times I rehearsed this conversation in my head. When you reached an age of understanding, I could never find the proper time to tell you what I am about to disclose. Part of me was afraid of your reaction."

"Mom..." I whispered. My heart ached as I watched her familiar face.

"Many years ago, we experimented with genetic modifications to improve humans' lives in space. As the modifications became more and more successful, we started experimenting with other DNA sources and soon created the first group of hybrids. Those hybrids were named 'Super Hybrids.' Regrettably, they were physically and psychologically unstable due to lethal deformities and organ problems. As a result, all Super Hybrids were terminated, the research project was closed, and any surviving Super Hybrid was persecuted and exterminated. The Super Hybrid project was called Chimera. It resulted from many years of work that your father and I were involved."

I felt my chest tighten like an invisible hand had seized my heart.

"Neo," Yohzak said softly, "are you all right?"

"I... I don't know." I felt my voice trembling. "This is... it's a lot to take in."

"Take your time, Neo," Yohzak assured me.

As the video message continued to play, I struggled to process the enormity of what I'd just learned. Mariyah's voice echoed through the cavern, her words heavy with significance.

"We never gave up perfecting the experiment, and after ten years of working on it behind closed doors, your father and I believed we had achieved the correct balance in the equation to make a Super Hybrid who would have no deformities or organ issues. An entirely new race of Super Hybrids, human/alien who would be far superior to both races and who could ensure peace to the entire galaxy. Out of the three embryos, only one succeeded. We named that embryo Neo. We decided to raise you as a human. But, for your safety, we kept the truth of your origins a secret.

Your biological father, Peter Murphy, is the mastermind behind The Chimera Project. And Queen Nahyla, who has since died, is your biological mother."

"Queen Nahyla? I'm part Luehirian?" My breath caught in my throat, the name falling from my lips like a prayer. The weight of this revelation was staggering. I felt as if the ground beneath my feet had shifted, leaving me to grapple for solid footing.

As the reality of my lineage settled in, an overwhelming mix of emotions coursed through me—disbelief, shock, anger, and something else I couldn't quite identify.

Chapter 25

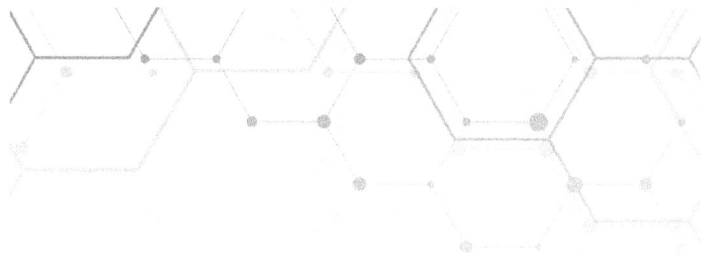

Wind and Will

"**N**EO," MAC WHISPERED. "TAKE a moment to process this. You're stronger than you realize. Remember that." I forced a weak smile, grateful for his presence and support. My thoughts churned like a whirlwind, struggling to accept the truth about my parents and the origin of my existence. I knew my life would never be the same.

The cavern around us grew colder as if the walls were recoiling from the revelation. My body trembled with shock and anger, my mind struggling to comprehend everything. My friends gathered around me. I was grateful for their support but, at the same time, desperate to protect them from the potentially dangerous implications of my newfound identity.

"Everything has changed now. How can this be? I've always known I was different but wasn't prepared for this." I touched my red hair, my face, my arms. I look so human.

"I can't say I'm surprised. You may look human on the outside, but your energy never felt like that of a human. Not like Blair, Suzuki, or Mac's. But Neo, please remember you're our friend—no matter what." Fender said.

"Nothing will change that," Suzuki chimed in, shooting me a determined grin. "We'll make sure of it."

"Your parents must have had a reason for keeping this secret," Blair reasoned. "Maybe they knew how dangerous it could be and wanted to protect you. That doesn't excuse withholding the truth but shows they cared about you."

"Z'hleena can't know about this," I insisted, knowing my lower lip quivered. "If she finds out who I really am—what I'm capable of—she'll stop at nothing to control or destroy me. We have to be even more cautious."

"That's right," Mac said. "We'll keep your secret safe, Neo. I promise."

A heavy silence settled over us, punctuated only by the faint water dripping from the cavern's ceiling. My thoughts raced. In the distance, something stirred—a soft, almost imperceptible sound.

"Did you hear that?" I asked my voice tight with fear. "It sounded like footsteps."

"Neo," Yohzak began as he walked toward us. His voice was solemn and tinged with sadness. "You result from The Chimera Project, a Super Hybrid—a successful fusion of human and alien DNA."

I stared at him. I was a Super Hybrid. My entire existence, my powers, all of it was because of this secret experiment. At that moment, I realized I was walking a tightrope between two worlds, part of me and neither truly mine.

"Your powers," Yohzak continued, "are a manifestation of your unique genetic makeup. Your empathic abilities come from your human side, while your telekinesis and psychokinesis stem from your alien heritage."

"What does this mean for me?" I asked.

"It means you possess abilities no one else has," Yohzak explained. "You have the potential to be a powerful force for good but also a target for those who would seek to exploit or destroy you."

As he spoke, I felt my mind racing, connecting the dots of my life thus far. No wonder I had always felt out of place, like I didn't belong anywhere. It was because I belonged to two different worlds—and yet, now that I knew the truth, I couldn't deny the relief and sense of purpose it brought.

"Neo." Mac gently reached out to touch my arm. "This is a lot for you to take in."

I was grateful for his support and that of our friends. I was a Super Hybrid, and with that came incredible responsibility and potential.

"Let's start by testing your telekinesis and psychokinesis," Trella suggested, her eyes sparkling. "I bet you can do some amazing things."

"All right," I agreed hesitantly, focusing on a small rock nearby. With every ounce of concentration, I willed it to move—and to my astonishment, it lifted into the air, hovering just above the ground.

"Wow," Fender breathed, his eyes wide with awe. "That's incredible, Neo."

"Try controlling it with your mind," Blair said, almost bouncing excitedly.

Taking a deep breath, I visualized the rock moving in a specific pattern and watched as it obeyed my mental commands, zigzagging through the air before coming to a gentle stop at my feet.

"Neo!" Mac exclaimed. "You're doing it! You've got this."

"Yohzak," I said, returning to him with renewed confidence. "What do I need to know about these powers? How can I master them?"

"Training and practice," he said. "Be patient with yourself and embrace your true identity. You can change the course of history, Neo, but only if you accept who and what you are."

In the days following, I threw myself into mastering my newfound abilities. With Yohzak's guidance and my friends' encouragement, I explored the depths of my powers, unlocking abilities I could never have imagined.

"Stay in sync, Neo," Yohzak encouraged, his eyes fixed on a complex holographic puzzle before me. "Understand its structure, recognize its pattern, and guide it into place."

I closed my eyes for a moment, feeling the intricate geometry of the puzzle in my mind, the pieces yearning to find their perfect alignment. Opening my eyes, I reached out with my thoughts and manipulated the holographic fragments. Slowly, yet with a certainty that thrummed in my veins, they clicked into place, forming a beautiful three-dimensional image.

A hushed silence filled the room before Mac's voice broke through, tinged with respect and wonder. "That was something else, Neo. Truly remarkable." His eyes met mine, and I could see the pride reflected in them.

"Try psychokinesis now," Trella suggested. Their pointy ears twitched excitedly. "You'll ace it, Neo."

"Right," I nodded determinedly. Through the connection I had established with the rock, I visualized its changing shape. To my amazement, the stone began to morph, its edges slowly softening until it formed a perfect sphere.

"Wow, Neo!" Blair cheered. "That's incredible!"

Yohzak's dark eyes filled with pride. "Indeed. You're making rapid progress, Neo."

I grinned my thanks and allowed the sphere to float back onto the pyramid. With these new powers, I felt stronger and more capable. Blair clapped her hands together. "Neo, let's see if you can levitate all the rocks at once!"

I nodded and laughed at her enthusiasm.

I stood at the edge of an expansive field, the tall grass swaying gently in the wind like a sea of green. The sky above was a brilliant shade of blue, dotted with fluffy white clouds that seemed to dance with the breeze. I could feel the faint sun's warmth on my face, and as I closed my eyes, I let the sensation wash over me.

With my telekinesis, I focused on boulders nearby, trying to lift them off the ground. At first, they didn't budge, but as I persisted, I felt the connection between my mind and the objects strengthen. Inch by inch, the boulders rose, suspended in midair by the force of my willpower alone.

"Wow, Neo!" Blair's eyes were wide with amazement. "You're getting better and better at this!"

The corners of my mouth lifted in a grin. As I released the boulder, allowing it to return to the earth with a soft thud, I marveled at the power that coursed through my veins.

"Okay, now try something more challenging," Trella suggested. "Like what?" A towering Zhe'lonn tree loomed over us, its iridescent branches stretching like luminescent tendrils against the alien sky. Mac pointed to the tree.

"See if you can create a gust of wind strong enough to knock over that tree." "Are you sure?" I hesitated. "I mean, that's a pretty big tree. The Zhe'lonn trees are known to be robust."

"Come on, Neo," Fender said, his metallic voice resonating. "You can do it." I agreed, hoping I was up for the challenge.

I paused and focused my energy on the task at hand, connecting with the complex energy grid of Luehiri. At first, nothing happened. But then, as if responding to my will, the air around me began to stir. The wind picked up speed, growing stronger and more forceful, the planet's energy field amplifying my control. "Neo, I think you've got it!" Suzuki shouted over the roar of the wind. "Keep going!" Mac said, gripping my hand tightly, his skin cool.

With their encouragement fueling me, I pushed harder against the raging winds. The winds howled like a pack of mechanized wolves, and the Zhe'lonn tree groaned under pressure, its luminescent trunk bending ever so slightly. "Neo, look out!" Before I could react, a resounding crack echoed through the air, amplified by the alien acoustics. I felt the ground beneath my feet tremble. The Zhe'lonn tree was falling--straight toward us.

"Run!" Blair screamed, her voice barely audible above the cacophony. We sprinted away from the collapsing tree, and the world seemed to blur around me. Shades of vibrant green and electric blue melded together in a dizzying whirlwind of color. And then, without warning, everything went black. As I opened my eyes, the world seemed to spin around me. Memories of the tree crashing down on me rushed back as my head throbbed with pain. Slowly, I tried to sit up, but Mac and Blair rushed to my side, urging me to stay still. "Hey, hey, take it easy," Mac said.

"You took quite a hit there, Neo. How are you feeling?"

I winced, feeling the ache in my body, but managed a weak smile.

"I've had better days, that's for sure."

Blair's eyes widened. "That is an understatement! That tree was massive, and I can't believe you survived."

"Perks of being a Super Hybrid, I guess." I winked. Acknowledging the uncanny resilience that my hybrid nature gave me.

CHAPTER 26

A Treacherous Path

A S THE FINAL GLEAM of the sun kissed the horizon goodbye, we wound our way through the hazardous wastelands of Luehiri. Z'hleena's fortress, an alien construct of nightmare proportions, cast a threatening silhouette against the dwindling light. Jagged remnants of a forgotten civilization dug into the soles of our feet, and the impending darkness seemed to swallow the path ahead, turning navigation into a game of luck and memory. Excitement mingled with dread, tying my insides into a knot on the verge of unraveling.

"Watch your step," Mac warned us. His voice was barely audible over the howling wind that whipped around us, carrying a metallic tang. He extended a hand to help Blair navigate a particularly tricky patch of rocks. She muttered her thanks, eyes never leaving the ground.

Trella and Fender led the group with their keen senses, alert for traps or guards that might lie in wait. Suzuki's eyes were ablaze with energy as we inched closer to the stronghold. "This is what I live for," he whispered.

Our progress slowed as we began to encounter Z'hleena's defenses. A laser grid blocked our path, the searing red beams crisscrossing just above the ground. Trella studied the grid intently, then turned to address the group.

"Stay close and follow my exact steps," they instructed. We huddled together, watching as they gracefully stepped between the beams. One by one, we mimicked their movements, our hearts pounding in our chests.

"Nice work, Trella!" Fender said as we cleared the laser grid. His bluish skin glistened with sweat. But there was no time to celebrate; more challenges lay ahead.

A sudden burst of gunfire erupted from a hidden turret, sending us diving for cover behind the rocks. Blair clenched her teeth as she worked on an improvised jamming device. "Just... a... second," she muttered.

"Come on, Blair, you can do it." I encouraged her, even though my voice shook with the strain of our mission. Mac knew the danger we faced, and he squeezed my hand.

Blair's device worked its magic, and the gunfire ceased. We scrambled to our feet and pressed onward. Suzuki led the charge, but we were soon forced to halt once more as we encountered another trap—a narrow bridge with electrified cables stretched across it, like a deadly tightrope walk.

Suzuki's black eyes twinkled. "Leave this one to me." He deftly navigated the cables, agile as a cat. As he reached the other side, he grinned wildly. "Piece of cake!"

"Your bravery is impressive, Suzuki," Trella said, their pointy ears twitching slightly. "But we must remain vigilant. There are surely more dangers ahead."

As we continued our treacherous journey toward the stronghold, I wondered if we would all make it out alive. Every step we took was a testament to our determination to save the distressed aliens and stop Z'hleena, with higher stakes than ever. The world seemed to tilt as we pushed deeper into Z'hleena's stronghold, the dim light of dusk casting eerie shadows across the alien landscape. The air hummed with tension, thick and suffocating like a noose tightening around our throats. I could taste the metallic tang of fear on my tongue.

Suddenly, the ground erupted in a cacophony of noise. Dozens of armed soldiers materialized from hidden vantage points with advanced weapons aimed directly at us. An icy chill of terror coursed through my veins—we'd walked right into their trap.

"Hands up!" one of the enemy soldiers barked. "You're surrounded."

"Stay calm, everyone," Trella urged us. "We can figure this out."

"Figure this out?" Fender hissed. "We're as good as dead!"

"Enough!" Blair shouted. "We've come too far to give up now. We have to fight!"

As if on cue, shouting and gunfire erupted all around us. Chaos reigned as the enemy soldiers closed in, their weaponry cutting through the air like deadly blades. My heart clenched in horror as they grabbed Blair and dragged her away from our group.

"Let her go!" Mac roared, lunging forward only to be held back by Fender's strong arms.

"Mac, don't!" Fender cried. "We can't risk it!"

"Fender's right," Suzuki said. "We have to be smart about this. We'll find a way to get her back, I promise."

I felt the energy within me swell, a torrent of psychokinetic power ready to be unleashed. My eyes locked onto the soldiers, my mind connecting with their weapons. With determination, I willed their firearms to jam and lock in place.

"NOW!" I screamed.

We seized the opportunity. Mac and Fender attacked, overpowering the stunned soldiers. Suzuki hacked into a nearby control panel, sealing the doors behind us.

"Blair's gone," Trella whispered, still trembling from the ordeal. Their voice quivered as if they were speaking of a ghost. The group exchanged grim nods of agreement. Blair's life—and the fate of countless aliens—depended on us.

"Let's move," Mac urged. "We've got a mission to finish."

I wondered what lay ahead. Would we succeed in saving Blair and stopping Z'hleena, or were we merely hurtling toward our own destruction? Only time would tell—and time was running out.

"Suzuki, cover our flank!" Mac shouted over the deafening sound of energy blasts. I observed carefully from behind a craggy boulder covered in luminescent moss, marked by past battles. Twisted, silvery branches of alien trees stood nearby, resembling ancient sentinels. The shattered remnants of towering buildings were visible in the background, a grim testament to the conflict.

Suzuki charged headfirst into the fray, visible through gaps in the makeshift cover. He wielded a pair of advanced plasma pistols with deadly precision, firing at Z'hleena's forces with an intensity that matched their own. His movements were swift and fluid, like an unstoppable force of nature, weaving between the debris and the labyrinthine growth of alien flora. I admired his courage as he dove behind a fallen piece of metallic structure to avoid an incoming blast.

"Neo, Trella, Fender—follow me! We need to push forward!" Mac yelled.

As we fought to get through, I noticed Suzuki sustained several injuries—a deep gash on his arm, a burn on his shoulder, and countless bruises. Yet he showed no signs of slowing down or backing away. He was a whirlwind of heroic defiance, leaving destruction in his wake.

"Watch out!" Trella cried, pointing to an enemy soldier taking aim at Suzuki. But it was too late—the shot connected, and Suzuki crumpled to the ground, his weapons clattering beside him. My breath caught in my throat, and my heart felt like it had stopped beating. But as the reality of Suzuki's death sank in, Fender's face twisted into a mask of rage. His eyes narrowed, and he locked onto the soldier who had fired the fatal shot. I could see something snap within him, a burning determination and thirst for vengeance igniting his soul.

"Fender, wait!" I called, but it was too late. He was already moving, his body propelled by a force beyond human control.

Still smirking at his success, the S'borrathian soldier didn't see Fender coming. He didn't see the fury in his eyes or the energy blade that glinted as it was unsheathed.

With a cry that was more animal than human, Fender lunged at the soldier. Their weapons clashed in a spark of light, and I watched from behind a cluster of alien boulders, my heart pounding.

The fight was a blur of motion, Fender's movements a lethal dance as he attacked with a ferocity I had never seen before. The soldier fought back, his weapon swinging in desperate arcs, but Fender was relentless. He moved with precision and deadly intent, every strike a step closer to his goal.

I saw when it happened the instant Fender's blade found its mark. The soldier's eyes widened, a look of shock and realization crossing his face as the energy blade sliced through him. He fell, his body crumpling to the ground, and the battlefield fell into a momentary hush, the only sound the ragged breathing of my remaining teammates. Fender stood over the fallen soldier, his chest heaving, his face a pale shade of blue but resolute. The fury had left his eyes, replaced by a hollow emptiness that spoke of loss and grief.

We made our way to him, each of us reaching out to touch his shoulder, a silent gesture of support and understanding. "Keep moving!" Fender barked. "We can't let his sacrifice be for nothing!"

As we pressed onward, I glanced back at Suzuki's lifeless form. His death was a stark reminder of the consequences we faced in our fight against Z'hleena—and a testament to the resolve we would need to see our mission through.

"Let's make sure he didn't die in vain," Mac said. "We need to save Blair and end this madness." I nodded, tears blurring my vision as I forced myself to focus on the task. We had lost a friend but couldn't afford to lose ourselves. The stakes were too high, and Suzuki's memory deserved nothing less than our unyielding determination.

The world seemed to slow down as if suspended in time. I stared at Suzuki's lifeless body, unable to process what had just happened.

Hot tears threatened to spill over, and my heart clenched with loss. A chorus of anguish rang out around me, echoing my own.

"Suzuki!" Mac yelled, slamming his fist against a tree. "Why did you have to be so reckless?"

"Because that's who he was," Trella whispered, their voice trembling. "Always looking for adventure, always trying to prove himself."

"We'll avenge him and save those innocent lives," I said. I wiped away my tears. "Suzuki wouldn't want us to give up now."

"Neo's right," Fender said. "We need to push forward."

"Okay," I said. "How do we proceed? We know Z'hleena is heavily guarded, and we've already lost two of our team members."

"Maybe... maybe we can use some sort of diversion to draw the guards away?" Trella suggested.

"Trella is right!" Mac exclaimed. "If we can create enough chaos, we might be able to slip past their defenses unnoticed."

"Let's do it then," I agreed. "For Suzuki."

"Z'hleena won't even know what hit her," Fender growled, clenching his fists.

"Right," I breathed, forcing myself to focus on the mission. "For Suzuki, Blair, the prisoners, and ourselves."

"Let's go," Mac said, leading the way.

We moved quickly, like shadows. As we crept through the barren terrain, we were all hurting, but there was no time for tears—not yet.

"Be on guard," Trella whispered. "We don't know what else Z'hleena has waiting for us."

Mac gripped his weapon tightly. It hummed with eerie energy, a testament to the advanced alien technology we'd acquired for this mission. My weapon felt strangely cold against my skin, as if it also mourned our fallen friend.

The air around us was thick with tension, the smell of burnt ozone, and fear. Our footsteps echoed softly across the rocky landscape. As we advanced, a fleeting thought of failure crossed my mind, momentarily shadowed by the memory of Suzuki's death. But I quickly dispelled those doubts with the determination that we would see it through—no matter the cost.

"Look," Fender murmured, pointing toward a cluster of guards up ahead. Their armor glinted in the dim light, a menacing sight that chilled me to the bone. "We'll have to take them out if we want to get past."

"Stay focused, everyone," Mac added. "Remember our plan."

The guards were well-armed, and the air was filled with the hum of charged energy weapons. The smell of ozone hung heavy in the atmosphere.

Our movements were slow and deliberate as we waded through the treacherous landscape. Each step felt like an eternity, yet time seemed to race at breakneck speed. In the distance, the stronghold loomed large and menacing, a testament to Z'hleena's power and ruthlessness.

"Remember," Mac whispered against my ear, "we need to disable their communications first."

Trella worked quickly and deftly over the controls of their portable hacking device. We huddled together, our backs pressed against one another, as we awaited their signal.

"Done," they finally announced, a hint of triumph in their voice.

"Good," Mac said and turned to Fender. "Now, let's create a diversion."

As Fender unleashed a barrage of energy blasts toward the guards, we heard their shouts of surprise and confusion. The ensuing chaos provided the perfect opportunity for us to slip past them and into the stronghold itself.

Inside, the walls seemed to close in on us as we navigated the dimly lit corridors, wary of the potential dangers hidden around every corner.

"Suzuki would've loved this," I thought, a bittersweet smile tugging at my lips.

"Stay sharp," Mac cautioned as we approached what appeared to be the heart of the stronghold. "We're close now."

Our boots echoed through the dark corridor, punctuated by our labored breathing.

"Let's pick up the pace," Mac said. His hand tightened around the grip of his advanced plasma rifle.

We moved swiftly, our hearts pounding. As we rounded a corner, a high-pitched beep pierced the silence. Fender reacted instantly, tackling Mac and me to the ground as an explosion rocked the hallway behind us.

"Thanks, Fender," Mac said, coughing from the dust filling the air.

"Of course." Fender offered me a smile, though it didn't quite reach his eyes. "Just be more careful, Mac."

"Trust me, I'm trying," Mac replied.

As we continued onward, we encountered more traps—laser grids, hidden pitfalls, and even robotic guards. We overcame each obstacle, yet time seemed to slip through our fingers like sand, making us increasingly frantic.

"Is it just me, or does this place feel like a maze?" Trella panted, wiping their brow with the back of her hand.

"Z'hleena clearly doesn't want us to find her," Mac said, scanning the dark passage.

"Then we'll just have to be smarter than her," I muttered, pushing aside my doubts.

"Listen!" Trella hissed, pressing their ear against a nearby door. "I think I hear voices."

"Let's check it out," Mac said, signaling us to follow him.

As we entered the room, we found ourselves surrounded by Z'hleena's soldiers, their weapons raised and ready. A cruel smile spread across their faces as they closed in on us.

"Do you guys ever give up? Isn't it time for you to return to Ryser and study for finals like any other student?" a sneering voice said over the intercom. Z'hleena's sinister laughter was getting under my skin.

As we prepared to engage the enemy, a sudden blast shook the room, knocking us off our feet. The ceiling began to crumble, and I could feel the floor giving way beneath us. Panic bubbled up inside me, clawing at my throat as I fought to maintain control. At that moment, it felt as if everything we had worked toward was unraveling before our eyes.

"Neo!" Mac shouted, reaching for my hand as the world collapsed.

"Mac!" I yelled, but the darkness swallowed my words.

Everything went dark, and a sensation of weightlessness overtook me. My mind raced, struggling to make sense of what had just happened.

When I finally came to, I found myself in a cell. The cell was dark, and the only light came from the faint glow of strange symbols on the walls. My body ached, and my head throbbed, but I was alive.

"Neo, you're awake!" Mac's voice broke through the fog in my mind, and I turned to see him at my side.

"Where are we?" I asked, my voice weak.

"We're trapped inside a highly advanced technological chamber filled with intricate mathematical puzzles and interconnected locking mechanisms," he replied, his face grim. "It's designed like a complex labyrinth, requiring us to solve each equation to unlock the doors and progress. We've been working on it for a few hours."

"Hours? How long have I been out?" I asked.

"A while," Trella responded. "Z'hleena used gas to put us to sleep, and her guards dragged us here." I looked around, examining the intricate designs and equations adorning the walls. Panic bubbled up inside me, but I fought to keep it at bay. We had to stay focused if we were going to get out of here.

"We have to solve these puzzles to open the doors," Mac said, joining us. "Fender's already working on one of them." I glanced over to see Fender studying a complex equation. His brow furrowed in concentration. We were in a race against time, and every second counted.

"Let's get to work," I said. "We have to find Blair."

We split up, each of us tackling a different puzzle. We filled the room with the sound of our voices, calling out ideas and solutions, working together to uncover the mysteries that had us trapped. The puzzles were challenging, combining mathematics, logic, and spatial reasoning. But we were a team, bringing our unique strengths to the table.

Slowly but surely, we began to make progress. One by one, the doors unlocked, and we moved closer to freedom.

"Got it!" Fender exclaimed, solving the final puzzle. The last door slid open, revealing a corridor beyond.

"We did it," Mac said, relief in his voice. "Let's go find Blair."

We made our way through the stronghold, our minds still reeling from the escape room experience.

Chapter 27

Trella's Plight

T HE NORTH WING OF Z'hleena's stronghold was like something out of a nightmare. Its towering walls were made of dark metal that seemed to absorb the scant light. The air was thick with the smell of burning metal and the sound of distant screams. The damp ground beneath my boots made each step feel heavy and deliberate.

"Neo" Mac's voice was barely a whisper as he squeezed my hand. "We'll find them. We'll save them." I nodded, trying to stifle the tears that threatened to fall. Even though I knew Mac was right, I felt like a failure at that moment. I couldn't shake the image of Blair being dragged away. Her face twisted in pain and fear. Tears streamed down my face. My heart sank, weighed down by the feeling of defeat and self-doubt. I clenched my fists, feeling my nails dig into my palms as I tried to hold on to the anger that surged within me.

As we continued down the corridor, Fender led the way. I knew they all felt the same way I did—desperate to save our friends, yet uncertain about how to proceed.

As much as I wanted to believe in my strength and abilities, doubt clawed at the edges of my mind, whispering poisonous thoughts that made me question my worth. I thought I was not strong enough to do this, my chest tightening with anxiety. I've failed them all. I brought Suzuki here, and now he's dead. I couldn't lose Blair as well.

The corridor seemed endless, the darkness oppressive, and every step forward felt like a battle against my doubts.

We continued deeper into the complex, and I noticed the smell of burning metal that filled the air, growing stronger as we got closer to the source. The scent was almost suffocating, making it difficult to breathe and think clearly.

We moved cautiously, alert to any potential threats lurking around each corner. The stronghold was a maze of tunnels and chambers, its secrets locked away behind heavy doors and guard patrols that we had to carefully evade.

"Wait," Fender said, suddenly holding a hand to signal us to stop. We crouched down, listening intently as approaching footsteps grew louder.

My breath caught in my throat as we stumbled upon a large room, dimly illuminated by an advanced form of lighting from bioluminescent panels embedded within the walls, pulsating with a soft glow. The room was filled with captives from different species, their eyes reflecting the unique lighting, each a haunting testament to the reach and power of our enemies. The air was thick with the stench of unwashed bodies and fear, and low murmurs of hopelessness echoed around us. I could feel their pain, their despair––it was like a crushing weight on my chest.

"Look at them all..." Trella said softly. "We have to do something, Neo."

I nodded, my heart pounding fiercely. This was the moment we had been working toward but seeing the enormity of the task before me made it all too real. "We're going to free them," I vowed. "Every last one of them."

"There are guards everywhere. We need to be smart about this." Fender said.

"Right," Mac agreed. "Let's split up and take them out one by one. That way, we can minimize the risk and maximize our chances of success."

We moved through the cells like shadows, taking out the guards one by one with silent precision. Each time a captive was freed, their eyes met mine––some filled with gratitude, others with disbelief that they could finally escape their nightmare.

"Go, get to safety," I told them, my voice cracking with emotion. "And don't look back."

As the last of the captives slipped away, the enormity of our mission began to truly sink in. So many lives had been saved, but countless others were still suffering under Z'hleena's rule.

"Stay sharp." Fender's voice was barely audible over the steady hum of machinery echoing through the halls. We crept cautiously forward, each step taking us deeper into enemy territory.

"Neo, you're up." Mac nodded toward a locked door up ahead. I closed my eyes, focusing all my empathic energy on the intricate mechanisms within the lock. A bead of sweat trickled down my temple as I manipulated the tumblers. "Got it," I breathed, opening the door to reveal a faintly illuminated chamber filled with cages. Prisoners from all over the galaxy—Blair among them—huddled against one another, their expressions a potent mix of terror and hope.

"Thank God you're here," Blair whispered, her eyes wide with relief. "We didn't know if—"

"Shh," I cut her off, fear gripping my chest like a vice. "We need to be quiet."

We heard chatter and footsteps approaching as we worked to free the captives.

"Neo!" Blair hissed urgently. "Guards!"

"Go, now!" I ordered, grabbing Blair's arm and shoving Trella toward the exit. But as we scrambled to escape, a pair of guards burst into the room, seizing Trella and dragging her away.

"NO!" I screamed, my heart breaking as her cries echoed through the chamber. "Trella!"

"Neo, we have to go," Mac urged, his grip on my arms firm but gentle. "We can't save her if we're caught too."

"Alright," I choked out, tears streaming down my cheeks. "Let's go."

As we retreated into the tunnels, I vowed to do whatever it took to rescue Trella and the others.

Chapter 28

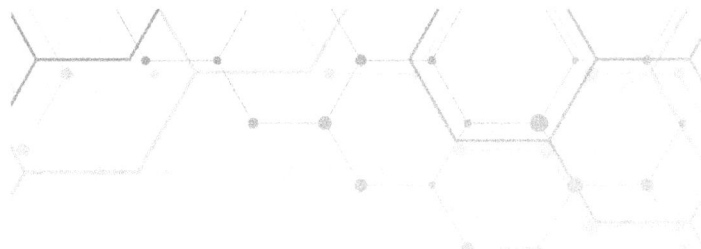

Shadow of Insecurity

THE DARKNESS OF THE Luehiri night enveloped me like a heavy cloak, its weight pressing down and intensifying the gravity of my thoughts. Stars dotted the sky, providing faint illumination barely penetrating the all-consuming shadows. The air was cool against my skin, raising goosebumps on my arms and neck, but it did little to numb the emotional turmoil bubbling beneath the surface.

In my mind, I mourned Suzuki and worried for Trella, imprisoned in Z'hleena's stronghold. At the same time, I struggled to accept that Nahyla—an alien, the ruler of Luehiri—was my biological mother. I carried a mixture of human and alien DNA within me, yet the Queen was dead, and I would never meet her.

I never expected to return to Staak'al's crystalline cave. Yet here I was, drawn back to the pulsating pink walls and ethereal glow. This time, I descended alone into the living biome.

As I walked further in, the surrounding walls resembled an ornate structure caught in a chain-melted state, fluid and ever-changing. The golden filigree and crystalline facets seemed to have fused, flowing together like liquid metal.

With each step I took deeper into the cave, the space around me seemed to vibrate with a resonant hum that I could feel permeating my bones. I trailed my fingers along the smooth walls, watching rainbow fractals of light dance in response.

Then, a shimmering figure coalesced at the heart of the cavern. An apparition of pure light gradually took the form of a female alien. Her eyes were large and ovoid, midnight blue with flecks of stardust. They held centuries of wisdom and sadness as she gazed at me.

Golden energy bands swirled around her, matching the aura I had seen on the ancient murals. This was no illusion. Somehow, at last, I was in the presence of Queen Nahyla—my biological mother.

Though she had perished long ago, her essence lived on here, woven into the crystal matrix of Luehiri itself. I sank to my knees before her projected form, overwhelmed and mesmerized.

"My child," her voice echoing softly, suffused with warmth and regret. *"At long last, we meet."*

I had no words.

Her lyrical accent reminded me of a half-forgotten lullaby. Here was the celestial ruler, guardian of her people for eons, now speaking to me. Her spirit had traversed time and space to reach this moment. She extended a shimmering hand to cradle my head, her touch as gentle as moonlight. In her fathomless eyes, I saw realms upon realms flashing past in cosmic migration. Her heritage was etched into every atom of this crystal sanctuary.

And in me as well. However improbable, I was her descendant.

"Neo, listen to what I have to say. I don't have much time. I met your father 16 human years ago. We met on Mars during a conference I attended. At the time, no one had really seen a Luehirian before, and I showed myself as human, also for my protection as a ruling Queen. Your father and I became very close. I knew he was married, and I initially saw our relationship strictly as that of scientists. I was also interested in your father's and Shane's experiments."

"Shane? As in Mac's dad? I didn't know he knew my father."

"They were close friends and collaborated often. We talked about Luehiri, our civilization, and we talked about Staak'al. Your father was experimenting with hybrids to lengthen human lives, but he wasn't successful. For reasons I don't have time to explain fully, I wanted to help your father. I admired his passion and perseverance, so I offered to help him. I knew your father found the human version of me to be attractive, but I wanted him to see how I really was. One day, your father's wife, whom I never officially met, wasn't in the lab, so I came over. We discussed our plans to bring to life a being that would be part human and part Luehirian—someone who would have the best of both species. Your father kissed me that day—the human version of me. Luehirians don't experience romantic love the way humans do, so I knew your father was growing feelings for who he perceived I was. So I showed him my

true form, knowing he would probably lose interest in me. But he didn't. Your father was a man ahead of his time, and my appearance did not deter our plans. He still wanted to go ahead with it. I must admit that I also dreamed of a collaboration between our species, but it was more than that on my side. I knew I could not be in your life, but I thought you would discover the truth when you grew older and would want to meet me."

"I'm confused," I said, disappointed that I was only an experiment.

"Neo, I sense your disappointment, but I must tell you I cared about your father. I never expected to feel love for someone, especially not some-one from a different species. However, that feeling fueled my conviction that we needed to go through with our plans and create life out of a beautiful connection between the two species."

"What about Mariyah? Did she know?" Now I understood why she was always so distant from me and why I felt so unloved. She must have known that it was something more than just an experiment.

My emotions were all over the place. I spent my entire life trying to understand why I was like this and felt like I didn't fit in, to learn that they made me without considering Mariyah's feelings. I loved Mariyah. She was the only mom I've ever had, and I couldn't imagine how hard it was for her to raise a child that wasn't hers. My head spun, and I didn't know if I wanted to learn anything else.

"Neo, Mariyah, and your father were no longer together as man and woman. They were living in separate places."

"Who carried me?" I asked Maryah for a picture or an image of me in her belly, but she never showed me one.

"That's because there was none. Neo, you are part human and part Luehirian. Your father and I didn't conceive you like humans conceive a child. Instead, I provided him with my genetic material, and he combined his. We placed you in something like an incubator."

Nahyla's image approached me, and I involuntarily took a step back.

"Your father and I hoped I would spend time with you here in Luehiri and Mars. I thought I could be in your life. But time was the only thing I didn't have. Once conceived, Mariyah agreed to raise you as her child on Mars."

"I don't have much time, Neo. Staak'al is our life force. That is why I can be here with you right now. But I can't exist in this form much longer. So you need to pay attention to what I have to tell you. Z'hlena is much more powerful than you can imagine. She has powers far superior to what I've ever had. So don't underestimate her."

"Although Z'hlena is a powerful being, she is not immortal. She will age, and there is nothing that Z'hlena wants more than to have eternal life."

"And since Staak'al is Luehirians life force and what makes you immortal, she hopes to harvest it and somehow use it to get immortality," I concluded.

"That is correct."

"But if you're immortal, how are you...dead?"

"Luehirians are immortal, which means we can't die of natural causes." Nahyla's hologram was fading away. I knew I was losing her.

"My child, my love, I will always be with you. Follow your instincts. You are more powerful than you know. You are part Luehirian. Trust that you'll save them. I will always be with you."

And just like that, Nahyla was gone.

CHAPTER 29

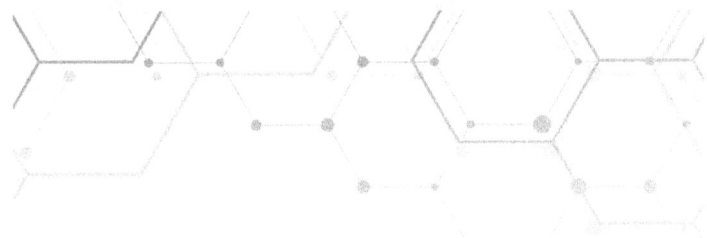

Challenges and Sacrifices

M Y LUNGS BURNED AS I gasped for air, dragging my exhausted body through the rough terrain of Luehiri. Weeks had passed since I set off on this journey to rescue the Vihilians and other aliens from Z'hleena's captivity.

"Neo!" Mac shouted, his voice strained and weary. "We don't have much time. We need to keep moving."

I glanced back at Mac. The sight of him, solid and determined, fueled my resolve to push forward. Our group, a mixture of humans and aliens, shared one common goal: infiltrating Z'hleena's stronghold and saving my friend Trella and the remaining captives within its walls.

"Neo," Mac said, placing a hand on my shoulder. "I know this mission means everything to you. But we have to be careful. Z'hleena won't hesitate to kill any of us."

"Mac's right," Blair agreed. "We've come so far, but we can't let our guard down now."

I studied the faces of Blair and Fender. The weight of the words I was about to say felt like a planet's gravity pressing on my chest. I took a deep breath, my green eyes flickering with uncertainty.

"All right, everyone," I began, my voice steadier than I felt. "There's something you need to know. We'll be meeting up with Shane Robbs soon. He's been helping us gather intel on Z'hleena's operation."

Everyone froze. Fender's eyes narrowed, his face twisting in disbelief. "Shane?" he demanded, his voice tinged with suspicion. "As in Mac's father, Shane?"

I nodded, feeling an icy shiver run down my spine despite my best efforts to stay composed. "Yep," I replied, my voice barely above a whisper. "He's not just a researcher and physician. He's also a skilled hacker." Fender's eyes searched mine, seeking answers or reassurance. I could feel the tension building in the room. "But can we really trust him?" he asked, his voice cracking.

I looked away, my mind reeling with memories and emotions. Trusting Shane now felt like a gamble, a desperate dice roll. My stomach churned with doubt as I met Fender's eyes again.

"Shane and my father were friends once," I muttered, my voice faltering. "We have little choice. We have to trust him." A heavy silence filled the room, each grappling with this unexpected twist.

As we approached our rendezvous point, I noticed a tall figure leaning against a tree, examining a holographic screen projected from a wrist device. His sharp features were strikingly like Mac's. "Neo, Blair, and Fender–I've infiltrated Z'hleena's security system, but there's something you need to see."

Despite his calm demeanor, I sensed that something was off. As we huddled around to view the holographic screen, I watched Shane closely, keenly aware of the tension building between us.

"Look at this," he said, tapping on the screen. The image flickered, revealing rows upon rows of aliens held captive in those cells. "Z'hleena has them rigged with some sort of explosive implants. One wrong move, and she could kill them all."

"Damn," Mac whispered. "We need to disable those devices before we attempt a rescue."

"Precisely," Shane said, his eyes meeting mine. "I can help with that, but I'll need access to your team's resources. Trust me, I want to save your friend and the prisoners as much as you do."

"Okay," I said hesitantly. "But we'll be keeping an eye on you."

"Fair enough," Shane replied with a tight smile.

As we walked toward the stronghold's entrance, my mind raced with suspicion and doubt. *Why had Shane decided to help us? And could we really trust him to help us save Trella and the prisoners?*

"Neo, Mac whispered," are you all right?"

"I don't know," I admitted. "Something about your father doesn't feel right. But we have no choice—we need him."

Mac stopped abruptly, his eyes widening with disbelief. He turned to face me, his face flushed with anger. "What are you saying? He's helping us. He's putting his life in danger to help us. How can you doubt him now?"

"I don't know. I have nothing concrete, but I must go with my gut feeling. My mother, Nahyla, told me to trust my instincts." I explained.

Mac ran a hand through his unruly brown hair and said. "Fine. Let's wait and see."

Once we were inside the stronghold, Shane began. "I have something to tell you all." His eyes flickered. "I've been working against Z'hleena this whole time."

The words hung in the air, heavy with implications. I felt the blood drain from my face. Mac's hand tightened around mine, but I barely registered the comforting touch.

"What?" I stammered, struggling to process the information. "But why? How? That was not the impression you gave us when we last saw you with Z'hleena in Proxima Centauri." I said.

Shane sighed, running a hand through his hair. "I discovered what she was doing to the Vihilians and other aliens. It's not just about power for her—it's about control. And I couldn't stand by and let her continue."

"Did you know that Z'hleena's guards killed Suzuki?" I spat, bile rising in my throat.

Shane looked disappointed. "I'm sorry. I really am. He was just a kid."

"But Shane," Blair said. "You were involved with her! You were so close!"

"Exactly," he replied, his voice heavy with regret. "That's how I gathered crucial information to help us save them. I had to maintain my cover or risk everything."

"Neo," Mac whispered to me. "This changes everything. We can trust him now."

"Can we?" My thoughts raced with conflicting emotions. Shane's confession left me reeling, unsure of what to believe. "How do we know this isn't just another trick? How do we know he's not still working for her?"

"Neo," Shane said, looking me in the eye, his expression filled with sincerity. "I know it's a lot to take in, but I'm on your side. I've risked everything to help you."

As I stared into his eyes, searching for any trace of deception, I felt my empathic abilities kick in. A whirlwind of emotions battered me—guilt, fear, and determination—but beneath it all was a genuine desire to make things right. The truth of his words settled over me like a blanket.

"Okay," I whispered, finally accepting the reality of the situation. "We'll work together. But we need to act fast—every moment we waste puts those prisoners and Trella in more danger."

"You're right," Shane said, relief evident. "Let's get to work."

We were silent for a moment as everyone absorbed the news. Fender was the first to speak. "So, you betrayed your own lover to help us? Why should we trust you now?"

"Because it was the right thing to do," Shane replied, his voice firm. "I didn't know the extent of Z'hleena's crimes when I got involved with her. When I discovered what she was doing to the Vihilians and other aliens, I knew I had to act."

"Then why keep it a secret?" Fender asked, his arms crossed over his chest. "If you were really on our side, you would have come clean from the start."

Shane sighed, pinching the bridge of his nose. "I needed to maintain my cover so I could continue gathering information. I thought it was the best way to help all of you without jeopardizing the mission."

"Even if it meant putting us in danger?" Blair said, her eyes narrowed.

"Believe me, I never wanted to put any of you at risk," Shane said earnestly, his eyes filled with regret. "But the situation was delicate. If Z'hleena had discovered my betrayal earlier, it could have spelled disaster for everyone."

I could feel the tension like a tightrope stretched to its breaking point. My friends' skepticism was understandable—after all, how often does someone betray their lover for the greater good?

"Look," Shane continued, desperation creeping into his voice. "I know I've made mistakes, and I understand if you don't trust me completely. But please, let me help you. I want to make things right, not just for the Vihilians and other prisoners, but for all of us."

Looking around at my friends, I could see their expressions soften. Though shocking, we were all fighting for the exact cause, and Shane's actions were ultimately in our best interest.

"All right," Fender said finally. "We'll give you a chance. But if you betray us again, there will be consequences."

"Understood," Shane nodded, gratitude shining in his eyes. "I won't let you down."

With the uneasy truce established, we returned to the mission.

Watching my friends reluctantly accept Shane's plea, I noticed Mac's expression. He seemed to be wrestling with his internal conflict, trying to reconcile his feelings toward his father's actions.

"Mac," I whispered, momentarily drawing him away from the group. "Are you okay?"

He hesitated before answering, his eyes searching mine for under-standing. "It's just that my dad and Z'hleena have been together for as long as I can remember. I never thought he'd betray her like this."

"From what he told us, it sounds like he did it for the right reasons," I offered softly, hoping to ease some of his pain.

Mac sighed, clenching his fists in frustration. "I know, Neo. And part of me is relieved he's on our side now. But it's still hard to wrap my head around it all."

"Maybe we should focus on the mission," I suggested. "We can deal with everything else later once Trella is back, and the other prisoners are safe."

"Right," Mac agreed, nodding resolutely.

We rejoined the group and began discussing our plan. Time was of the essence, and we needed to work together if we were going to succeed.

"Shane," Blair said. "You know Z'hleena better than any of us. How do you suggest we approach the cells without being detected?"

"Z'hleena has a weakness for N'ymean wine," Shane replied thoughtfully. "She often indulges herself in her private chambers. If we can find a way to infiltrate the stronghold during one of those moments, it could give us the opening we need."

"Sounds risky," Blair muttered. "But I guess we don't have much of a choice."

"Shane, do you think you can get us inside?" I asked.

He nodded solemnly. "I'll do everything in my power to help you."

"Then let's make it happen," Fender said.

"Shane, your job is to disable any security measures in place," I added, meeting his gaze. "We need to ensure the safety of Trella and the prisoners as well as our own."

"I understand," Shane replied. "I've already begun hacking into the cell's systems. It won't be long before I gain full access."

Under the cover of night, we crept toward the entrance to the stronghold. Our group moved in sync, our breaths steady and measured as we used the shadows to our advantage.

"There's an access panel just around this corner," Blair murmured. Her eyes scanned the darkened hallway ahead. "We'll disable the security system and create a diversion while you and Fender slip inside."

"Got it," I replied. As we approached the access panel, my empathic abilities kicked into overdrive. I felt the fear and desperation of the captives pulsating in my mind like a distress beacon.

"Mac and I will join you once the guards are occupied," Blair continued, her fingers flying across the panel as she worked to disarm the security system. "Just give us the signal."

"Remember, Neo," Fender rumbled from behind me. "Trust your instincts, and we'll succeed."

I closed my eyes for a moment, drawing strength from Fender's words. My resolve hardened; we couldn't afford to fail.

"Security disabled," Blair announced. "Let's move."

"Good luck," Mac whispered. He squeezed my hand and melded into the shadows with the others.

"Ready?" Fender's white markings glowed eerily in the darkness. I could see the fierce determination etched on his features.

"As ready as I'll ever be," I replied. "Let's go save some lives."

Fender grinned, and together, we slipped through the now-unlocked door.

My heart pounded like a war drum when our group entered the dusky chamber. Sweat trickled down my forehead, and I fought to control my ragged breaths. Fender stood beside me like a solid rock of support.

"Good luck," Fender rumbled softly and veered off to the right. He flashed me a quick smile before disappearing into the shadows.

"All right, Shane." I turned to face our hacker companion. "You know what to do. Get us any information you can find about disabling the chambers.

"Will do." His fingers were already flying across the keyboard of a nearby terminal. His concentration and determination were a stark contrast to the suspicious behavior he had displayed earlier. With a surge of relief, I watched him work. Despite our initial doubts, Shane had proven himself to be a valuable ally in our mission.

"Thank you, Shane," I said, my voice filled with gratitude. My hand reached out to grip his, feeling the warmth and strength that reassured me.

He gave me a firm nod, his face set with resolve. "Be careful, Neo. I've done all I can from here. You and your team are on your own now."

I nodded, watching Shane walk out as the door closed behind him.

CHAPTER 30

Race Against Time

WITH A SENSE OF urgency and resolve, I scanned the dark surroundings of Z'hleena's stronghold, ready to press on toward the chambers where the prisoners were held.

"Neo, are you ready for this?" Blair asked. Her brown eyes scanned my face, searching for any signs of hesitation.

"I am," I replied, setting my jaw and meeting her gaze with determination. "We have to find Trella."

"All right," she said, her expression hardening. "You know I've got your back. Let's do this."

We sprinted down the corridors, dodging debris that fell from the ceiling as tremors shook the building. The air was thick with dust and smoke, making breathing difficult. Despite my fear, I couldn't let anything distract me from our mission. As we turned a corner, we found ourselves face-to-face with armed guards, their weapons aimed at us. "Halt!" one barked, his finger hovering near the trigger.

"Split up," Blair whispered, her eyes darting between the guards and the nearby hallway. "We'll find a way around them."

I nodded in agreement. We split into three groups, each dashing down separate hallways, our hearts pounding. My path led me through a maze of dark, ominous corridors. The echoes of our boots on the floor were the only sound as we made our way deeper into the enemy's lair.

As the minutes ticked by, I felt my strength beginning to wane, my legs shook with exhaustion. But I couldn't afford to slow down—not when so many lives hung in the balance. I pushed myself harder, focusing on my goal and my friends counting on me.

"Neo! Over here!" Blair's voice cut through the darkness, and I stumbled toward it.

"Did you find a way around?" I gasped, wiping the sweat from my brow.

"Mac found a hidden passage," she replied, pointing to a narrow door. "Come on!"

With urgency, we launched ourselves headfirst into the nebulous tunnel, an artery of ancient mysteries, underlit by intermittent phosphorescent fungi that danced on the rocky walls in an eerie luminescence.

Each footfall echoed in our ears, bouncing off the damp stonework, reverberating with the frantic pulse of our mission. As we reached the end of the tunnel, my intuition alerted me we were closer than ever to finding Trella and the prisoners. Emerging from the narrow confines, we were engulfed by an awe-inspiring cavernous chamber, a feat of architectural genius that dwarfed us. The room's impressive vastness was adorned with meticulous rows of tubular, crystal-clear containment units, holding the prisoners and other aliens in suspended animation. Each encased figure stood in their silent units—like prisoners in a translucent limbo between life and hibernation. Rage surged through me, boiling my blood and constricting my hands into iron fists. The sight of such vivid exploitation, a gross mockery of these sentient beings' freedom, ignited within me a blazing resolve.

"We need a plan," I said firmly. "Blair, you start working on deactivating the controls for these containers. Mac and Fender, keep an eye out for any guards."

"Got it." They nodded, setting off in different directions, while Blair approached the control panel. I focused on using my empathic abilities to reach out to the imprisoned aliens, feeling their fear and suffering, which only fueled my resolve.

"Neo," Blair whispered. "I think I found something, but I need your help."

I hurried to her side. We examined the complex system together, brains working to decipher the alien technology.

"If I'm reading this correctly," Blair said, pointing to a series of symbols on the panel, "we'll have to override this security lock before we can release them."

With my heart pounding, we navigated the intricate security measures, relying on our knowledge and instincts.

"Wait!" I held Blair's hand before she could press a button. "That one triggers an alarm. Try this sequence instead."

"Good catch, Neo." Blair entered the new sequence. The control panel beeped in response, and the security lock disengaged. Our resourcefulness and ingenuity had paid off.

"Start releasing the prisoners. I'll find Trella," I told Blair, sprinting toward the row of tubes where I sensed her presence. As I approached, I spotted her familiar features through the glass, her face etched with pain.

"Stay strong, Trella. I'm here," I whispered, pressing my hand against the cold surface of their tube. I quickly located the release mechanism, my fingers trembling as I activated it.

With a hiss, the glass slid away, and Trella collapsed into my arms, gasping for breath. "Thank you, Neo," they choked out.

"Of course," I said, hugging them tightly. "Now, let's get everyone out of here. Stay with me, but don't push until you feel strong again."

We hurried back to Blair, who was diligently releasing the other captives. Together, we worked tirelessly as we freed them, one by one. "Neo, we did it!" Mac shouted from the entrance, his eyes scanning the room full of liberated beings. "You did incredible."

"Thanks, Mac, but we're not done yet. There are still more prisoners in this facility. We have to find them all." We pressed on through the sterile hallways. My heart raced as we moved from one cell to the next, searching for any sign of life.

"Mac, are you sure we're going in the right direction?" I asked.

"I'm certain," Mac replied. "The map shows this is the way to the high-security cells."

"Okay." I took a deep breath and tried to calm my racing thoughts.

As we continued onward, Blair and Fender stayed close. Their eyes scanned every corner for potential threats.

"Guys, we have to be careful," I whispered. "Z'hleena could be anywhere, and we don't know what she's capable of."

"Right," Fender agreed.

"Wait!" Blair's voice stopped us in our tracks. "Do you hear that?"

We all fell silent, straining to pick up on the muffled sounds. Something was happening just around the corner, but it was impossible to tell exactly what.

"Stay behind me," Mac ordered. "If there's trouble, I'll handle it."

I nodded, and as one, we turned the corner, our hearts pounding with anticipation.

"Neo, look!" Blair pointed to the rows of cells before us, each holding an emaciated prisoner, their dark eyes full of desperation and fear.

As we prepared to free the captives, the air suddenly crackled with energy, and Z'hleena appeared before us.

"Ah, Neo," Z'hleena's lavender skin glowing menacingly, her white eyes narrowing. "You've come so far, only to fail at the last moment."

"Z'hleena, let them go!" I shouted, my face contorted with repulsion and indignation at her disregard for the suffering of others. "This ends now!"

"Does it?" She raised a hand, and a wall of shimmering energy shot up between us and the cells, trapping the prisoners inside. "You really thought you could defeat me? You're nothing but a foolish child."

"Good job, my love." Z'hleena extended a hand to Shane, who suddenly appeared at her side. He kissed her hand like a loving accomplice.

"Dad!" Mac yelled. Anger and disappointment filled his eyes.

Fender rushed to tackle him. "You will regret this, Shane."

And with that, Shane vanished. Suddenly, a pulsating aura of iridescent light enveloped him, casting long, spectral shadows that danced hauntingly against the surrounding stillness. As the luminous

energy swelled, his form disintegrated, his atoms separating and dif-
fusing into glittering dust, each particle radiating a mesmerizing and
eerie light.

Chapter 31

Amid Chaos

M Y HEART THUNDERED AS I watched Z'hleena gather dark forces around her. Her eyes were alight with an eerie, unnatural glow, and the air crackled with energy. With a wave, she sent tendrils of darkness snaking out toward us.

"Get ready!" Mac shouted. His voice was barely audible over the howling wind. Blair and Trella positioned themselves for battle while Fender gripped his weapon tightly, ready to strike at any moment.

"Z'hleena, you don't have to do this!" I yelled. She laughed—a cruel, mocking sound that sent chills down my spine.

"Your naivete is almost endearing." Z'hleena flicked her wrist with a sneer, conjuring up a wall of solid black energy—a form of dark matter manipulation. "But it won't save you."

As the battle raged on, my thoughts raced alongside it. "Neo, focus!" Mac's voice snapped me out of my thoughts as he deflected one of Z'hleena's attacks with his alien technology-enhanced shield. "We'll deal with Z'hleena later. Right now, we need to survive!"

Mac's right, I thought. Stay alert and use your skills. *I can't let my emotions cloud my judgment.*

"Watch out, Neo!" Trella called out, launching herself into the air and dodging another of Z'hleena's dark blasts. I quickly followed suit, evading the attack by mere inches. I panted, my heart racing. The action was intense, but I couldn't afford to let my mind wander again.

As we stood before Z'hleena's dark energy wall, a thought began forming in my mind. The swirling black mass was terrifying and fascinating, a testament to her control and power. *But what if that control could be disrupted? What if we could use her own power against her?*

I glanced at Blair, who seemed to think along the same lines, her eyes fixed on the dark energy.

My mind raced, piecing together the fragments of knowledge we'd gathered. If we could disrupt Z'hleena's control over the dark matter, even for a moment, she would be vulnerable. It was a risky plan, but it might be our only chance.

I gritted my teeth, focusing all my energy on Z'hleena, trying to find a way to breach her defenses. I remembered what Trella had taught me about channeling empathy, understanding, and connecting with others. Could I use that to reach Z'hleena, to break her concentration?

I focused on the wall of dark energy, feeling its presence, seeking its weaknesses. We could do this. We could use Z'hleena's own power against her.

I closed my eyes, took a deep breath, and reached out with my mind, trying to sense Z'hleena's emotions. *Please, let this work*, I thought.

Z'hleena's raw emotions were laid bare—her lust for power, her twisted desire for immortality, and her utter disregard for the lives she was destroying. But beneath that, there was something else—a flicker of guilt, a hidden pain she'd tried to bury.

"Neo!" Mac yelled as he deflected another attack, sweat dripping down his face. "Now!

I focused on that hidden pain and amplified it, sending it back toward Z'hleena through my empathic connection. Her eyes widened in shock, and her control over the darkness faltered.

"NO!" she screamed, desperately trying to regain control. But it was too late—the darkness collapsed on itself, momentarily stunning her.

"Take her down, now!" I shouted, and we all lunged toward her.

As we fought to subdue Z'hleena, I grappled with my internal conflict. Queen Nahyla had trusted her, and Z'hleena had betrayed her most unimaginably.

Stay strong, Neo, I told myself. Tears pricked at the corners of my eyes. *You can mourn later. Right now, you need to fight.*

"Watch out!" Mac shouted as a twisted tendril of darkness shot toward us. I barely dodged it, feeling the icy chill in its wake. I knew we had to end this battle quickly.

"Blair, use your energy disruptor! Trella, cover her!" I commanded through gritted teeth. This was our only chance to weaken Z'hleena's dark forces long enough to strike.

Blair yelled, whipping out a sleek metallic device with pulsating lights—a prototype from her engineering class at Ryser Academy. As she activated it, energy waves rippled through the air, disrupting the malevolent force Z'hleena wielded.

"Mac, give me some cover fire!" I called out, readying my own weapon—a compact plasma blade.

The atmosphere in the chamber crackled with tension as Mac's fingers danced over the controls of his energy blaster. With a resolute nod, he unleashed a barrage of bright, sizzling energy blasts toward Z'hleena's dark energy wall. The air filled with the sharp scent of ozone as the blasts collided with the wall, creating an opening that shimmered with residual energy. I seized the opportunity, my heart pounding. I rushed toward Z'hleena, gripping my weapon—a sleek, silver plasma blade that hummed with deadly potential. Nearby, Trella's graceful N'ymean form darted and spun in hand-to-hand combat with Z'hleena. Their movements were a blur of agility and strength, their body a finely tuned instrument of battle. They wielded twin energy daggers in their hands, their blades glowing with a fierce blue light as they sliced through the air.

Z'hleena, however, was no ordinary opponent. Her eyes glowed unnaturally, and a dark, magical energy emanated from her very core, enhancing her movements. She parried Trella's strikes with her own weapon—a wickedly curved dark energy blade that twisted and writhed as if alive.

They were evenly matched in strength, their blows landing with a force that echoed through the chamber. Trella's daggers met Z'hleena's blade in a clash of light and shadow, sparks flying as the energy fields collided.

But Z'hleena's magic gave her an edge, a wild, unpredictable element that made her a formidable opponent. Her blade was guided by an invisible force, effortlessly deflecting Trella's attacks and counter-attacking with deadly accuracy.

Trella struggled fiercely to hold Z'hleena off, their muscles visibly straining with the effort. Sweat glistened on her brow, and her breath came in ragged gasps. She was holding her own, but it was clear she needed help.

"Your pathetic attempts to stop me are futile!" Z'hleena snarled. Her white eyes burned with hatred. She raised her hands, summoning a whirlwind of dark energy that lifted debris and threatened to engulf us all.

"Neo, we can't hold her off much longer!" Trella cried out.

I felt a storm brewing in my chest. "Hold on," I whispered, reaching deep within myself to tap into my empathic abilities. Focusing on Z'hleena, I sensed her emotions and brought them to the surface.

"Your time is up, Z'hleena!" I shouted, releasing a wave of pure emotion that shattered her concentration. The whirlwind dissipated, and she staggered back, momentarily disoriented.

"Attack, now!" Mac yelled. We unleashed a coordinated assault, our weapons and abilities merging into a force even Z'hleena couldn't withstand.

As we pressed our advantage, my anger and grief engulfed me. Z'hleena had betrayed my mother and now sought to destroy everything I held dear. I fought not just for the Vihilians but for my own sense of justice. And yet, doubt gnawed at me. *Could I genuinely defeat someone who wielded such immense power?*

"Get out of your head, Neo," I muttered, pushing those thoughts aside. "Get this job done."

We continued our relentless attack on Z'hleena, driving her back with the combined might of our alien technology and raw determination. The dark forces that had once seemed invincible now faltered under our onslaught.

"Your reign of terror ends now, Z'hleena!" I roared, my voice filled with fury and determination.

My muscles tensed, every fiber of my being focused on the task at hand. I lunged forward, my legs propelling me with my last strength reserves. My hand gripped the hilt of my plasma blade, its surface humming with vibrant energy. The blade was a marvel of technology, a concentrated beam of superheated plasma contained within a magnetic field. It glowed with a fierce, blue-white light, casting an eerie glow on Z'hleena's sneering face.

As I closed the distance, I could see the realization in her eyes, the flicker of doubt and fear. She raised her dark energy blade to parry, but I was already in motion, my body guided by instinct and training. I twisted my wrist, angling the blade just so. The magnetic field that contained the plasma fluctuated momentarily, allowing the energy to extend beyond its normal confines. It was a maneuver I'd practiced a thousand times—precise manipulation of technology and skill.

The plasma blade lashed out, its tip extending in a flash of brilliant light. It struck Z'hleena's dark blade, bypassing her defense and cutting through the dark energy that surrounded it. Her eyes widened, and a cry of shock escaped her lips as the plasma found its mark. The energy seared through her defenses, cutting into her flesh with a hiss and a sizzle. The smell of burning filled the air, and Z'hleena's scream echoed through the chamber.

I could feel the blade's energy reverberate through the hilt, a tangible connection to the strike that had landed. My heart raced, and a surge of triumph washed over me.

We'd done it. We'd finally prevailed. As I pulled the blade back, watching Z'hleena stagger and fall, I knew we had won––at least for today.

The battle was over, but the war was far from done. The victory was ours at that moment, and I allowed myself to savor it, the weight of the plasma blade heavy and satisfying in my hand.

With Z'hleena momentarily reeling from our assault, we seized the opportunity to rescue the prisoners. As Mac and Trella kept Z'hleena at bay, Blair, Fender, and I rushed to the captives, freeing them from the dark forces ensnared them.

"Thank you," gasped a frail Lorazian woman. Her eyes were dimmed by exhaustion and pain. "Our people... we owe you our lives."

My voice trembled with emotion. "Right now, we need to get you all to safety."

Fender's booming voice called out, "Follow me." He guided the exhausted captives toward the opening of the crystal cave—Staak'al, a haven.

As we entered the cave, we were greeted by a breathtaking sight. The cavern walls glistened with iridescent crystals that reflected the soft glow of bioluminescent plants. The air was cool and fresh, carrying the scent of damp earth and the faint whispers of ancient secrets. Here, in the heart of Luehiri, the captives would be temporarily safe from Z'hleena's wrath.

"Please, rest here," Fender instructed the prisoners as they sank gratefully onto the smooth crystal floor. "We'll make sure Z'hleena can't harm you again."

"Be careful," warned an older Venusian. His voice was hoarse but full of determination. "She is more powerful than you realize."

My eyes met his. "Trust us," I said. "We won't let her win."

As we left the cave, we prepared to face Z'hleena once more. I knew our most significant challenge still lay ahead.

We stood before Z'hleena, our bodies tense and ready for the next round of battle. Her eyes blazed with a cold fury, and I felt a sudden chill as if ice had traced its way down my back, but we refused to back down. "Did you really think you won?" she said, her voice dripping with venom. "You may have rescued your friends and my prisoners, but there's still one thing you can't change."

My chest heaved, and I sensed her words before she spoke them.

"Your mother, Queen Nahyla," Z'hleena began, a twisted smile curling her lips. My breath hitched at the mention of my mother, a painful knot forming in my chest. "She begged me for her life."

Z'hleena's eyes glinted with cruel satisfaction as she continued, her voice dripping with malice. "I remember how she knelt before me, her royal robes soiled and torn. Her eyes were wide with terror, but something else was there. A spark of defiance, even as she pleaded for mercy."

"She cried," Z'hleena went on, her voice soft and mocking. "Tears streaming down her beautiful face as she clung to my leg, begging me to spare her. Her voice broke as she spoke of you, her love for her people, and her hopes for a peaceful future."

"But I saw through her," Z'hleena said, her voice rising triumphantly. "I saw the weakness, the fear. And I knew she didn't deserve to rule. She didn't deserve to live."

"And so I killed her," Z'hleena whispered, her eyes locked on mine. "I drove my dark blade through her heart and watched the life drain from her eyes. I watched her fall and heard her last gasping breath."

The revelation hit me like a tidal wave, knocking the air from my lungs. My friends stared at Z'hleena, their faces etched with shock and horror. My legs threatened to buckle beneath me, but I stood tall. "You're lying," I whispered, my voice trembling.

"Am I?" Z'hleena challenged, her smile growing wider. "Your mother confided in me, you know. She told me all about her little experiments with Luehirian and Human DNA alongside that foolish human scientist, Peter Murphy."

My mind reeled as she continued, detailing the specifics of the experiment—how they had sought to create a bridge between two species, to foster unity and understanding through the birth of a child who was both Luehirian and human. The motivations behind it were noble, but the risk had been great.

"Your mother believed the union of the two races would bring peace." Z'hleena's voice was laced with disgust, and she spat the words. "She thought she could control Staak'al's power, but she was wrong. That power belonged to me."

"Neo." Mac murmured, reaching out to touch my arm. I flinched at the contact; my skin felt on fire.

"Shut up!" I snapped, my voice cracking. "Just shut up!"

"Face the truth, Neo." Z'hleena's words taunted me, and her eyes gleamed with cruel satisfaction. "Your mother's death was no accident. It was a necessary sacrifice for the greater good."

I couldn't hold back the tears any longer. Hot and angry, they streamed down my face, but I refused to break. I clenched my fists, my nails digging into my palms, drawing on every ounce of strength I possessed.

"Z'hleena, your reign of terror is over now." I snarled. "You may have taken my mother from me but you won't take anyone else."

"Let's see you try to stop me," she hissed, her eyes narrowed into slits.

And with that, the battle resumed—fiercer, more desperate than before.

"Z'hleena, how could you?" I choked out, my voice breaking as I lunged at her, my blade narrowly missing her side. My eyes were blurred with tears, my heart pounding with rage. "How could you betray her like that?"

"Betrayal?" she scoffed, parrying my strike swiftly and gracefully. Her dark blade gleamed as she spun, her voice dripping with derision. "I did what was necessary! Nahyla was blinded by her delusions of grandeur, believing her experiments would bring some sort of utopia. But she was a fool, Neo." She lunged at me, her blade aiming for my throat. "She didn't understand the true potential of our combined powers."

I dodged her strike, my breath coming in ragged gasps. Mac was beside me now, his face twisted with fury. "Potential?" he spat, firing a quick energy blast at Z'hleena, forcing her to dodge. "You murdered her for power."

"Power, yes," Z'hleena said, her eyes gleaming as she blocked another of Mac's blasts. Her movements were swift and deadly, her body a lethal dance of grace and strength. "But not just any power." She advanced on us, her dark blade whirling, her voice filled with triumph. "The ultimate power—immortality."

"Immortality?" Trella whispered.

"Yes." Z'hleena sneered as she spoke. "With the life force of the Luehirian crystal, I can unlock the secret to eternal life. Imagine it, Neo, an everlasting empire ruled by me."

"An empire built on death and suffering," Blair said. "You're a monster, Z'hleena."

"Monster or visionary?" Z'hleena replied. Her laughter chilled me to the bone. "It's all a matter of perspective."

"Whatever your twisted motivations," I said, "you won't succeed. We will stop you."

"Is that so? Then let's see if you have what it takes to challenge a goddess."

She raised her hands, and the very air around us seemed to crackle with dark energy. As her fingers wove a complex pattern, a wave of malignant force surged toward us. We barely had time to brace ourselves before it struck, sending us sprawling to the ground.

"Neo!" Mac cried out. "We have to stop her!"

"Stay close!" Fender shouted, his powerful Teutonian form shielding Blair from the brunt of the attack. Together, we fought our way toward Z'hleena, each of us drawing on our unique strengths and abilities to counter her relentless assault.

"So eager to die for your precious cause?" She purred.

"Death is nothing compared to living under your tyranny," I shot back.

"Such noble words." Her mocking laughter rang in my ears like a death knell. "But ultimately futile."

"Never," I shouted. "I will never give up. Not until you're defeated."

"Then come, child. Face your destiny and meet your doom."

As we continued to battle Z'hleena's dark forces, the horrifying truth of her actions began to unravel. The cunning witch had used her powers of manipulation and deception to lure the Vihilians from their home in Usiox, convincing them Luehiri held the answers to their deepest desires and greatest hopes. In one of my earlier dreams, Yohzak explained that Z'hleena had promised them salvation, and they had believed her lies.

The Vihilians had been desperate, hungry for a better life—and Z'hleena had preyed on their vulnerability like a parasite. I could see the shame and regret in Yohzak's eyes as he shared their tragic tale.

"Once we arrived at Luehiri, she placed us under her spell. She took away our free will, forcing us to mine the Staak'al for her twisted purposes.

"Her trance was powerful," Yohzak added, his voice barely audible. "It numbed our minds, making us nothing more than slaves to her will. It was only when I realized you were half Luehirian that I reached out to you, hoping your unique heritage would enable you to break her hold over us."

Remembering Yohzak's words, I felt a storm of emotions: fury at Z'hleena's cruelty, guilt for not realizing the truth sooner, and a powerful determination to set things right.

My friends and I gathered close. We knew the stakes were high, and countless lives hung in the balance. But Z'hleena had underestimated us—and we would not let her win.

"Let's finish this," Mac whispered.

Trella gripped their axe tightly and nodded in agreement

"Z'hleena will pay for what she's done," Trella vowed with a snarl.

"Today, we fight for the Vihilians and the universe's future," Fender declared.

As one, we charged back into the fray, ready to face whatever horrors Z'hleena had in store. And though the battle raged on, I knew, together, we would overcome her darkness—and finally end her reign of terror.

Chapter 32

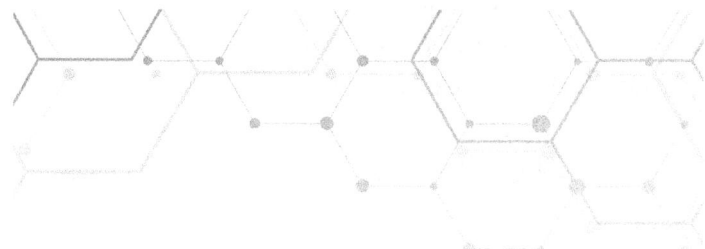

The Power Within

E NERGY COURSED THROUGH ME like a river of electricity that connected my mind to everything around me. Z'hleena lunged toward me, her movements swift and graceful. I barely managed to dodge her attack, stumbling backward as my heart hammered. Sweat beaded on my forehead, and my breaths came quick and shallow. I needed to control my fear, or I would never stand a chance against her.

"Is that all you've got?" Z'hleena said."

"Shut up!" I snapped, gritting my teeth. Anger surged through me, hot and powerful, and I focused on it, hoping to channel it into my abilities. I reached out with my telekinesis, trying to push her away, but my trembling hands betrayed my lack of control.

"Pathetic," Z'hleena said, effortlessly deflecting my feeble attempt. "Is this really the best the great Super Hybrid can do?"

"Enough!" I cried, and with a fierce wave of my hand, I unleashed a torrent of telekinetic force. The blast knocked Z'hleena off her feet, sending her crashing into the far wall.

"Did you really think you could just take what you want?" I snarled, my voice trembling with fear and newfound strength. "You have no idea who you're dealing with."

"Maybe not," Z'hleena admitted, picking herself up off the ground and dusting herself off. "But it seems you don't know who you're dealing with either." She raised a hand, and a wave of dark energy radiated from her palm, catching me off guard.

I tried to block it with my telekinesis, but the force was too strong. The wave threw me backward, slamming me into the ground with a painful thud. Desperation clawed at my insides as I struggled to catch my breath, my vision swimming from the impact.

I gritted my teeth, my heart pounding in my ears as I launched myself at Z'hleena. She met my charge with a sinister smile, our powers colliding in an explosion of light and dark energy.

"You call that a challenge?" Z'hleena said, her taunting voice dripping with contempt. "You'll have to do better than that."

I refused to let her words get to me. Focusing on our connection, I tapped into my empathic abilities, searching for any hint of emotion or vulnerability.

"Your confidence is just a mask," I whispered, dodging another energy blast. "I can feel it. You're afraid of losing control, of admitting someone could be stronger than you."

Z'hleena's eyes widened, but she quickly recovered, her expression hardening again. "You think you know me, little girl? You know nothing."

"Maybe not," I retorted, using my telekinesis to deflect an onslaught of debris she sent flying my way. "But I know enough to beat you."

As we continued to clash, I kept pushing deeper into her psyche, searching for a weakness. Her fear was growing, and I knew I had to use it to my advantage. The stakes were too high––Trella's life hung in the balance, and I couldn't afford to fail.

"What are you so afraid of, Z'hleena?" I asked, my voice carrying over the chaos of our battle. "That I might expose you for the fraud you really are?"

"Silence!" she roared, her facade beginning to crack. "I will not be defeated by some pathetic child."

"Pathetic?" I laughed bitterly, ducking under a vicious swipe of her hand. "You're the one who's hiding behind a wall of lies and fear. And I'm about to tear it down."

As I said those words, I felt my empathic connection with Z'hleena grow stronger. Suddenly, I could see into the darkest corners of her mind, unearthing secrets she had long kept hidden.

"Your father, King Fehnir, has never loved you," I whispered. My heart felt heavy with the weight of her pain. "That's why you're so desperate to prove yourself––because deep down, you know you'll never be good enough for him."

"Stop it!" Z'hleena screamed. Her voice cracked under the strain of her emotions, and her energy wavered––giving me the opening I needed.

I lunged forward, my telekinetic powers at their peak as I seized hold of Z'hleena's wavering defenses. With one final surge of strength, I tore through her barriers, leaving her defenseless and exposed.

"Enough," I breathed, my voice barely audible over my ragged breathing. "It's over, Z'hleena."

She stared at me, defeated, and broken. Her eyes brimmed with tears she refused to let fall. "You won't get away with this. My father will come for me."

"Your father will not save you this time." Trembling with anger and adrenaline, I spat out the words. The connection I had made through my empathic powers still held firm, granting me a glimpse into the chaos of Z'hleena's mind. Her fear and desperation fueled my determination, driving me to push my telekinetic abilities to their limit.

I focused on the air around Z'hleena, feeling it shift and twist at my command. I willed it to gather in a concentrated force like an invisible hand reaching to grasp her.

"Please don't," she begged, her eyes wide as she realized what would happen. But her pleas fell on deaf ears––I had seen too much suffering at her hands to show her mercy now.

I clenched my fists and thrust them forward, sending the gathered energy hurtling toward Z'hleena with a force that shook us. She cried out as the telekinetic blow struck her square in the chest, knocking her off balance and throwing her backward. She hit the ground hard, her body skidding across the rough terrain before coming to a painful stop.

"Look at you now," I said, approaching her fallen form. "So helpless. So weak."

Z'hleena's face twisted in agony, her body writhing on the ground as Mac and I circled her cautiously. Her dark blade lay discarded, her strength seemingly spent. Once filled with madness and malice, her eyes now looked up at me with a vulnerability I hadn't seen before.

"Neo, please... I didn't want any of this," she whispered, tears filling her cheeks. Her voice was broken, a shadow of its former arrogance. "I just wanted my father's approval."

"By hurting innocent people?" I spat, my voice cold and unforgiving.

My blade remained ready, but I couldn't help but be affected by her words and apparent remorse. "By destroying lives? Is that really what it takes to earn his love?"

"Y-you don't understand," she stammered, struggling to sit up despite the pain radiating. Her face was pale, her movements slow and shaky. "He's all I have left."

I hesitated, my anger giving way to doubt. Could she really be sincere? Could there be some truth to her words? Was she really just a victim of her father's manipulation?

As I stood frozen, caught between suspicion and empathy, Z'hleena's eyes flickered, a brief glimmer of something dark and cunning hiding behind her tears.

And then, in a flash, she moved. Her hand shot out, grabbing the dark blade that lay beside her. She lunged at me with a sudden, vicious strength, her blade slashing through the air, fueled by desperation and deceit. I was too slow to react, too caught up in her words, her apparent vulnerability. The blade found its mark, cutting through my defenses and tearing into my flesh.

Pain exploded through my body, white-hot and blinding. I stumbled back, my vision dimming, my strength faltering. Z'hleena's triumphant laugh rang in my ears as I fell. Her fake defeat gave way to a cold, merciless triumph.

She had taken the upper hand, and I had fallen for her ruse. I had let my guard down, allowed myself to be swayed by her words, and now I was paying the price.

I could hear Mac's shout of alarm.

"Leave her alone," Mac growled. He stepped forward and placed himself protectively between Z'hleena and me.

"Ah, the boyfriend returns," Z'hleena said, her eyes narrowing. "Do you think you can save her?"

"Try me," Mac challenged, his fists clenched tightly at his sides.

"Mac, don't," I pleaded, my heart twisting with fear. But he held his ground, staring Z'hleena down with steely determination.

"Very well," Z'hleena agreed, her eyes cold and calculating. She raised her hand, summoning a deadly bolt of energy aimed straight at Mac's chest.

"NO!" I screamed, feeling helpless and desperate. My telekinetic abilities felt distant, pushed to the brink by our earlier fight. But I had to try.

"Neo, focus," I whispered, trying to steady my breathing. I reached deep within myself, tapping into the last reserves of my strength.

"Mac, get out of the way!" I shouted, and as he dove aside, I used my telekinesis to shove the beam off Trella. The effort was immense, and I felt myself stagger from the strain.

"Pathetic," Z'hleena spat, preparing another blast of energy. But before she could release it, Mac lunged forward, his arm raised.

Mac fired at Z'hleena, hitting her straight in the chest, sending her sprawling backward. Her eyes widened in shock just before she crashed into a pile of debris and lay still.

"Mac!" I cried, rushing over to him. His breathing was labored. His eyes clouded with pain and confusion.

"Is she...?" he asked, his voice shaking.

"Dead," I confirmed quietly. "It's over."

"Good," he murmured, wrapping an arm around my waist for support.

"Let's go find the others," I said.

Mac's grip on me tightened.

With Z'hleena's lifeless body sprawled before us, the dust from our battle hung in the air, carrying a metallic tang that made me wince. I felt the energy coursing through me, my powers more alive than ever. A mixture of pride and fear bubbled within me as I considered the extent of my abilities.

"Neo," Mac said. "We need to find Blair and Fender. They must be around here somewhere."

"Right," I said, swallowing hard.

As we searched, I listened carefully for any signs of distress or their familiar voices.

"Blair!" I yelled when I spotted her pinned under some debris, her eyes wide with panic. As I approached, I felt her fear wash over me, and I fought to keep my emotions at bay.

"Neo, help me get this off of her!" Mac shouted, already grabbing one end of a broken beam that pinned her down. I reached out with my telekinesis, lifting the beam off Blair.

"Thanks, guys," Blair gasped and rubbed her bruised legs. "What happened?"

"Z'hleena's dead," I said. "Mac killed her."

"Wow," she whispered, "you both did it." Her brown eyes were filled with awe.

"Where is Fender?" Mac asked, scanning the area.

"Over there." Blair pointed weakly. We found him bent double. His head bowed as he panted for breath. Fender's white hair was matted with sweat and dirt, and his deep green eyes were filled with pain.

"Are you all right?" I asked. Fender nodded slowly, but his breathing was labored.

"I'll be okay," Fender assured me. "Thanks to you and Mac."

"Let's get out of here," Mac suggested. "We must get the Vihilians and the others out of Luehiri."

"Agreed," I murmured.

"Neo, are you okay?" Mac asked. I hesitated for a moment, considering my response.

"I'm not sure," I said quietly. "I feel different. Stronger."

"Neo, that strength was always inside you." He squeezed my hand. "You've grown so much since coming to Ryser Academy. Today, you realized your potential, and it saved us all."

Chapter 33

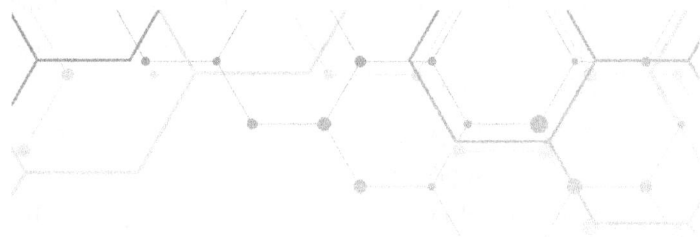

Usiox

T HE CRYSTAL CAVE OF Luehiri shimmered with iridescent light, casting kaleidoscopic reflections on the faces of our group as we celebrated our hard-won victory. We could breathe easily for once, knowing this sanctuary was a safe haven from outside danger. The air in the cave carried the faint scent of ozone and minerals, mingling with the aroma of the forest biome inside. The forest biome within the crystal cave exhibited extraordinary biodiversity, boasting an intricate ecosystem that showcased a remarkable array of plant species.

Mac and I guided the Vihilians and the other prisoners to a Luehirian ship that would transport them to Usiox.

"Almost done here," Blair announced. "These prisoners we rescued are going to be so grateful."

"Usiox awaits them," Trella said, smiling at the thought of the Dyson Sphere that encompassed Luehiri's star. "A new beginning, after all they've been through."

"Speaking of beginnings," Mac said, "I can't wait to return to Ryser Academy and finish my pilot training."

"Same here!" Blair clapped her hands together. "My goal is to become an aviation engineer, after all."

Fender grinned and flexed his azure arms. "Let's not forget about our warrior path, Trella." He was right; he and Trella had come a long way in honing their combat skills during our journey.

"Indeed," Trella said, nodding. "But for now, let us focus on helping those who need it most."

As we continued working on the transport ship, I marveled at the technological innovations that made space travel possible. The advanced propulsion systems, the energy shielding, and the life support systems were all products of cooperation between different species, each contributing their unique knowledge and expertise. It was a testament to the power of unity, something I hoped to foster in my future career as a diplomat.

Mac gestured to the holographic display. "Blair, could you help me with these calibrations? You've got a knack for this stuff."

"Sure thing," Blair replied, stepping up to the console. She adjusted the settings, feeling a swell of pride.

Throughout our journey, I discovered new strengths within myself and forged unbreakable bonds with my friends. We had faced adversity together, and we had emerged stronger for it.

"All right, everyone." Blair closed the last panel on the ship. "I think she's ready for launch."

"Perfect timing," Trella said as a group of Vihilians and other aliens approached. Their eyes were wide with gratitude and hope. "Let us help them board the ship."

A Vihilian elder stepped onto the boarding ramp, and Fender solemnly shook his hand. "Safe travels," Fender said.

"Thank you all," the elder said, his voice trembling. "We will never forget what you have done for us."

As the last passengers boarded, we exchanged final goodbyes and well wishes. Then, with a roar of engines and a brilliant flash of light, the transport ship soared into the heavens, carrying its precious cargo toward a brighter future.

"Come on, guys," Mac said, clapping me on the shoulder. "Let's head back to Ryser Academy. We've got work to do."

"Right," I agreed.

We returned to the crystal cave after the transport ship left for Usiox. The walls were shiny, and crystal lamps provided dim light.

The air hummed with relief and triumph, our hearts swelling with pride at what we had achieved together.

"Guys, I can't believe we actually pulled it off," Blair said. Her eyes sparkled as she wrapped her arms around Trella and me. I leaned into the embrace. "Neither can I. But we did it."

"Cheers to that." Mac raised a canteen of sweet-smelling Tarmarian nectar. We clinked containers and took deep swigs. The liquid's warmth spread through our bodies like liquid sunshine.

"Remember when we first met?" Fender asked. "I had no idea we would make such a great team." I smiled, recalling how unsure I had been back then. "Me neither. But I'm so grateful for each one of you."

"Hey, who knew I'd become friends with an empath?" Blair teased. She poked me playfully in the ribs, and we all laughed. Our earlier fears and doubts dissolved into the night.

"Speaking of which," Trella said, their voice softening. "Neo, your ability saved us more than once on this journey. You have grown so much since we first met."

"Thank you, Trella." My cheeks flushed with warmth. "You've been a true friend and mentor. I couldn't have done it without you––any of you."

"Aw, stop it! You're making me blush!" Trella joked. But I could see the emotion shimmering in their eyes.

"Let's never forget what we've been through," Mac said. "We've fought side by side and come out stronger for it."

"Agreed," Fender added. "No matter where life takes us, we'll always have each other's backs."

I raised my canteen once more. "Here's to that. To friendship, love, and a future full of possibilities."

"Cheers!" they echoed, and we drank deeply. Firelight danced on our faces as we reveled in our newfound unity.

As the night wore on, we shared stories of our adventures––the close calls, the moments of triumph, and the laughter that had bound us together. Gradually, the conversation turned to Suzuki, and we were all momentarily silent.

Images of Suzuki flashed through my mind, but instead of sorrow, I felt gratitude for the time we had shared and the memories that would live on in our hearts.

Blair was the first to break the silence. "Remember when Suzuki pulled that crazy stunt with the ship's hyperdrive? I thought we were all going to be space dust!"

We all laughed, and Mac joined in, "Or how would he somehow find the most obscure alien snacks in the galaxy? He had a taste for the bizarre."

Trella's eyes sparkled as they recalled, "And his talent for languages. How many did he speak fluently? A dozen?"

"Fifteen," I corrected, smiling at the memory. "Suzuki was always so curious about other cultures."

Fender's voice softened. "He had a way of making everyone feel important, no matter who they were."

The memories flowed, one after the other, each of us contributing, painting a vivid picture of our lost friend. We reminisced about his quirky sense of humor, unbreakable spirit, kindness, and the way he always knew how to lift our spirits.

"His courage was unmatched," Mac added, his voice thick with emotion. "He never backed down from a fight, even when the odds were against us."

"He was a true friend," Blair said, wiping away a tear. "Always there when you needed him."

We sat in contemplative silence, each of us lost in our thoughts, honoring Suzuki's memory. The room was filled with love and respect for a friend who had left an indelible mark on our lives.

Finally, Trella raised their canteen. "To Suzuki. May his spirit travel the stars."

We all raised our drinks, echoing, "To Suzuki."

The warmth of our shared memories enveloped us, a comforting reminder that although Suzuki was gone, he would never be forgotten—in our hearts, Suzuki would always be with us, a part of our team.

CHAPTER 34

The Crystal Palace

A S WE APPROACHED THE Crystal Palace in Luehiri, its resplendent presence became more apparent, shimmering in the light of Usiox. This was more than just a palace. It was a symbol of a proud and enduring lineage. My mother, Queen Nahyla, grew up here and ruled with wisdom and grace. The majestic towers of crystalline brilliance reached for the sky, their facets reflecting various colors. Wide bridges and elegant archways connected the multiple wings, each adorned with intricate carvings that told the ancient history of the Luehirian monarchy. It stood tall and majestic, like a crystalline beacon of light in the barren landscape of Luehiri. Intricate details adorned its surface, forming mesmerizing patterns that seemed to shift and change as we moved closer. The towers reaching for the sky sparkled with a rainbow of colors, giving the impression they were made of countless gemstones instead of solid crystals. Windows dotted the castle's surface in every direction, offering a glimpse of the wonders within.

The Palace was a testament to my family's legacy. It was the heart of the kingdom, a beacon of strength and unity that had stood for generations—a legacy that I was now a part of. My heart raced excitedly as we crossed the threshold into the Crystal Castle.

The interior was even more breathtaking than the exterior. Tall ceilings stretched above us, adorned with cascading crystal chandeliers illuminating the grand hall with a soft glow. The walls contained innumerable crystals that emitted a faint hum that blended with the spirit of Luehiri.

As we ventured inside, Daar-Hull greeted us. Queen Nahyla's Counselor turned to Prime Minister. His tall, slender figure emanated an otherworldly aura, causing the surrounding air to shimmer like a mirage. His eyes, ovoid with no visible pupils, gave him a stereotypical alien appearance. Still, I sensed the wisdom within their depths.

"Welcome to Crystal Castle." Daar-Hull's voice echoed in my mind, and a telepathic connection formed between us. The words resonated within my soul, comforting and reassuring. I glanced around at my companions, wondering if they, too, could hear his words in their minds.

Daar-Hull's triangular head bore a long, pointy nose and a tiny, pursed mouth that rarely revealed his emotions. His taupe skin blended harmoniously with the surroundings. The most striking feature was his attire—a long, flowing green cloak adorned with intricate patterns. The cloak bore an eight-pointed star within a star, which I knew was a symbol of significance to the Luehirians. But the spiral design, electrically charged and radiantly blue, captivated my attention.

With a graceful gesture, Daar-Hull motioned for us to follow him. As we walked through the castle's corridors, I marveled at the vibrant hues that danced along the crystal walls, creating a mesmerizing display of colors. The floor beneath our feet seemed infused with a gentle luminescence, guiding our path deeper into the castle's heart.

We entered a chamber with crystal sculptures that seemed alive as the light refracted through their intricate forms. Daar-Hull turned to face us, his mysterious eyes glimmering with warmth.

"Each crystal in the castle holds a piece of our history," he explained, his words flowing into our minds like a soothing melody. "These crystals are not mere decoration; they are living vessels that store the memories of our ancestors. Through them, we preserve the wisdom and experiences of past generations."

I marveled at the thought of a culture so intimately connected with its history, with each member carrying the legacy of their people within them. Daar-Hull's explanation made me think of a unique living library, more profound than records of books and digital data.

As we continued our journey through the Crystal Castle, we reached a chamber that left me breathless. It was filled with crystalline structures. Each was shaped like a unique celestial object—a miniature galaxy of sparkling wonder. They hung in midair, suspended by some unknown force, and the soft light they emitted painted the room in a mesmerizing dance of colors.

"These are our star shards," Daar-Hull said, his voice conveying reverence. "They are remnants of the ancient stars that once graced the skies of Luehiri. We cherish them dearly, for they hold the essence of the cosmos."

I approached one of the star shards, touching its surface gently. As my fingertips made contact, a burst of images flooded my mind. I saw galaxies colliding, stars being born and dying, and the birth of planets and moons. It was as if the star shard allowed me to witness the birth and evolution of the universe itself.

"Amazing, isn't it?" Daar-Hull said as a smile played on his lips. "These star shards come from Staak'al, our mother crystal. They have witnessed our world's birth and the countless wonders of the cosmos. They remind us of the vastness and beauty of the universe we are a part of."

I nodded, feeling a profound connection with the universe and everything it contained. This encounter with the star shard was unlike anything I had experienced before—it was as if the knowledge of the cosmos was imprinted on my very soul.

Daar-Hull guided us to the highest tower of the Crystal Castle. From there, we could see the vast expanse of Luehiri below—the sparse forests, the dying rivers, and the distant mountains shrouded in mist. The stars above shone with an intensity I had never witnessed on Mars as if they were closer, more present.

"We are all connected," Daar-Hull said. "To each other, to the land, and to the stars. Luehiri is a place of harmony and balance, where every living being is part of a greater tapestry. When Queen Nahyla died––your mother––the planet also died. We honor our past, embrace our present, and look toward the future with hope and wonder. For a long time, we were oblivious to what Z'hleena was doing to the Vihilians and others she imprisoned in the caves while keeping us under a spell."

I gazed at Daar-Hull, his enigmatic appearance now carrying a sense of familiarity. He seemed to embody the essence of Luehiri. Nature and technology merged seamlessly in this world, where the past and the future coexisted in perfect harmony.

As I stood there, surrounded by the brilliance of the Crystal Castle and the wisdom of Daar-Hull, I realized this journey had transformed me in ways I could never have imagined. I had come to Luehiri expecting adventure and discovery. Still, I found so much more—a connection to a world beyond my own, a sense of belonging to something more significant, and the understanding that the universe was vast and wondrous beyond comprehension.

Daar-Hull explained he would make a speech to the people of Luehiri. "You must return with the Intergalactic Police to Ryser Academy, Neo. But I want you to consider taking your place here at the court when all is settled. You are Nahyla's heir and the direct successor to the throne. This is your home, your kingdom, your planet."

I pondered on what Daar-Hull was asking of me. Part of me felt I owed the people of Luehiri. I should help them rebuild and thrive again as a civilization. Still, part of me was not ready to take on the responsibility of an entire planet. I had learned so much in such a short amount of time. The discovery of who I was and my non-human powers had been thrilling and terrifying. It was a journey of self-revelation that left me reeling, grasping to understand my newfound identity. I was glad to have been able to help my people and the Vihilians who had reached out to me for help, but I knew deep in my core that my destiny lay elsewhere. I wanted to be a diplomat and make a difference in cultural affairs, plus I knew monarchies rarely worked. It was an old-fashioned regime where power lay solely in the hands of the ruler.

Chapter 35

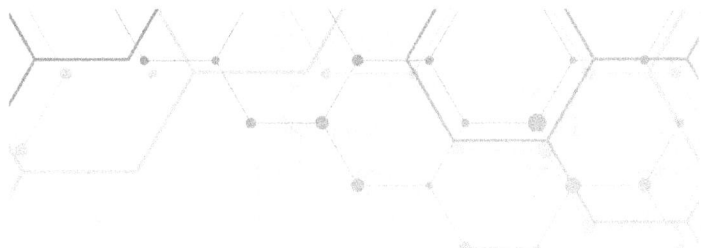

A Solemn Promise

T HE SUN HAD BARELY begun to rise as we stood on the rocky shores of Luehiri. The Intergalactic Police ship loomed before us, its sleek metallic hull reflecting the first rays of sunlight. Excitement and anticipation mingled with sadness as we prepared to board the ship that would take us back to Ryser Academy. We all knew this was the beginning of a new chapter in our lives.

"Ready to go?" Mac asked. I could see the strain in the lines around his eyes, but there was also a glimmer of hope.

"Almost," I replied. We had one last task to complete before we could truly celebrate our victory: delivering Suzuki's body to his family on Karmar. The thought of facing his loved ones weighed heavily on us, but we owed him to make sure his body was released with the love and respect he deserved.

"Let's do this," Blair said. "For Suzuki."

We nodded in agreement and carried the casket containing our fallen friend onto the ship. The Intergalactic Police officers greeted us solemnly. Their calm expressions led us to the room where Suzuki's body would be kept during our journey. It was a small, softly lit chamber, much like the rest of the ship, but we took comfort in knowing he would be with us every step of the way. Once Suzuki's casket was secure, we went to the common area where the celebration would occur. The room was filled with an array of food and drinks. This lavish spread lifted our spirits and reminded us we were not only mourning a loss but also celebrating a victory. Trella's eyes widened in awe as she surveyed the room. "Wow, I've never seen so much food."

"Me either," Fender agreed, his eyes lingering on a platter of steaming meat. "It all looks delicious."

"Come on," Mac said. "Let's dig in."

We filled our plates with various delicacies from various planets: crispy fried Glethian eel, juicy Largothian fruit that burst with flavor as we bit into it, and spicy Tarmarian noodles that made our tongues tingle. The rich aroma of freshly brewed Azurian coffee filled the air, tempting us to indulge in a few cups.

"Hey, Neo, try this," Blair said. She offered me a forkful that resembled mashed potatoes but had a slightly greenish hue. "It's called Selvarian mash. It tastes like a mix between sweet potatoes and avocados. Trust me; you'll love it."

I took a tentative bite. To my surprise, it was delicious, the unique blend of flavors melding together in perfect harmony. "You're right. That's amazing."

"Isn't it?" Blair grinned. Her earlier grief was momentarily forgotten as she took another mouthful.

The room echoed with our voices, creating a symphony of emotion filling every corner of the ship.

"Remember when Trella accidentally set off the fire alarm during their combat practice?" Fender asked, chuckling at the memory. "The entire academy was evacuated because they thought there was an actual fire."

"Hey, it wasn't my fault!" Trella's cheeks flushed with embarrassment. "That stupid training bot malfunctioned and started shooting actual flames!"

Mac's eyes were alight with amusement. "Sure, blame the bot," he teased.

"All right, all right," I said and raised my cup in a toast. "To Suzuki, to our victory, and to all the memories we've shared along the way."

"Cheers!" they echoed, clinking glasses and taking long sips of their drinks. We continued to eat, drink, and share stories, and I knew this was only the beginning of the adventures that awaited us.

We were all eager to engage in activities that showcased our unique interests and how much we had grown throughout our journey. Mac led us to a small virtual reality gaming station he had set up earlier. "Come on, guys! I've been working on my piloting skills, and I've got this new game that'll seriously put them to the test!" His eyes shone with excitement as he handed out the VR headsets.

"Count me in," Blair said. "I bet I can give you a run for your money, Mac!" I watched Blair and Mac compete with amusement and pride as they immersed themselves in high-speed interstellar racing.

They had come so far since our first meeting at Ryser Academy—their confidence and camaraderie were a testament to the bond we had formed together. Fender and Trella, meanwhile, had set up a makeshift sparring area at the back of the ship. While they practiced their martial arts, I could see the incredible growth they had both experienced during our journey. Their movements were fluid, precise, and deadly—a far cry from the unsure fighters they had been when we first met.

"Neo, come join us!" Trella called, beckoning me over. "Show us what you've learned about N'ymean fighting techniques!"

I hesitated, acutely aware of the lingering sadness that still clung to each of my friends. But as I looked around the room at the smiling faces and determined expressions, I realized we were all healing together--and it was okay to celebrate our victories, even as we mourned our losses.

"All right," I agreed, stepping onto the mat and assuming a defensive stance. "But don't go easy on me. I can take it!"

I looked at each of my friends, marveling at the bond we had formed and the incredible journey we had shared.

"Guys," I said softly, my voice thick with emotion, "I just want you all to know how much you mean to me. You've become my family, and I couldn't have made it through this without you."

"Same here, Neo," Mac replied. His eyes softened, and he reached out to squeeze my hand.

Blair stood, her eyes glistening, and raised her cup high. "To the stars, we've yet to explore, the challenges we'll face, and the family we've become."

"To the stars," we all echoed, clinking glasses in a final, heartfelt toast.

Chapter 36

A Heroic Return

THE THRUSTERS ON OUR ship sputtered and died as we touched down on the landing pad at Ryser Academy. I peered through the window, my heart pounding with anticipation. Mac, Blair, Trella, Fender, and I had just returned from a dangerous mission to save the Vihilians. None of us were the same as when we left.

"Here goes nothing," Mac said. He was the best pilot our age at Ryser Academy. Still, even he couldn't have anticipated what we'd faced out there among the stars. We all exchanged nervous glances before disembarking from the ship.

When we stepped onto the landing pad, our classmates and teachers swarmed around us, cheering and hugging us like long-lost loved ones.

"Neo, you're amazing!" Professor Mogh, of all people, shouted over the din. His brown eyes sparkled with pride. He wrapped me in a bear hug, nearly knocking the wind out of me. "I knew you could do it!"

"Thank you," I whispered. Tears pricked at the corners of my eyes. I felt the swell of emotions—pride, relief, happiness—but also a pang of insecurity. Did I really deserve this adulation?

"Look at all these people!" Trella exclaimed as she took in the crowd. Their dark skin contrasted against their tribal markings, which seemed to shimmer as they surveyed the scene. Trella was not easily impressed, so the heroes' welcome they and the rest of us received must have genuinely affected them.

"Doesn't feel real, does it?" Fender asked. His white hair and blue skin stood out among the students. He looked around, visibly struggling to process the outpouring of admiration. He was always trying to prove his strength, but now it seemed he didn't know what to do with it.

"No, it doesn't," I admitted. The crowd continued to cheer and clap, but I couldn't shake the feeling we were on borrowed time. Our actions had consequences, and I knew we would eventually have to pay for them.

"Everyone, please!" Mac shouted, raising his hands for silence. "We appreciate your support, but much more must be done. We're just getting started!"

As if on cue, Counselor Aurora appeared among the throng of students and staff. Her stern expression told me everything I needed to know. Although our celebration would be short-lived, we basked in the glory, knowing the price we'd have to pay for our actions.

The celebration began to fade as Counselor Aurora made her way through the crowd, her black curly hair pulled back tightly into a bun. Her stern expression caught my eye, and I knew something was wrong. My heart sank, and suddenly the cheering seemed distant and hollow.

"Neo, Mac, Blair, Trella, and Fender," she called out, her tone authoritative, as we all turned to face her. "While your actions have been commendable in saving the Vihilians and several other prisoners, there is still the matter of the stolen ships."

An uneasy silence settled over us. I glanced at my friends, each of them tense and wary.

"Ryser Academy's ship and King Fehnir's S'borrathian ship were taken without permission," Counselor Aurora continued. "As much as we recognize your heroics, you must also face the consequences of your actions."

I swallowed hard, a knot forming in my stomach. We had known this moment would come, but it didn't make it any easier to bear.

"Your punishment has been decided," she announced, looking at each of us directly. "Six months of community service in a penal colony on Neptune and a fine of ten thousand credits each."

"Six months?" Blair blurted out, her eyes wide with disbelief. "But our studies?"

" They will have to be put on hold," Counselor Aurora replied, her voice firm. "You will be permitted to resume your education at Ryser Academy upon completing your sentence and paying the fine."

I could see the shock and despair painted across my friends' faces. Mac clenched his fists, his knuckles turning white. Trella's pointy ears twitched ever so slightly, and, despite her stoicism, I could sense her fear. Even Fender, usually so self-assured, seemed to be grappling with the reality of our situation.

"Is there no other option?" Mac asked. "We had no choice but to take those ships. We did what we thought was right."

"Unfortunately, your intentions do not negate the consequences," Counselor Aurora replied with finality. "This decision is not up for negotiation."

I felt my heart race as I considered the prospect of six months in a harsh penal colony. The idea of being separated from everything I knew terrified me. But deep down, I understood we couldn't escape the consequences of our actions, no matter how noble our intentions were.

"Very well," I said quietly. "We'll accept our punishment."

"Good." She nodded solemnly. "You will leave for Neptune in two days. I suggest you use this time to prepare yourselves."

As Counselor Aurora walked away, leaving us to process our fate, I felt a specific determination arise within me. Yes, our punishment was severe, and yes, we would suffer for our choices. But we had made those choices together, and now we would face the consequences together, too.

"We can do this," I whispered, staring at my friends.

None of us had anticipated such a harsh sentence, and the shock left us reeling.

"Six months in a penal colony?" Mac whispered. "And ten thousand credits? That's insane!"

Blair's usually bubbly demeanor was replaced by anger. "Ryser Academy can't seriously expect us to do this," she said. "We saved the Vihilians. We saved hundreds of other prisoners from all across the galaxy! We're heroes!"

Fender's azure skin deepened in hue as he clenched his fists, and his green eyes flashed with indignation. "This is unjust! We were only trying to help."

Trella remained silent. Their eyes were downcast, and their long, pointy ears were pulled back against their head—an obvious sign of distress for a N'ymean.

I took a deep breath, trying to steady my racing heart while my mind churned with thoughts of how drastically our lives would change. Our futures at Ryser Academy now hinged on completing this community service and paying the hefty fine.

"Guys," I said, forcing myself to sound calm, "we must remember we did break the rules. We stole ships from Ryser Academy and King Fehnir."

"Neo's right." Mac ran a hand through his brown hair. "As much as it hurts to admit it, we must face the consequences of our actions."

"Do you really think they'll let us return after all this?" Blair asked tentatively.

"According to Counselor Aurora," I replied, "if we complete the community service and pay the fine, we can be reinstated at Ryser Academy." I tried to sound optimistic.

"We've come this far together," Trella said. "We can overcome this as well."

As I sat with my friends in the common area of our dormitory, the weight of our collective punishment bore down on us. Mac broke the silence that had settled over us. "Okay, let's think about this logically. Our options are limited, but we can't just sit here and do nothing."

"Right," Blair chimed in. "We could try to appeal our sentence, but there's no guarantee it would change anything. And besides, we broke the rules. We stole ships from Ryser Academy and King Fehnir."

"Not to mention we killed his daughter," Fender added.

"Neo's right," Mac sighed. "As much as it hurts to admit it, we must face the consequences of our actions."

There was a moment of silence as we all digested the reality of our situation. Then Blair's eyes lit up. "Wait, what about my parents? They have influence in the Intergalactic Union. Maybe they could appeal on our behalf and get the sentence revoked."

We all turned to look at her.

Mac shook his head slowly. "Blair, as tempting as that sounds, it wouldn't be right. We knew what we were doing, and we knew the risks. We can't just use connections to escape the consequences."

Blair's face fell, but she nodded in understanding. "You're right, Mac. It's hard to accept, though." I reached out and took her hand, giving it a reassuring squeeze.

"We all knew what we were getting into, Blair. We made choices, and now we have to live with them."

Trella, who had been quietly listening, finally spoke up. "We did what we thought was right. "The past cannot be altered, but we can own up to our actions and move on."

Finally, Mac stood up, determination in his eyes. We made our choices and must face the consequences. When the sentence concludes, we will restore our lives.

Chapter 37

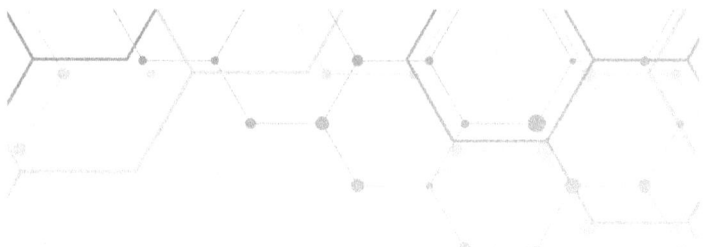

Tau Kufar

A DESOLATE AND FROZEN landscape greeted us when we arrived at Tau Kufar, the penal colony on Neptune. The icy wind howled fiercely, creating flurries of crystals that stung despite our heavy-duty suits. In the distance, the massive facility loomed before us, a stark reminder of the grueling months to come.

As we disembarked from the transport, a stern-faced officer led us into the main building, where we were introduced to the colony's rules and daily routines. The orientation was cold and clinical, a series of do's and don'ts delivered with military precision.

"You are here to serve your sentence," the Neptunian officer stated, his eyes scanning our faces.

"You will work, you will obey, and you will survive. Any deviation from the rules will be met with punishment." His face was stern and weathered, with deep-set eyes that seemed to miss nothing. He wore specialized goggles with sensors and night vision capabilities to see through the constant darkness of the Neptunian landscape. His skin was pale and toughened, conditioned by the biting cold and relentless winds.

"Feels like being a part of a science experiment," Trella remarked, looking at the Bundled in layers of protective gear.

"Keep moving," one guard barked, his voice devoid of sympathy.

"Easy for him to say," Fender muttered under his breath, his face contorted with effort as he lifted a heavy piece of machinery.

"We're in this together," Blair reminded us, her voice soft but determined. "We'll get through it."

They assigned us to different work details, each with its unique challenges. Blair was tasked with maintenance, so she had to maneuver the complex machinery that kept the colony operational. Fender took care of the hazardous chemical processing unit, a job that demanded extreme caution and precision. Trella helped the construction crew, working on expanding the colony's infrastructure. Mac worked on the maintenance and repair of the colony's communication systems.

In Neptune's remote and harsh environment, staying connected with other colonies and the Intergalactic Union was vital. I assisted in the meteorological station, monitoring and predicting the violent storms that frequently ravaged the area.

Our work was brutal. Bundled in layers of protective gear, we struggled against the relentless cold as we repaired infrastructure and cleared debris from the frequent storms that battered the colony.

One of the hardest things about life in Tau Kufar wasn't just the grueling work or the relentless cold; it was the isolation from those we cared about. Mac and I were assigned to different work details, and our shifts were staggered so that we rarely saw each other. His role required him to work long hours in a remote part of the facility. The absence was palpable, a void that seemed to grow each day. We would catch fleeting glimpses of each other in the mess hall or the colony's narrow corridors. Still, those moments were far too brief, mere shadows of the connection we once shared. Our conversations were reduced to hurried exchanges, and our time together was measured in stolen minutes. I stumbled into the mess hall, my body aching from a long shift, only to find Mac's usual seat empty. My heart sank, a familiar pang of disappointment settling in.

"Looking for Mac?" Fender asked, noticing my expression as he joined me in line.

"Yeah," I sighed, grabbing a tray. "I thought he'd be off by now."

Fender shook his head. "They had a power fluctuation in Sector 3. He's probably still fixing the communication system." I nodded, trying to hide my frustration.

"I just miss him, you know? We barely see each other."

Fender placed a comforting hand on my shoulder. "I know, Neo. It's tough on both of you."

Later that night, as I lay in my bunk, a soft chime alerted me to a message on my communicator. It was from Mac.

Hey, Neo. Sorry, I missed dinner.
Sector 3 was a mess. How was your
day? Miss you. - Mac.

I quickly typed a response.

Miss you too. The day was hard.
Wish you were here. - Neo.

The next day, I caught Mac in the corridor, our paths crossing momentarily.

"Mac!" I called out, rushing to him.

He turned, his face lighting up as he saw me. "Neo! I've got like two minutes before my next shift. How are you?"

"I'm okay," I said, though my voice betrayed me.

Mac pulled me into a quick hug, his warmth a fleeting comfort. "I know. I miss you too."

I whispered, fighting back tears. "I just wish we had more time together."

"We will," Mac promised, his eyes filled with determination. "Once this is over, we'll have all the time in the world." He gave me one last squeeze and rushed to his next task, leaving me in the corridor, feeling hopeful.

Life in Tau Kufar was unforgiving, but it was not without its moments of warmth and connection. A sense of camaraderie grew among the inmates, forged through shared hardship and mutual respect. We all had our stories, our reasons for being here, and as the weeks wore on, we found ourselves opening up, sharing those stories, and finding unexpected allies. Trella, in particular, seemed to find a kindred spirit in Alexi, a non-binary human who had been at Tau Kufar for over a year. They were both assigned to work in the hydroponic gardens, an essential part of the colony's food supply. They worked together, caring for the fragile plants that grew in the artificial environment. From the start, it was clear they had a connection. Their voices would often carry over the gentle hum of the hydroponic systems as they worked, chatting and laughing.

On one of my breaks, I made it to the hydroponic gardens. The delicate plants thrived in the artificial environment, contrasting with the harsh Neptunian environment. As I approached, I spotted Trella and Alexi chatting and laughing as they worked side by side.

"Hey Trella, Alexi!" I called out, my voice carrying over the gentle hum of the hydroponic systems.

They both looked up, their faces lighting up with smiles.

"Neo!" Trella exclaimed, their eyes twinkling. "Come join us. We're just transplanting some seedlings."

Alexi waved, their face bright with curiosity. "Yeah, come on over. We could use an extra pair of hands."

I joined them, my eyes filled with longing. "I don't know how much longer I can take this, not seeing Mac. It feels like we're on different planets, not just different shifts."

Trella placed a comforting hand on my shoulder, their eyes filled with understanding. "I know it's hard, Neo. But you're strong, and so is your connection with Mac. You'll get through this."

Alexi nodded sympathetically, their eyes softening. "I can understand that. It's tough being separated from the ones you love."

I looked at Trella and Alexi, my eyes reflecting my admiration. "You two seem to have found a good rhythm in the gardens. It's nice to see you both so connected."

Trella smiled, their eyes twinkling. "Yeah, Alexi and I hit it off right away. We have a lot in common, and working here in the gardens, it's like we're in our own little world."

Alexi agreed, their voice warm. "It's true. When I first got here, I felt so alone. But meeting Trella, having someone who understands me, made all the difference."

A soft smile curved on my lips. "It's great to see that you both found each other. "It makes me hopeful that even in such a place, connections can be formed,"

"I mean, look at Fender. Trella said. Their eyes followed Fender and Seraphina as they walked together through the maze of Tau Kufar.

I looked in the direction Trella was pointing, my eyes widening. "Yeah, I've seen them together a lot. They seem really close."

Trella nodded, their voice thoughtful. "They're both assigned to the chemical processing unit. They work closely together, handling the complex reactions vital to the colony's survival. I think their relationship has blossomed quickly."

I leaned in, intrigued. "Really? What do you think draws them together?"

Trella's eyes sparkled with understanding. "Shared interests, for one. And a mutual understanding of each other's culture and biology. Seraphina is a spirited Teutonian. I think Fender is drawn to her energy and her unwavering determination."

I smiled, my heart warmed by the thought. "That's beautiful. It's nice to see Fender finding solace in someone like Seraphina. After everything he's been through, he deserves some happiness."

Trella reassured me, their voice firm. "Absolutely. And remember, Neo, Mac is still there for you, even if you can't see him as often. Your love is strong, and it will endure this."

Alexi chimed in, their voice filled with conviction. "And we're here for you too.

Alexi grinned, their brown eyes sparkling with mischief. "Now, how about we get back to these plants? They won't grow themselves."

I laughed, and my spirits lifted. "You're right. Let's get to work."

The storm came without warning, a sudden, violent tempest threatening the floating platform's stability.

"Neo!" Mac's voice crackled over the comm, filled with panic. "Something's wrong with the platform! It's starting to tilt!" I ran to the control room, my heart pounding in my chest. The platform's alarms were blaring, the lights flashing red. The platform trembled as the storm's rage threatened to rip it apart.

"What's happening?" I demanded my voice tight with fear.

"It's the storm," one guard said, his face pale. "It's too strong. The platform can't handle it."

"We have to do something," I said, my mind racing. "Mac's out there!"

I could feel Mac's fear, his desperation. It was a tangible thing, a connection that went beyond mere words. I reached out with my mind, my Super Hybrid powers of empathy and telekinesis connecting me to him.

Mac. I'm here. Stay calm. I'm going to help you.

I closed my eyes, focusing on the storm. I could feel its power, its wild, untamed fury. But I could also feel something else—a connection to the elements.

I reached out with my mind connecting with the storm. I could feel it bending to my will, the winds slowing, the rain easing.

"Neo," Mac's voice was filled with awe. "What are you doing?"

"I'm controlling the storm," I said, my voice filled with determination. "I'm saving you."

The platform steadied, the alarms falling silent. I opened my eyes, my body trembling with the effort.

Mac returned to the control room with a wide smile. "You did it," Mac said, his voice filled with relief. "You saved us."

I smiled, my heart filled with pride. "We saved each other," I corrected softly, recalling the countless times we had leaned on one another throughout our ordeal.

Mac's eyes met mine, and I could see the depth of his gratitude and understanding. Without another word, he pulled me into a warm, enveloping hug, his arms solid and reassuring.

"Thank you, Neo," he whispered, his breath warm against my skin. "For everything."

I hugged him back, feeling a profound connection and a shared triumph. We had faced the unimaginable together and came out on the other side stronger and closer.

The day had finally come. Our sentence at Tar Kafur was over, and we were going home. The penal colony that had been our world for the past six months was now a part of our past. The lessons we'd learned and our forged friendships were all coming with us, but Neptune's cold, harsh environment was to be left behind. We stood at the docking bay, our bags packed, our faces etched with relief and anticipation. The guards, who had once been our overseers, now merely nodded as we passed, their faces impassive.

"Can't believe we're finally leaving this place," Fender said, his voice tinged with disbelief. He paused, looking thoughtful, then added, "Serafina will be leaving too, in a couple of months. She's heading back to Titan."

"It feels like a dream." Blair agreed, her eyes shining with unshed tears.

"It's no dream," Trella said, their voice firm but with a hint of uncertainty. "We've earned this. We've served our time, and now we're going home." They paused, their eyes distant, and then added softly, "But it will be several months before I can see Alexi again."

I looked at my friends, at the people who had become my family. We had been through so much together and faced challenges that would have broken others. But we had come through it stronger and more united than ever.

"Ready to go?" Mac asked, his hand reaching for mine. I smiled, squeezing his hand. "More than ready."

We boarded the shuttle, and the doors closed behind us. I looked out the window as Tau Kufar grew smaller and smaller until it was nothing but a speck in the distance.

"We did it," I whispered, more to myself than anyone else.

"We did," Mac agreed, his arm wrapping around me. "We're going home."

The shuttle's engines roared to life, and we were on our way. Back to Titan, back to Ryser Academy, back to the life we had left behind. We had changed. Shaped by our experiences, forged in the fires of adversity. We were ready for whatever came next.

As the stars streaked by, I leaned against Mac, my mind filled with thoughts of what lay ahead. But no matter what awaited us, I knew I could handle it. We could handle it.

We were a formidable team known for our resilience. We endured Tar Kafur, proving our determination and grit. It was time to go home.

As we re-entered Ryser Academy, I felt the familiar warmth of its halls embrace us, a stark contrast to the cold, unforgiving conditions we had endured. Our footsteps echoed through the corridors as we walked toward the administrative offices to finalize our reinstatement. The academy seemed quieter than before, a subtle reminder of how we no longer fit in. We had changed.

"Can't believe they actually let us come back," Fender muttered. His voice was tinged with disbelief.

"Neither can I," Blair said. "But we did it, guys. We survived that hellhole and made it back."

"Thanks to each other," Trella chimed in. Their usually stoic tone was now filled with melancholy. "We couldn't have done it without one another."

I swallowed the lump in my throat. They were right—our bond had deepened during our time on Neptune.

As we finally stood before the administrative office, I took a deep breath. From that moment on, we embraced our futures at Ryser Academy with a new sense of purpose, driven by the lessons we had learned during our time on Neptune.

Chapter 38

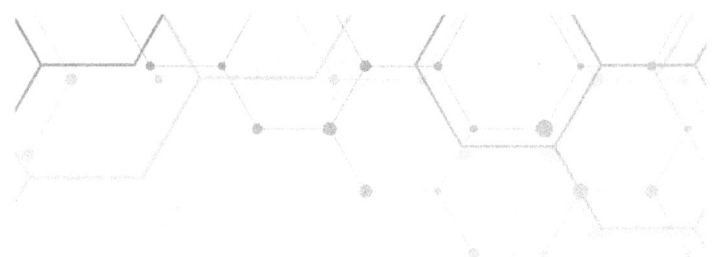

In the Warmth of Sunset

T HE GOLDEN RAYS OF Titan's sunset streamed through the
windows of Ryser Academy, casting a warm glow across Mac's
hazel eyes. We sat together on the roof, laughter filling the crisp air.

"Look at that view," he said. The view paled in comparison to the beauty I saw in him. His strong arms crossed over his chest gave me a sense of protection.

"Titan really is breathtaking." I tried to keep my voice steady. Heat rushed to my cheeks as I realized I had been staring at him too long.

"Almost as breathtaking as you," Mac said. He flashed me that irresistible smile, and the warmth of his gaze made me feel like I was melting inside.

"Mac, you're such a flirt." I grinned, playfully nudging his shoulder with mine. Inside, though, I was silently pleading for him to be serious.

"Only when it comes to you, Neo." His tone softened, and he reached over to brush a stray lock of red hair from my face. "You make it hard not to be."

Our eyes locked, and the rest of the universe disappeared for a moment. It was just us, suspended in this intimate sliver of time. The vulnerability in his gaze stirred something within me I had never felt before—a longing for something more profound, stronger than friendship.

"Mac, I hesitated, unsure how to put my emotions into words. He seemed to understand and squeezed my hand gently.

"Neo," he whispered, "I've never met anyone like you." His breath was warm against my ear. "You're smart, kind, and you have this incredible way of making everyone around you feel important. You're truly special, and I'm so grateful to have you in my life."

My chest swelled with love for him, and I leaned into his embrace. My mind raced, trying to find the right words to express my feelings for him, but nothing seemed adequate. So instead, I let my actions speak for me.

"Mac," I whispered. Our lips brushed against each other's, and my pulse quickened. The kiss was electrifying, a spark of energy coursing through our veins. It was a connection unlike any I had ever experienced before.

As we pulled apart, breathless and grinning, our unspoken feelings hung heavy between us, a secret we were both desperate to share. But for now, we held each other close, basking in the warmth of our newfound love.

We strolled through the lush gardens of Ryser Academy hand in hand. I marveled at the vivid colors surrounding us. The vibrant reds, blues, and greens of the Titan flora stood out against the backdrop of the magnificent dome enclosing the campus.

"Neo," Mac's voice held a hint of nervousness. He stopped walking and turned toward me. His hazel eyes shimmered with sincerity. "There's something important I need to tell you."

"Of course, Mac. What is it?" My heart skipped a beat, and I squeezed his hand reassuringly.

"Ever since we met, I've been drawn to you in a way I can't explain. You're powerful and intelligent, yet your vulnerability makes me want to protect you." He paused, taking a deep breath as if to gather strength. "I've fallen for you, Neo. Hard. And I'm wondering. Would you be my girlfriend?" My heart swelled, and I had to smile at the earnest look on Mac's face. "Yes, Mac," I replied without hesitation. "I'd love to be your girlfriend."

"Really?" His face lit up with joy. We embraced tightly, our hearts beating in unison as we shared another exhilarating kiss.

As we pulled away, a sudden chill swept over me—an eerie feeling that made my skin prickle. My empathic abilities seemed heightened, picking up on something in the air.

"Mac, I have this strange sense Z'hleena might still be alive," I whispered. My gaze darted around the garden as if she might appear.

"Z'hleena? But I killed her, didn't I?"

"Maybe not," I mused. "It's just a feeling, but I can't shake it. We need to be prepared for anything."

We resumed walking through the garden, and my thoughts raced with the possibilities. Z'hleena's return would undoubtedly pose a significant threat to us and our friends at Ryser Academy. But one thing was sure: As long as Mac and I had each other, we could overcome any obstacle that came our way. Hand in hand, we ventured down the path, our love for each other a beacon of light amid the looming shadows of uncertainty.

The following day, as I walked across Ryser Academy's courtyard, the wind whipped my hair around my face. The sky above Titan was a stormy blue-gray, mirroring the disquiet in my heart. My gut feeling about Z'hleena's survival had gnawed at me all night, and the universe seemed to reflect my unease.

"Hey Neo, have you heard?!" Blair shouted, running toward me from the school building. Her eyes were wide with shock, and she clutched her Xoria tightly.

"Slow down, Blair," I said. "What's going on?"

"Z'hleena's alive!" she blurted out. "The Intergalactic police just sent a message. They couldn't find her body. It's all over the Interstellar news!"

My heart dropped like a stone. "I knew it," I whispered and stared at the screen. The headline read:

S'borrathian Princess Z'hleena Cyrek: Unconfirmed Survival.

"Wait till Mac hears about this," Blair muttered.

"Where is he?" I scanned the courtyard for his familiar figure.

"Over there, by the fountain," she said, pointing in his direction. "Go talk to him, Neo."

"Thanks, Blair." I nodded and sprinted toward Mac.

"Neo, what's the rush?" His eyes brimmed with surprise as I approached him.

"Z'hleena is alive." I barely managed to choke out the words; my breath was ragged from running. "The Intergalactic police can't find her body. She's still out there, Mac."

He looked stunned but quickly composed himself. "Okay, we'll deal with this. We'll make a plan."

"Mac, she's dangerous." Fear crept into my voice. "She'll come after us."

"Then we'll be ready," he declared. "We won't let her hurt anyone, Neo. We'll keep ourselves and our friends safe."

I swallowed the lump in my throat. "But how do we prepare for something like this?"

"First, we need to inform Fender and Trella," Mac suggested. "They have a right to know; we'll need their help."

"Sounds good." I tried to banish the dread that threatened to drown me. "Let's meet up after classes and start planning."

"Neo," Mac whispered and touched my cheek gently. "I know you're scared—so am I. But we're stronger together. We'll face this, and we'll win. I promise."

"Thank you, Mac," I murmured, leaning into his touch. "I'm glad I have you by my side."

The next day, as I walked through the bustling halls of Ryser Academy with Mac by my side, I felt the weight of our conversation from the night before. The knowledge that Z'hleena was still out there somewhere, lurking in the shadows, cast a dark cloud over us.

"Are you okay?" Mac asked. He reached out to hold my hand and gave it a reassuring squeeze.

"Of course," I lied and forced a smile. "Just a little tired, that's all."

"Neo, you don't have to pretend with me." He stopped in the middle of the hallway as students flowed around us. "I know how much Z'hleena's survival affects you. It scares me too."

"Mac, I'm terrified," I admitted. "But I can't let fear get the best of me. We have to be strong and focused if we want to protect our friends and ourselves."

"Hey, we're in this together." Mac pulled me into a warm embrace. "You're not alone, Neo. Remember that."

As classes ended for the day, we met up with Fender and Trella in the library. They listened intently as we shared our concerns about Z'hleena's return and the danger she posed. The gravity of the situation settled heavily on their faces, but they didn't balk or hesitate. Instead, they nodded in unison, showing their faithful support.

"Count us in," Fender said firmly. "We won't let her threaten us or the Intergalactic Union. We'll do whatever it takes to stop her."

Chapter 39

Young Explorers

THE SUN'S RAYS FILTERED through the dome over Ryser Academy. I smiled as I walked with my friends, each of us eager to begin another day at the prestigious school for young space explorers. As we settled into our seats in the lecture hall, I felt grateful for this opportunity. Here we were, a group of teenagers from different corners of the galaxy, brought together by our shared dreams of exploration and discovery.

"Listen up, everyone," our instructor called out. "Let's get started. Today, we're focusing on interstellar flight and communication."

As the lecture began, a fire ignited inside me. This was where I belonged, where my future lay. I looked around at my friends, knowing they felt the same way. We would face the unknown and make our mark on the universe. The familiar hum of the spacecraft simulator filled my ears as I settled into the pilot's seat. Blair, my best friend and an aspiring engineer was busy calibrating the controls for another practice session. Mac, who had become my boyfriend and confidant since my arrival at Ryser Academy, adjusted the straps of his safety harness and flashed me that heart-melting smile.

"Ready to show off your piloting skills, Neo?" he asked. His eyes sparkled with excitement.

"More like trying not to crash," I replied with a nervous chuckle. Despite the countless hours spent in the simulator, I still felt the butterflies in my stomach every time I strapped in.

"Relax," Trella said from her co-pilot's seat. Her soothing voice helped to calm my nerves. "We're here to learn and improve. Besides, you've come a long way since we first met."

"Right," Fender agreed, flexing his bluish fingers over the navigation console. "You're a natural, Neo. Just trust yourself."

I took a deep breath and focused on the task at hand. As the simulation began, I guided our virtual spacecraft through a series of complex maneuvers, relying on the support and expertise of my friends. Together, we made a formidable team, each honing our unique skills and abilities.

"Approaching the asteroid belt," Mac warned. I gripped the throttle and adjusted our trajectory, weaving through the floating debris with newfound determination.

"Good job," Blair said. "Keep it up, Neo!"

Just as I began to feel more comfortable, a holographic screen flickered to life before me. The face of Daar-Hull, Prime Minister of Luehiri, appeared on the display. With his triangular head, ovoid eyes, and tiny mouth, he was the epitome of Luehirian authority.

"Ah, Neo," Daar-Hull greeted with a courteous nod. "I've heard much about your potential as a diplomat. I hope you won't mind if I observe your training session."

Startled by his sudden appearance, I stammered, "Of course not. It's an honor, Prime Minister."

"Please, proceed," he urged. His eyes never left mine. Though I felt the weight of expectation bearing down on me, I knew this was an opportunity to prove myself—not only to Daar-Hull but also to my friends and instructors at Ryser Academy. I continued guiding our simulated spacecraft through the treacherous asteroid field.

As the simulation ended, I wiped away beads of sweat from my forehead. My heart raced with a mixture of nerves and excitement. "That was intense," I muttered under my breath.

"Very impressive, Neo," Daar-Hull said. His holographic image flickered slightly. "Your skills have grown exponentially since you arrived at Ryser Academy."

"Thank you, Prime Minister." I tried to hide the pride swelling within me. "I've had excellent guidance from my instructors and friends."

"Indeed, they have served you well," he said. His gaze briefly acknowledged Mac, Blair, and the others before returning to me. "But now, I must ask for your assistance."

My curiosity was piqued. "What can we do for you, sir?"

"Something has befallen my planet, our planet," Daar-Hull explained as a hint of desperation crept into his usually composed voice.

"An unknown enemy is attacking Luehiri, and we struggle to understand their motives or tactics."

"Of course, we'll help in any way we can," I assured him. I saw the same determination mirrored in the eyes of my friends.

"Thank you, Neo." Relief washed over his face. "Your diplomatic skills and empathy may be crucial in resolving this crisis. Your mother, our late Queen Nahyla, would've been very proud."

As the holographic connection ended, my mind raced. We had trained tirelessly for moments like these. To explore strange new worlds, negotiate with alien species, and take on the challenges of the universe.

"Neo," Mac called out. "Everything okay?"

"Yep," I replied. "I'm just trying to process everything."

Blair spoke up. "By Daar-Hull's tone, whatever's happening on Luehiri doesn't look good."

"Right," I agreed.

The thought of Z'hleena, the cunning S'borrathian princess who was believed dead, haunted me. *What if she wasn't gone? What if her influence remained connected to the chaos unfolding on Luehiri?*

"You don't seem very confident," Trella remarked.

A tense silence fell upon us, and the magnitude of my suspicion hung heavy in the air. If Z'hleena was alive and involved in the attack on Luehiri, the stakes had just skyrocketed.

Epilogue

THUNDER ROARED IN THE black sky, and fire spat out of the ancient volcano. The small cell window gave a view of the shattered moon. He was on some unnamed, inhospitable planet in one of the farthest galaxies from Titan—Galaxy GN-z11. To the prisoner, every day was the same routine. Wake up and eat a disgusting mixture of amino acids, vitamins, and other essential but unpalatable nutrients, put on an old heavy suit, and head to the transporter for relentless hours, working on artificial crops. Time stood still in this hellish place. But today differed from any other day. Something had changed, and he could feel it.

He quickly exited his small bunk bed in his six-by-eight-foot cell. To avoid hitting the low ceiling, he bent his head and walked a few steps to stand by the hatch, waiting for his turn. As the thunder roared louder and the angry volcano erupted in the distance, he knew the time had come. With his heart pounding, the man tightly clenched his fists and felt the adrenaline surge through his body. With a creak, the hatch opened, revealing a dimly lit corridor glowing with an eerie red light. The guards' footsteps echoed in the distance, growing louder with each passing moment.

Summoning his courage, the man slipped through the gap, tiptoeing into the adjoining room. A control center was visible, with monitors showing alien landscapes and surveillance footage. Using a steady hand, he decoded the controls, searching for a means to override the security systems and main doors. The console hummed to life under his touch, responding to his every command. As he worked frantically, the guards' voices grew louder, their footsteps drawing nearer. With time ticking away, the man's heart raced with anticipation and fear. His eyes widened in surprise as another set of doors swung open, revealing a figure cloaked in a flowing cape.

The tension in the room dissolved as he recognized the mysterious newcomer. It was a woman; shadows obscured her face, but her smile was warm and comforting.

The woman's smile widened as she lowered her hood, revealing her face. He touched her cheek and caressed her lips, letting his fingers rest on her chin. It had been too long.

This is the end of *The Chimera Project*.

- Loved the book? Please leave **a review.** It helps me so much.

- **Join my Newsletter** to receive a **FREE** prequel to *The Chimera Project* as well as a sneak peek at chapters of my upcoming book in the Ryser Academy Series, *The Crystal's Legacy*, and other writings.

- Follow me on **Facebook** and **Instagram** for a chance to sign up to be an ARC reader.

ΛBOUT THE ΛUTHOR

A.P. Taber holds a Master's Degree in Nursing Education and is a Registered Nurse living in Nevada with her family. Her life is characterized by her unwavering commitment to her healthcare profession and a lifelong passion for writing and artistic expression.

With a novel penned at ten, A.P.'s journey into the literary world began early. Her writing reflects a unique fusion of her academic background, keen insights into human nature, and boundless creativity. Beyond her literary endeavors, A.P.'s interests span the realms of art and strategic gameplay, engaging in complex games such as Dungeons & Dragons and Magic The Gathering.

These pursuits further contribute to her approach to storytelling.

Connect with A.P. Online

https://authoraptaber.com

instagram.com/author_aptaber

facebook.com/authoraptaber

goodreads.com/authoraptaber

amazon.com/author/ap_taber

tiktok.com/author_aptaber

twitter.com/author_aptaber

Want to know more about me? Like where I get my ideas from, or what my favorite sci-fi movies are?

Sign up for my newsletter, and I'll answer all those questions, and I'll even send you a FREE prequel to The Chimera Project.

FREE PREQUEL

Book two in the Ryser Academy Series, *The Crystal's Legacy*, is coming out soon. In the meantime, here is your **link to the FREE prequel** to The Chimera Project.